Results Will Vary

Courtney Duke Foster

Published by McQueen Road Press
First Edition

Library of Congress Control Number: 2024920817
ISBN: 979-8-9853774-2-2 (paperback)
ISBN: 979-8-9853774-3-9 (ebook)

Edited by: Trinette Hylton
Edited by: Alice Osborn
Cover art by: Rochelle Dickerson @laarocheart
Book Design by: Marie Leonard

To my parents, who inspired me to write stories.

*And to my nephew, Michael, who inspired me
to share them with the world.*

Chapter 1

Miami, Florida
2009

The aroma of saltwater, seaweed and sex, with hints of weed and liquor had Drew leaning almost completely over the hotel balcony trying to get closer to the sights and sounds of South Beach. He watched the people: fellow escape artists, looking for a respite from their reality. Ocean Drive was the flame, and these scantily clad individuals were the moths, drawn to an unseasonably warm December to brave the overcrowded sidewalk, hoping to recapture some summer fun, if only for one night. The street traffic was as bad as the foot traffic, jam-packed with flashy cars, blaring the best 2009's Top 40 had to offer in hip hop, Latin, rap, Caribbean, and pop. But one chart-topping hit stood out from the rest. A smile bright enough to compete with the art deco neon lights spread across Drew's face.

"To everything!" his bandmates cheered from behind the sliding glass door separating Drew's balcony retreat from the hotel hospitality suite. Then the door slid open, and the boring wrap party chatter spilled out, invading his oasis.

"Damn, it's hot out here! What the hell, dude?" his bandmate, Chris, barked, stepping onto the balcony with two shot glasses filled to the brim with brown liquor.

"Shhhhh," Drew hissed. "Listen."

Chris slid the door shut with his foot then, stood frozen until he caught the wavelength Drew was on just as Chris's explosive drum solo serenaded them from the street. His hundred-watt smile appeared instantly, and Drew knew exactly what he was thinking: *This will never get old.* Hearing yourself on the radio for the first time was one of the most thrilling experiences a musician can have; it meant the gatekeepers had let you in. But hearing fans blast your music from their cars was something else entirely. It meant you got to stay.

Chris joined Drew at the railing as Beyonce's anthem to all the single ladies drowned out their song. "You missed the toast." He handed him a shot glass.

"To everything," they said, clinking their glasses like they had been doing since they took their very first drink together in high school. Drew downed his whiskey as Chris poured his out over the balcony.

"I'm proud of you, man," Drew grunted as the burning sensation subsided.

"Thanks. It'll be three years next week, you know?"

Drew nodded, remembering the long drive to upstate New York the week before Christmas three years ago. The rehab place was only four hours from New Jersey, but it took three times as long to get there because Chris kept changing his mind. Drew shuddered, thinking about the pile of gray skin and bones trembling in his back seat, desperate to get out from under the crushing weight of addiction to drugs and alcohol, yet terrified he would fail again. It was hard to believe Chris had found his way back from that. He walked out of that facility three months later looking like himself again, sporting his normal swoon-inducing, perpetually tanned skin and a full head of coily brown hair gifted to him by his Black father. But he looked different too, stronger than ever before, like he was really going to make it that time. And he had.

They watched the crowd for a while, reminiscing about the days before stardom came calling. "You know, it wasn't that long ago we'd be down there roaming the streets after a show, instead of hiding out in a hotel suite with a bunch of suits who probably don't even listen to our music. Don't you miss that, man?" Drew asked.

"Yeah, I do. But I think you're forgetting how those nights usually ended with us sleeping in the van or on the beach. Is that why you bailed on the party? Ready to give up everything we've worked for to go sleep on the beach?"

"You call that a party?"

"You call that an answer?"

"Relax. I just needed some air. I'm not gonna do anything drastic."

"It looked pretty drastic when you walked out on that reporter mid-question."

"You know I hate interviews. They all ask me the same questions over and over: 'Where'd you come up with the name Wiretap? Where does the inspiration for your songs come from?'" Drew said as his gaze drifted back to the live people show below. "Why don't they ever ask you guys any questions? Mike and Travis can play like eighteen instruments between the two of 'em, Randy's a kick-ass bass player, and you can beat the piss out of a drum kit. They act like I'm a solo artist and I'm not."

"No. You're the 'pretty boy front man with the wild, jet black, curly mane and piercing blue eyes.'" Chris fluttered his eyelids. He had a special talent for filing away the most embarrassing quotes from articles about the band and regurgitating them at random times. Drew gave him a taste of what his piercing blue eyes could do with a hard look that, unfortunately, had zero effect. Chris threw his arm over Drew's shoulder and went in for the kill. "They don't wanna hear from us losers. They wanna hear from *The Son of Rock and Soul.*" Drew shoved him off and they fell into a fit of laughter.

The title was flattering, and much better than the dreaded *Blue-Eyed Soul* that the people in charge of that kind of thing often slapped on white singers with a rich tone and gritty texture, but it didn't fit any better. And knowing his true origin story, it was impossible for Drew and his bandmates not to laugh at how ridiculous it sounded. *The Son of Rage and Sweetness* would have been a far more accurate moniker to describe where (and who) he came from in a nutshell.

Drew glanced over his shoulder into the hotel suite. Randy was talking a mile a minute to the reporter he had left hanging. And if his wild hand gestures were any indication, the poor guy was getting a blow-by-blow account about the time a grilled cheese sandwich saved his life. "Randy's got that guy on the edge of his seat. He won't even remember I left."

Chris looked back and shook his head. "He's telling the grilled cheese story, isn't he?" They laughed again.

"So, you gonna tell me what's really goin' on with you, bro?" Chris asked as their laughter subsided.

Drew shrugged. "Feeling weird about the tour being over, I guess. I've never been too good at transitioning back into normal family life. I always feel like I'm in the way at first until everybody gets used to having me around again. And I dunno." He wrung his hands together. "All this feels like it's happening so fast, you know?"

"Are you kidding? This is our third album, man. We've been grindin' for fifteen years and people are just now starting to know who we are."

Drew's gaze drifted from the street to the ocean. "I guess I didn't realize how much I'd miss being a nobody."

Chris gave him another hardy pat on the back. "Well, you better get used to it. Everybody's sayin' we're gonna get Album of the Year and that you're gonna get Song of the Year. Mel says once that happens, we'll be able to write our own ticket." He shrugged. "Giving up anonymity is the price of making our dreams come true."

Drew stared at his friend, shaking his head. "You never worry about anything, do you?"

"Don't need to. Not as long as I have *The Droid* for a best friend, slash front man. I know you got everything covered." He chuckled.

Drew didn't. He never liked the nickname. Chris started calling him *The Droid*, short for *Drew the Droid*, in ninth grade after their evil biology teacher called on him on his first day as a mid-year transfer student to list the five kingdoms of living things. Drew showed him and rattled off not only all five kingdoms, but all their subgroups as well. Most of his classmates were unimpressed by Drew's display of academic excellence, but not Chris. He chased Drew down after class and asked if he was some kind of robot because he talked like he had been programmed with facts. The nickname came out of that conversation, and it stuck, so did Chris. Drew didn't have the heart to tell his new best friend that his android-like qualities were born out of survival, not in a factory or a laboratory. He had learned early in life that being perfect at school, and everywhere else, kept his father's rage at bay and made his mother happy, which amplified her sweetness. Chris would find that out soon enough on his own, then he would embark upon a lifelong mission to yank the stick out of Drew's ass.

"Look, man. Your work ethic is off the charts. And we all know we wouldn't be here without your annoyingly relentless pursuit of perfection, but you can turn the robot off now," Chris said, still on his mission. "Just chill for a minute and bask in the glow of our success." He stood up straight, spreading his arms out wide. "I'm sure April and the kids would appreciate it if you took it easy for a little while."

"I wish I could, but I can't. Mel wants to build on the momentum from this album. We gotta get back in the studio and start workin' on the next one."

"Ugh... I know," Chris groaned, dropping his head below his shoulders. Then he looked up at Drew with a raised brow and a crooked smile. "But not tonight."

Drew knew that twinkle in his friend's eyes. When they were in high school, it meant Chris had an idea that was going to get him grounded, or worse. These days, it meant they'd end up trying to talk a cop out of arresting them.

"I'm afraid to ask," Drew said.

"Fear not, my friend!" Chris said, sounding like he had just stepped off the set of the next *Harry Potter* movie. "I have acquired the use of a time machine. And as my best friend, you shall have the privilege of riding shotgun."

"No way. Mel's lettin' you borrow the Aston Martin? He just got it yesterday. D'you see him murder somebody or somethin'?"

"I don't know what to tell you. I've been blessed with the power of persuasion. I even offered to drive it up to New York for him—free of charge."

"Cool. What'd he say?"

"He said, and I quote, 'I've been running a record label for over thirty years. I know better than to trust a musician's sense of time. If I let you drive my car from Miami to New York, I won't see it for at least a month,'" Chris said, imitating Mel's heavy New Jersey accent. Chris was a master at mimicking accents, but he had Mel's down pat, as it was only slightly thicker than his own.

"Well, that's offensive."

Chris's deep frown morphed into a broad smile. "And it's completely accurate!" He threw his head back, offering a maniacal guffaw to the night sky. "So, what say you, my good man? This is your only chance. Because when I'm finished breakin' that baby in, Mel won't let any of us borrow a pen, much less his $200,000 car." He glanced at his watch. "It's two a.m. now. The highway should be clear enough to open her up."

Drew was torn. He wanted to join his best buddy on the ride of a lifetime, but he was worn out. The tour had taken its toll, making him feel closer to eighty than thirty-two. All he wanted to do was fall into bed and pull a Rip Van Winkle. But Chris never got tired. He had a thirst for adventure that he could never seem to quench and the two hours they had spent at the so-called after-party most certainly had left him parched. Sleeping was always the last thing on his mind anyway. "I'll sleep when I'm dead," was his favorite saying.

"Nah, man, I'm gonna pass. I have a ten o'clock flight. And I gotta be fresh when I get home."

"Right, right, right. Of course," he said, giving Drew a few sympathy pats on his shoulder. Then he trotted over and slid the door open. "Yo, Randy! You're in luck! Drew decided to be lame tonight! Mike, Trav, let's roll!"

Drew watched his bandmates rush out of the suite, shoving and jabbing at each other like a group of unruly teenagers unable to contain their excitement on their way into an amusement park. He chuckled as he scanned the room, planning a way more discrete exit. His eyes skimmed past a woman leaning against the bar and did a double take, homing in on her tight black dress, or rather the tight figure it accentuated, then his eyes traveled up to her face. She flashed a warm smile—a warm, familiar smile—and made her way across the room. His heart rate sped up like it was sending out an alert, while his brain kept saying, *"It can't be her."* But his heart beat even faster in protest the closer she came to the sliding door, and when she stepped out onto the balcony, it shot off the charts.

"Andy Simon," she said, pointing at him. "Oh, I'm sorry... it's Drew now, isn't it?"

"Victoria Russo." He narrowed his eyes. "It's always been Drew, actually. But, if I recall, when I met you, you said, 'Ew. Drew is my lying, cheating, douche ex-boyfriend's name. I'm going to call you

Andy. It tastes sweeter on my tongue, anyway.'" He winked, just like she had nearly twenty years ago.

She covered her face with her hand. "Oh my God! Did I really say that? I was such a bitch back then. I can't believe I had the nerve to change your name like that. I don't know how—or why—you ever put up with me?"

Drew smirked. "I was a skinny freshman with a buzz cut and a face full of acne, on top of being the new kid on the block. When your smokin' hot, next-door neighbor tells you your name tastes sweet in her mouth, you go with it. Even if it's not really your name."

"You've certainly grown up a lot since then." She smoothed down a curl that had lost its way from the mass of hair on his head. "I don't see any hint of that lanky army brat." Her hand slowly grazed the length of his tattoo-covered bicep. "Those beautiful baby blues of yours haven't changed, though."

The temperature had nothing on the heat rising in Drew's cheeks. He was that skinny freshman trying to find his words all over again. "You look great, Vicki," he said, finally. "I almost didn't recognize you as a blonde. How do you manage to look even better now than you did in high school?"

"Good genes, I guess. My mom's in her sixties and still looks pretty hot in a bikini." She smiled while they stared into each other's eyes well past the point where things should have gotten awkward.

"So, how've you been?" Drew asked, breaking the trance. "I always wondered what happened to you after your, um, family moved away."

"You don't have to sugarcoat it, Drew. You can say what really happened. My dad cheated on my mom with my English teacher. And then, to maximize the humiliation of the experience, he moved her into our house after my mom left Jersey with me and my little brothers." She shook her head. "I haven't been back to that house since." Her words had no emotion, like she was repeating a story she heard on the news, but the brightness in her eyes dimmed a little.

"Uh, okay, so how have you been since... all that, then?"

Vicki's eyes lit up again. "Great! I've been at Biggs and Brighten for five years now. And I'm already up for partner."

"The entertainment law firm? Wow," Drew said with wide eyes. "That's awesome."

"You look surprised."

"Not surprised. Impressed. You always talked about being a lawyer. Everybody doesn't get to live out their dreams."

"That's true. And speaking of livin' their dreams, look at you, man! I can't even tell you how crazy proud I am to say I knew you when."

His cheeks went hot again. Hearing his teenage crush say she was proud of him inflated his ego more than performing for arenas full of screaming, adoring fans. He couldn't stop smiling while they reminisced about their old neighborhood and friends.

"So, how's my dad doing?" she asked, the carefree girlish quality suddenly absent from her tone. "Haven't seen him since we moved."

Drew shrugged. "I haven't been home in a while myself," he said. "It's kinda hard to be there since my mom died."

"Oh, Drew, I'm so sorry. I forgot your mother passed away." She placed her hand on his shoulder. "Remember all those times your mom insisted my brothers and me come over for dinner when all that stuff was going down with my father? She always seemed to know when my mom needed a minute to herself just to breathe."

"Yeah. I remember you guys eating with us a lot," he said with a nod, keeping to himself how often he insisted his mother invite them over.

"I think part of me has never really accepted that she died."

"Tell me about it," he said, massaging his temples.

"What's wrong?"

"I'm getting a headache. Shit. I hope it doesn't turn into a migraine."

"You get those too?" She winced, and then her eyes brightened up again. "Hey, I've got the perfect pill for migraines. My herbalist turned me on to them—all natural," she said as she rummaged through the flat, sparkly purse she had been holding under her arm. "Damn. I must have left them in my travel case."

"That's okay, Vic. I just need to get some sleep."

She poked out her bottom lip. "Are you sure? Those little pills work wonders. If I get even the tinge of a migraine, all I have to do is take one and I'm a new woman." She moved closer to him. "I'm staying in this hotel... on two," she said softly, twirling the same wayward curl around her finger. "Why don't you escort me to my room, and I'll get you one," she whispered in his ear.

"I don't want you to go to any trouble. I'll be alright," he grunted, squeezing his eyes shut tightly as a throbbing pain pulsated from his temple to the back of his eye.

"It's no trouble. Really." She threaded her arm through the crook of his elbow. "Come on, Drew. Let me help you."

Chapter 2

Sleep came on fast and intense, but rest was elusive. Drew tossed and turned as his migraine harnessed a memory and twisted it into a nightmare in which the well-lit New Jersey neighborhood street his family moved to in his early teens shifted to a dark endless stretch of highway.

Drew glared at Chris, silently berating himself for trusting a kid he had only known for three days.

"Stop lookin' at me like that, dude," Chris said. "How many times do I have to apologize?"

"I don't need your apologies. I need to be at home right now!"

"And if I had a magic wand or a time machine, I could arrange that for you! But since I ain't got neither one of those things, our only option is to keep walking."

Drew fumed as they continued briskly down the two-lane highway. He had been so anxious about making friends with civilian kids he didn't ask enough questions when Chris invited him to a party. *How far away is it? What time do the buses stop running around here? Are there buses around here?* would have been good ones. They also would have exposed him for the ROTC geek he really was to the coolest fourteen-year-old he'd ever met.

"Look on the bright side," Chris said. "At least we'll know better for next time."

"Next time?" Drew's mid-pubescent voice normally sounded like a cross between a lost goose and an out of tune trumpet, but his heightened anxiety had put him dangerously close to the shrieking zone. "If I don't get home before my dad's shift ends, there won't be a next time for me. He's going to murder me," he said, remembering how his father had gone ballistic the one and only time he was late for curfew.

"*Twenty-two hundred hours means TWENTY-TWO HUNDRED HOURS NOT TWENTY-TWO O FIVE, ANDREW!*" he had roared in his face.

Chris slowed down and looked over at his new friend. Drew put his head down and hastened his pace. There was no way he was going to let Chris get a glimpse of the fear or the tears brimming in his eyes.

"Why are you freakin' out, man?" Chris asked, catching up. "I blow off my curfew all the time. It'll be okay."

"No, it won't! My dad's state police."

Chris shrugged. "So what?"

"You don't get it. He just retired from the Army," Drew said. "He was military police, now he's state police. He gets off on policing people, especially me. And he never cuts me any slack—ever. You do as you are told, or—" He shook the thought out of his head. "You just do as you're told." He looked over his shoulder. "He'll be driving down this road soon on his way home. When he sees me, I'm toast." He took off running.

Chris caught up with Drew again and grabbed his arm. "Follow me. I know a shortcut."

The next thing he knew, they were on a train bridge with a big one heading their way. It was far enough away to give them plenty of time to reach safety. But the bridge was longer than it looked, and the train was going faster than he calculated. They ran for their lives.

Drew kept pace with Chris before passing him as they approached the end of the bridge.

"Come on, man! We can make it! Let's go!" Drew shouted over his shoulder. He expected at least a grunt from Chris as his competitive nature pushed him to outrun both Drew and the train. But he heard nothing except for hundreds of thousands of pounds of steel barreling down on them.

"Let's go!" he shouted again, glancing over his shoulder. But he saw nothing. He looked again. The train was gone, and so was Chris.

"Ugh!" Drew sat straight up on the bed, sweating and panting like he had really been running for his life. His heart pounded so hard he felt it in his toes. He looked around as his eyes began to focus in the dimly lit hotel room. The only light in the room was daylight glowing around the perimeter of the drapes.

"Look who's finally awake," Vicki said as she approached the bed. The hotel bathrobe hung off her right shoulder, exposing most of her breast. She crawled onto the bed and straddled his lap. "Now we can start back up where we left off before you passed out." She sucked on his bottom lip and fiddled with his belt buckle.

"What? Whoa. Wait. Stop." Drew lifted her off his lap and scrambled to his feet, holding his spinning head. "What time is it?"

"Elevenish."

"Shit! What was in that pill you gave me?"

"Not sure." She shrugged. "But don't worry. It's all natural. How do you feel?"

"I feel like this can't be happening. Did we... have sex?" he whispered.

"Not yet." She licked her lips as she, all at once, slid out of the robe and off the bed. Putting her arms around his waist, she pressed her naked body against him and pulled up the back of his T-shirt.

"Stop." He pushed her away, more forcefully than before, and she fell back on the bed.

"Hey! What's your problem!"

"Vicki, I'm married."

"Is that what you're worried about? I don't care. I'm married too." She stood up again and stepped toward him. He stepped back.

"I gotta go," he said and flew out the door as she hurled obscenities and insults at his back. He ducked into the nearest stairwell and climbed the stairs two by two, but getting away from Vicki brought him little relief knowing the wrath that awaited.

Back in his own room, Drew plugged in his lifeless cell phone and pulled the hotel phone closer. His stomach churned as the wheels turned in his head, trying to think of how to explain missing his flight home. *Hey babe, funny story. After you left Miami to make sure you'd be home when the kids woke up, I got myself drugged by a groupie—again—and I overslept.*

He sighed as he dialed.

"Hello," April answered before the first ring. Her voice was strange, raspy, like she had just woken up, but she should have been up with the kids for hours by now.

"Babe? It's me."

"Drew! Where have you been? I've been calling you all morning!"

He had planned to tell her the truth. It was a promise he made and had kept since they first started dating fourteen years ago. It was better if she heard tales from the road directly from him before they got stretched and embellished beyond recognition by third, fourth, and hundredth parties. And there was no way his exit from the suite with Vicki in the wee hours of the morning went unnoticed. But April sounded like she was on the verge of hysterics.

"What's wrong! Are you okay? Are the kids... okay?"

His cell phone buzzed to life, then. All the missed text messages and voicemails came through back-to-back, causing the phone to vibrate relentlessly off the nightstand and onto the floor.

"Drew." Her voice cracked. He could almost feel her trembling through the phone. "Chris and Randy... they're dead," she sobbed. "Where were you? I thought you were with them. You're always with them."

"I'm sorry, baby. I ran into an old friend. We got to talking. I overslept. My phone died. I missed my flight," he said, deciding a watered-down version of last night's events would do until he got home. He hadn't heard what she said. He couldn't hear what she said.

"Drew! Are you listening!" she shrieked through her sobbing. "There was an accident. Chris and Randy were killed last night!"

He sat on the bed, trying to listen to his wife tell him what details she knew about the accident. He didn't catch everything she said. His mind reeled with flashes of memories from the night before: The concert, "They were going too fast," the party, "Chris and Travis pulled Mike out," the balcony, "it caught fire," his last conversation with Chris, "Chris went back to get Randy out," bits and pieces of what happened with Vicki, the dream, "Explosion."

Drew's body went numb. He could control his words and movements, but he couldn't feel anything.

"Where are Mike and Travis?" he asked.

"They're at the University Hospital," she said. "Drew, I'm flying back down."

"Yeah, yeah. Okay," he said, but he didn't recognize his voice. He passed his hand over his face and pulled it away quickly. He stared, confused and disoriented by his wet palm glistening in the sunlight streaming into the room. The robot was crying.

Chapter 3

Los Angeles, California
2010

"You both look amazing this evening, absolutely stunning," Lena Rocha from *Rolling Stone* gushed. "Who are you wearing?" she asked, sticking a microphone in Drew's face.

He glanced at it, then looked over at the crowd, his attention snatched away by someone yelling his name. The corners of his mouth curved up, belying the sorrow in his eyes. He gave a head nod as he held his hand up in an odd half wave, half salute gesture, triggering a flurry of screams.

"WE LOVE YOU, DREW!!!!" a voice squealed as the reporter waited for an answer, shifting from one sparkly stiletto shimmering against the red carpet to the other.

"We're both wearing Dolce and Gabbana," April said, jumping in to save the day, like she had been doing from the minute they stepped out of the limo, really from when she came back to Miami to bring him home.

"Thanks, April. You both look positively stunning tonight," Lena reiterated. "So, Drew," she said, bringing his attention back to her mic. "I'm sure this is, um, pretty bittersweet, being here at the Grammys tonight. Most people think Wiretap is a shoo-in for Album of the Year and you for Song of the Year, and you'll also have your first Grammy performance. That's pretty much the pinnacle for any recording artist. But I can't imagine how hard it is to be here after experiencing such a devastating loss less than two months ago. I mean, the drummer and bass player are, inarguably, the backbone of any band. Can you tell us what's going through your mind right now?"

Drew locked eyes with Lena. For a fraction of a second, she looked afraid. He was far from an interviewer's dream before the accident. Since then, his reputation as a "temperamental artist" had reached new heights. He was unpredictable. No one knew how, or if, he would respond to even routine questions, not even him.

Drew sighed and transferred his glower to April. *She didn't even say their names*, he thought. April gave him an encouraging smile as she made a heart shape on his lower back with her finger. Then she tilted his head down gently to her lips and kissed the side of his face close to his ear. "It's *Rolling Stone*. Be nice. We don't have much farther," she whispered quickly.

He sighed again. "I'm thinking that I would give all this up in a second, if I could have my friends back," he said. Then he remembered what his manager said: "Be as dark as you want, but always end with light."

Drew smiled. "I'm also thinking that Randy and Chris would look way better in this tux than I do," he said and managed to produce a noise resembling a chuckle.

April smiled, nodding vigorously. "They definitely would!" she giggled.

"Well, thanks, Drew, April. And good luck tonight!" she called out as they walked away.

"You did good, baby," April said as they entered the Staples Center.

Once inside, a production assistant and an intern greeted them. Drew kissed April goodbye and the intern whisked her off to the VIP reception area. The production assistant and a security guard escorted Drew back to the band's dressing room where Travis and Mike waited with their management team. Wiretap wouldn't perform until the end of the show, but they needed to meet with the production assistant to go over the logistics one last time.

"How'd you do?" Mike asked after the PA and their managers left the dressing room.

Drew shook his head. "Not great. If April hadn't been there..."

"I'm sorry we couldn't walk with you, man," Travis said, looking down at the floor. He rarely made eye contact anymore. Since the accident, he showed signs of post-traumatic stress disorder; large crowds freaked him out. The red carpet was out of the question. There would be no VIP reception or afterparties for him either.

Mike limped over to his guitar. He had injured his tailbone and fractured his arm when the car flipped. The performance was going to be painful for him in every way. But he was lucky. He was unconscious when Chris and Travis dragged him from the car. He didn't see what Travis had.

"You guys wanna run through it again before the show starts?" Mike asked as he carefully lowered himself onto a chair.

"Sure," Drew said, even though they never rehearsed right before a show. After sound check, they usually busied themselves doing whatever they needed to do as individuals to prepare for their performance. Then, right before showtime, they all sat backstage with their road crew, busting each other's chops and generally cutting up. The three of them alone in that dressing room made Chris and Randy's absence even more unbearable. The void needed to be filled with something; music was the obvious choice.

Drew handed Chris's tambourine to Travis as Mike pulled out one of Randy's guitar picks and began playing the intro of the acoustic arrangement of their song, "Force Field." There would be no light show, no smoke, and no backup musicians. Without their drummer and bass guitarist, acoustically was the only way they could perform. It was the only way they would perform—three musicians, three instruments, and two empty stools.

A few months later

"Drew, honey, I can see you have your heart set on disengagement today, but you have visitors," April said flatly as she flung open their bedroom curtains. "Hey look, babe, it's daytime outside!" she said sarcastically.

He winced as light flooded the room. "I'm not expecting anybody."

"Oh, I think you were very much expecting these visitors, Drew."

"Tell 'em to go away."

April narrowed her eyes. "Am I your secretary now, Mr. Simon? Can I get you a cup of coffee too?"

"Sorry, April. Shit. I don't wanna see anybody. Tell them to fuck off... please."

She continued glaring at him, shaking her head. "I will not say that to Mike and Travis. Besides, from the looks on their faces, they're not going anywhere until they talk to you—or see your head on a stake. So, get up."

"Fine!" he growled, and he threw the covers off.

"And please do us all a favor and jump in the shower before you come downstairs. You're starting to smell like a zoo animal," she said as she scooped up from the floor the sweatpants and T-shirt he had been wearing for five days. Before he could protest, she darted out of the room so fast her hair billowed behind her like a shiny blond cape.

He sat on the side of the bed for a few minutes grumbling obscenities under his breath, then he yawned and stretched. A blast of what April was talking about hit him in the face. "Whoa."

The shower did some good. Drew headed down to greet his uninvited guests, feeling a little more human, or at least smelling a little more human.

"What's up, guys?" Drew asked as he plopped down on the sofa.

Mike pinched the skin between his eyes. "Unbelievable."

"What's up, guys?" Travis said slowly. "That's all you have to say to us?"

"We waited for you for two hours," Mike snarled, his nostrils flared wide enough to drive a truck through them.

Drew hung his head and focused on a loose string hanging from his ratty old sweatpants.

"All you had to do was sit there. You didn't even have to talk, but you have to show up when the record label calls a meeting, Drew," Travis said.

"What did they say?" Drew asked without looking up.

Mike stepped toward him. "You fucking son of—"

Drew looked up as Travis blocked Mike with his body. "It was a quick meeting. Mel said to tell you that if you don't get your shit together, like pick another drummer and bass player and get your ass back in the studio, he's gonna drop us from the label," Travis said as he pushed Mike several feet back.

For a second, Drew thought he was dreaming because there had never been a time when Travis could move Mike. Travis was the smallest guy in the group. He wasn't a weakling; he could hold his own. But Mike was the biggest guy in the group, not fat, but broad and thick. Drew studied his friends, trying to make sense of what had just happened. Then he saw it. Travis had bulked up significantly since the last time he had seen him. A flashback popped into Drew's head of the severe panic attack Travis had at the hospital after the accident. Between gasps for air, he kept saying, "If I was stronger, I could have gotten Mike out by myself... Chris would have had more time to get Randy out before, before..."

"Maybe dropping us isn't a bad idea," Drew said, twisting the scraggly hairs growing along his cheek.

Mike opened his mouth to speak, but nothing came out. He threw his hands up instead as he turned a concerning shade of red. If he had been a cartoon character, smoke would have been pouring out of his ears.

"After all that work we put in to get a record deal, you just wanna throw it all away?" Travis said. He appeared considerably calmer than Mike, but only half a shade less angry. "You don't really think they would want this, do you? Chris started talking to me about making a band when we were in third grade. We owe it to him, to keep his dream alive, even if he isn't—especially since he isn't. He was your best friend, man."

"He wasn't my best friend! He was my brother! And Randy was my brother! I can't look over my shoulder and see some random dudes on drums and bass! They were my family," Drew sobbed. "They can't be replaced."

The guys stood quietly, giving their silent permission for Drew to finally break down, something they had never seen him do. Instead, he sucked in a gulp of air and held it, cutting off the tears before they had a chance to fall, a survival technique he learned as a kid to stop himself from crying. It came in handy when his father ordered him to "quit your blubbering before I give you something to really cry about."

Drew looked up at Mike and Travis again. Mike must have been hitting the gym as hard as Travis. He looked good too. They had both been working hard to recover from their injuries—physical and mental. And they were eager to move forward with their lives and keep hold of the success that was quickly slipping from their hands. They needed him to push through the pain and lead the way. They needed *The Droid* back.

He dropped his gaze to the floor. He wasn't involved in the accident, but he had been paralyzed by it, by the grief and the guilt. "We moved around so much when I was a kid, I never really knew any family outside of my parents and my sister," he said. "And I never had any friends longer than a year or two before my dad got reassigned. But then he retired, we moved to Jersey, and everything changed. Chris was my first real friend. And now he's gone. Randy's gone. My mom's gone. So, what's the point?"

Mike moved toward Drew. Travis grabbed his arm, but he yanked it back and continued his approach. "The point is, we're your brothers too." Mike clamped his hand on Drew's shoulder. "And we're not dead—neither are you. Mel rescheduled the meeting for the day after tomorrow. I'll pick you up. Be ready at noon," he said, jabbing his finger into Drew's chest. Then he walked out.

Travis gripped Drew's shoulder, then followed Mike's path out of the door.

In the quiet of their absence, the desire to go back to bed came on strong, but not strong enough to convince his body to move.

"You're depressed," April said, appearing out of nowhere. She sat next to him.

He nodded. "Yeah."

"What are you going to do about it?"

He shrugged. "What do you think I should do?"

"You need to go back to Dr. Lee."

He shook his head slowly. "That didn't help when my mom died."

"Sure it did."

"I was still sad. It's been eight years and I'm still sad," he said quietly, staring at the vacuum lines in the carpet.

"Of course you're sad. You loved her. She loved you. Your mother was a tremendous force in your life." She ran her fingers through his damp hair. "You inherited so many wonderful things from her. Unfortunately, you got her sadness too, the kind that holds you to the bed for days at a time." She placed her hand on his. "It's time to see a doctor, Drew."

"I'll think about it."

"I also want us to go back to marriage counseling."

He furrowed his brow. "I'm sorry about earlier. I'm not mad at you for letting Travis and Mike in here." He lifted her hand and kissed it.

She tilted her head. "This isn't about you being mad at me, Drew. This is about you lying to me."

He sighed. "What are you talkin' about, April?"

She pulled his cell phone out of her pocket. "You got a text," she said, handing him the phone. "It was in your dirty sweatpants."

The message glowed on the screen.

Hi Drew. I've wanted to reach out to u for 6 months now but I didn't know what to say. I just hope ur doing ok and I'm truly sorry 4 what I did that night in Miami. Please believe I wasn't trying to drug u. I only wanted u to relax a little bit so we could enjoy our special night together. FYI ur lips are as sweet on my tongue as ur name. Love always, Vicki

Drew winced and blew out a long hissing breath. "It's not what you think."

"I think you ran into the subject of all your teenage wet dreams. I think you made out. I think she gave you something. I think you took it even though you know better than that. I think you passed out. I think you know that I would think those details were important. And I think you lied to me about what happened that night."

"I'm sorry, April," he said. "I swear. Nothing happened with me and Vicki," he insisted. "We don't need to go to marriage counseling again."

She frowned. "My dad was a guitar player, Drew. I know what happens on the road. And I grew up watching my mother get eaten alive by jealousy and suspicion. Losing her mind over his whereabouts and his 'what's he done nows,' his 'who's he done nows.' When I read that text, I felt like my mom. I wanted to kill you, and it scared me. We need to go back to counseling. Will you think about that too? Please?"

"Sure, babe. I'll think about it," he said and kissed her cheek.

That conversation was all the motivation he needed to heave himself off the sofa. He left her sitting there and trudged back up the stairs just as their eight-year-old son came barreling down, almost plowing into him.

"Slow down, Zach!" Drew barked, catching his upper arm.

"Sorry, Dad," Zach said, flashing a sheepish grin. His chubby, cherubic cheeks turned bright pink.

"Goin' out to practice shooting?"

Zach nodded.

Drew smirked as he snatched the basketball wedged under Zach's arm and spun it on his finger. "Looks like you need to work on your offense too, dude."

"Whoa, Dad! I didn't know you could do that! Will you teach me?"

"Sure," he said as he tousled his son's curly blond hair. "Let me change first."

"Sweet! Meet you outside!"

Drew smiled as he continued up the stairs and into the bedroom. He took off his pants and T-shirt and placed them neatly back on the shelf in his closet. Then he grabbed a basketball jersey and shorts as April's voice singing their clean up song floated into the room followed by the squeals and giggles of their four-year-old daughter and hard toys crashing into plastic bins. He sat on the bed and sucked in a ragged breath. Then the sound of Zach dribbling out back joined the noise from down the hall, getting louder and louder with every bounce, and his heart pounded harder and harder each time the ball hit the concrete slab. Dizziness set in as his breathing became more labored, so he lay down and closed his eyes for a minute. When he opened them again, the room was dark and quiet except for the gentle snoring coming from April way on the other side of their king-sized bed. He closed his eyes again, picturing the small efficiency they lived in when they first got married, wishing he could smell the fresh baked bread wafting up from the sub shop below. They slept in each other's arms in a tiny, full-sized bed back then. But they wouldn't have chosen to sleep any other way, even if they could. Drew stretched out his arm and sighed. He couldn't reach her. She was so far away.

Chapter 4

New York City
2018

Drew rolled his guitar pick over his knuckles and back again like a coin to give his fingers something to do while he baked under the heat of the studio lights, waiting for the next cue. The new gig was great. He had hit it off with the other guys in the house band right away, and he was getting used to the smaller audience, but the constant starts and stops made him antsy. Eight years away from the stage had taught him that it only took a moment of sitting still for thoughts of everything—and everyone—he had lost to creep in. He needed to let it rip and lose himself in the music to keep those thoughts from taking over.

"It's getting more and more bizarre, guys. I wake up in the morning these days like it's back in the day after a wild night. I got one eye open, looking at the news like 'what's the damage?' bracing myself to see what ridiculous tweet the orange creamsicle posted overnight," said Reid Cox, host of the *Latest Late Show*.

Chuckles reverberated through the audience.

"All I know is that in '08, everybody was like, yes! Yes! Yes, we can! Hip hip hooray! Anybody can be president! And then in 2016 it was like, weeelllll maybe not *anybody…*"

The audience burst into raucous laughter and applause.

"And I never needed America to be great, by the way. But I'm keepin' my fingers crossed that in 2018, it'll start makin' some sense again. Wha'dya think, Drew?"

"Don't hold your breath!" Drew shouted—like they had rehearsed—from his perch on the bandstand over the applause and cheers.

"Ha! Good advice! Look, we have a great show planned for you tonight. It's Ladies' Night! Since we have an audience full of smokin' hot chicks, I think it's only fitting we give you beautiful ladies a show you won't ever forget," Reid said, unbuttoning his shirt as Drew and the other members of the show's house band played Def Leppard's "Pour Some Sugar on Me." He took it off and flung it out into the audience. Women dove for it like it was a bridal bouquet. Then he stripped down to his red silk boxers. The audience screamed and shrieked. Some of the women threw dollars at him as he danced around like he was auditioning for *Magic Mike, III.* Suddenly, he stopped and the music also stumbled to a halt.

"Hey! You guys aren't gonna let me be naked out here by myself, are you?" He gestured toward the band. They all shrugged and looked around at each other. Then they ripped off their shirts and resumed the song. The women in the audience nearly blew the roof off the building, a few of them screaming at levels only dogs could hear.

Reid clapped and whistled along with them. "We have a great show for you ladies tonight. Nothin' but sexy men as far as the eye can see. Dwayne 'The Rock' Johnson, Kevin Hart, Hugh Jackman, and when we come back EJ Wallace is in the hooousssse!!!!! So, sit tight. Don't pass out. And no matter what you do, don't change that channel," he said, pointing straight at Camera 2. "We'll be right back!"

Reid danced toward the back curtain as the band increased the volume into the commercial break.

"And we're at commercial," Shanice, the producer, announced in Drew's earpiece as Reid rushed over from the left.

"Hey, man, when EJ comes out, can you guys play some stuff from his first album?" Reid asked as he slipped his pants back on. "The old stuff is way more hype than his recent stuff."

"Don't even think about it," Shanice said in the earpiece. Reid had an earpiece too, but he stared at Drew with a blank expression like she had never spoken.

"I can't do that, Reid. Shanice will murder me if I go off script," Drew said, giving Reid a quick head nod and a thumbs up he was confident she couldn't see.

Reid mouthed "Yes!" as he gave Drew a discreet fist bump. Then he darted backstage. Drew chuckled. Reid was five years older than him, nearly forty-five, and, other than a few gray strands in his sand-colored hair and some creases around his eyes that stuck around even when he wasn't laughing, he was still the same big kid he was when they met on the road twenty years before.

Once upon a time, Reid sang lead in a band from Arizona called Red Rover's Revenge. Wiretap opened for them a few times in the early years before their stars took off in different directions. Red Rover was Nu Metal, whereas Wiretap sat nestled in the middle of the vast spectrum of rock music, the sweet spot, freely drawing elements from both ends.

Drew met Shanice's glare from across the studio. She shook her head, adding emphasis to the displeasure conveyed by the death stare. But her curly afro didn't move a centimeter, her hair a physical manifestation of her unyielding conviction.

Drew flashed a grin. "What? I told him no."

"Whatever, Drew. Do I look stupid to you?" Drew opened his mouth to reply. "Don't answer that. Why can't we just get through a show without any of these little last-minute changes?"

"You know Reid likes to be spontaneous, read the crowd. He thinks it makes things interesting," he said, at the risk of annoying her further by answering another one of her rhetorical questions.

"No, it makes things messy and a nightmare to edit," she said through clenched teeth. "Enough goes wrong around here without people deliberately throwing a monkey wrench into the machine just for kicks and giggles. And if I may remind you both, the network doesn't have to renew us for a second season."

"Lighten up, Shanice," Reid said. "This is a rock 'n' roll show. People like their rock 'n' roll a little messy." He stepped out from behind the curtain and took his position on the platform with the chairs and couch where he interviewed his guests. The audience squealed with delight at the return of their bare-chested host.

Shanice rolled her eyes and threw up a hand signal to the light crew, then another to the sound techs. Drew shook his head, then told the other guys in the band about the change of plan for EJ's intro. They all shrugged and said, "Cool."

Drew smiled. He loved working with good musicians. They know how to go with the flow. And he was thankful every day that he had been smart enough to agree to do the show when Reid approached him a year ago. "It's gonna be rock 'n' roll madness, dude. Nothin' like those other late-night shows. I'm never wearin' a suit or sittin' behind a desk," Reid had said.

Drew was ninety-nine percent sold at "rock 'n' roll madness." But along with a ridiculously high salary and a promise they would only have to work four days a week, it was an offer he could not refuse. He was almost out of money. And this might have been his last chance to get back out there before the world completely forgot who he was. For the first time in a long time, Drew let himself believe he could put his life back together.

"Go," Shanice said.

Reid clapped. "Okay, alright, okay, alright! How are my lovely ladies doing!" The audience roared. "Are you ready for your first piece of eye candy! Put your hands together for multi-platinum, Grammy award-winning recording artist and producer, founder and CEO of Python Records, the hottest urban music company in the world, and my good friend, EJ Wallaaaace!"

EJ emerged from behind the curtain, shirtless, doing his own *Magic Mike* audition to his group, Latitude's, first number one hit, "Tripped Up." He got really into it, making his intro closer to sixty seconds than the agreed-upon fifteen as he descended upon the audience and two women jumped up from their front row seats and took turns grinding on him in the aisle. The details of the tattoo on his back were hard to make out against his brown skin from where Drew sat, but it was common knowledge the snake across his upper back was a python. As it rippled and bucked along with EJ whenever he flexed his traps and delts, the audience lost their minds. So did Shanice—for different reasons.

When EJ finally made his way over to the couches, he was sweating and out of breath. Reid was almost doubled over, clapping and laughing. He greeted EJ with a bro-hug before they sat.

"Okay, man. I have plenty of collarless shirts, but I don't think I've ever had a shirtless collar," Reid said, pointing at the white collar and purple bowtie encircling EJ's neck.

"You don't have one of these, man?" EJ asked. "Here, take mine." He pulled off the collar and handed it to Reid. The Velcro breaking apart made a loud ripping sound in the mic that was securely tucked in the black band around his upper arm.

"Aw, thanks, guy," Reid said as he put on the collar. "Well, I guess if this music thing falls through you can definitely be a stripper! You looked like you really knew what you were doing out there, man."

"Ha! There's a stripper in all of us! I may or may not have danced like that in my bedroom to that same song last night," he said, rubbing his chin. "I dunno. I'm gettin' old. I can't remember stuff." He smirked.

"Getting old, eh? You're lookin' pretty good for an old guy. Hey, what do you think they would call you? What's your stripper name?"

"Hmmmm," EJ hummed, rubbing his chin again. "It's clearly gonna be Chocolate something. Hot Chocolate? Chocolate Chip?" he suggested with a laugh. "Chocolate Thunda'!" he blurted out with a finger snap.

"Those are good ones! Maybe not 'Chocolate Chip' though."

"Yeah, that one can go," EJ agreed. "What would yours be?"

"Psshh, I don't know... Pasty White Boy?" Reid chuckled.

"Ha! That's hot!"

"I heard some years ago that to get your stripper name, all you have to do is put the name of your first pet with the street you grew up on."

"Okay, okay, then mine is Momo Birdsong," EJ said proudly. Reid and the audience burst into laughter.

"Oh, that's awful, but I think I have you beat for the worst stripper name. Mine would be 'Fishy Cummings!'"

"Ewwwww!" exclaimed EJ along with the audience, then they laughed hysterically again.

"Let's move on from the stripper talk now," Shanice said into the earpiece. "Take a commercial break. Then start fresh. Perhaps ask him something from the list of topics we agreed upon," she suggested with a tone of manufactured sweetness.

Reid patted the arm of his chair twice, which meant, "Got it."

"We're gonna take a commercial break. When we come back, I wanna talk about the new movie, the new wife, and any new music you have coming down the pike."

Shanice signaled the sound guy to cut Reid's and EJ's microphones off as the band played "Tripped Up."

"Okay, Reid, you and EJ ready?"

Reid tapped his chair, and Shanice signaled the sound guy to turn on the mics. Recognizing the cue, Drew cut the music.

"Go," Shanice said.

"So, EJ, you're a big movie star now?"

"Nah, man. I wouldn't say all that. I just got lucky and somehow this chance kinda fell in my lap. The only acting I had ever done was in music videos. I'm in no danger of an Oscar nod, but it's an excellent movie. The director and the real movie stars made sure of that."

"Wow, that's cool, man. What's it called? What's it about?"

"It's called *Homecoming*. And it's pretty much a comedy about a group of old college friends that meet up at their homecoming about twenty years after they graduate. They basically cast off their worries and life struggles to relive their wild college days over the course of one night. And things get wild, man."

"That sounds cool. You brought us a clip, right? Why don't you set it up for us?"

"Yeah, so, in this clip, my character is debating with his buddy about whether he should hook up with his college girlfriend. This part in particular is of me role playing with my buddy tryin' out different excuses he could tell his wife."

"Roll the clip," Reid said, looking up at the sound booth.

"Dude! That was funny!" Reid gushed after the clip had played on the drop-down screen and the audience's laughter died down. "I can't wait to see it. So, have you ever done that? Hooked up with an ex like that?"

"Uh, hell no! Not like that!" EJ swiped his hand across his neck, shaking his head. "You tryna get me killed, man?" he said, laughing as he reared back and playfully punched Reid's shoulder.

"Ha! No, no, no, I mean, you know, pre-marriage. Because you recently got married, right? To your lovely wife, Maya? Isn't her group on your label?"

"Yep, yep, that's my queen. She and her girls are in my double platinum club." He beamed. "And, for the record, she's the only ex I've ever hooked up with," he said, looking directly into the camera with a serious, wide-eyed expression, earning chuckles from the audience. "We got married a couple of months ago. Now we gettin' down with this happily ever after thing."

A wave of "awws" and applause spread across the audience.

"That *is* adorable." Reid nodded in agreement with his audience. "So, what's next for you, E? More movies? Space travel?"

EJ laughed. "I haven't gotten any more movie calls, so I'm just doin' my day job. Been back in the studio workin' on a reunion album."

Reid's mouth popped open. "Are you serious? Latitude's back together?"

"Yep, we been in the studio writin' and playin' and singin', just like old times. It's like we never stopped, you know?"

"Well, you heard it here first, ladies. One of *the* best hip-hop groups in the world is back in the lab, mixin' up something explosive, I'm sure. Will you come back with the rest of the fellas when you drop the album?" Reid asked eagerly, on the verge of drooling.

"Of course. No doubt."

"Awesome! Maybe, in the meantime, we can get you back on to jam with Drew and the boys over there sometime too."

EJ raised his eyebrows. "That's what's up. I would love that. I mean, if that's cool with Drew."

Drew sat motionless, awestruck. EJ Wallace was one of the most talented musicians in the world and an even better producer. His record label represented dozens of platinum artists, and his wife's group had plenty of company in his double platinum club as well. It was like everything he touched turned to gold—no, platinum. Drew had only talked to him once briefly at an industry party years ago. He remembered EJ being a cool guy. He had answered all the fanboy questions Drew fired at him about how he went from being a music industry puppet to one of the biggest puppeteers in the business. But he never would have imagined that EJ would be interested in playing with him and his little late-night talk show house band.

"Your mic is on, Drew, if you wanna say something. But if not, you might wanna go ahead and close your mouth," Shanice teased in his ear.

"I'd be honored," Drew managed to say in a reasonably even tone, despite how fast his head was spinning.

"Yes!" Reid said. "Thanks again, E." He shook EJ's hand. "Everybody, go see *Homecoming* this Friday! Hilarious movie! We'll be right back with Dwayne Johnson and Kevin Hart."

Chapter 5

"Good work, guys," said Brad Schwartz, the musical director of *The Latest*, as he approached Drew and his sax player, Javier Torres, backstage after they finished taping the show. "You fellas amaze me," he said, passing them. Then he disappeared around a corner.

"Phew! I thought he was gonna say we have to record the last segment again," Javi said. "My timing was off a little during the foosball tournament after that lady took her shirt off."

"That's one perk of having a musical director who's never played an instrument," Drew said. "His ear doesn't hear those subtle mistakes like we do."

Javi cast his eyes downward. "Yeah, I guess," he mumbled to the floor.

Drew gave Javi's shoulder a shake. "Look, man. It happens to everybody. If you feel like you're off, don't panic. It only makes things worse. All you have to do is remember to listen to Barry's kick drum. He's super solid; nothing rattles him."

Javi nodded, but he didn't look convinced. He was a young musical phenom Reid had found on social media. Having played more by himself for his video camera, he didn't have much experience performing with a band for live audiences. He had been a lot more than a "little off," but Drew refused to rake him over the coals for it. The kid was already beating himself up over his mistakes, and he was confident Javi would do whatever he needed to do to make sure it didn't happen again.

Drew gave Javi a pat on the back. "Okay. Go on and get outta here. I'll see you tomorrow."

Javi headed to the exit, and Drew headed in the opposite direction toward his dressing room. He turned the corner and EJ appeared, fully dressed, with his bodyguard and a production assistant.

"Oh, good! There you are," said Terrance, the PA. "When you weren't in your dressing room, I was afraid you had slipped out. Mr. Wallace wanted to talk to you before he left."

Drew's heart kicked into overdrive, and his head started doing that spinning thing again. *Dude, be cool.*

"Really? I didn't know you were still here. Most people cut out right after they finish their segment. What's up?" Drew asked, trying hard to sound nonchalant.

"I just wanted to tell you I really like what y'all are doin' up in here," EJ said. "This show is like a big party, man. I had a blast."

"Thanks. Reid's a good host. He likes to go against the grain, and he's made it his mission to make this show different from other late-night guys."

"Oh, I definitely see that! I tell him all the time he's hilarious, but to tell you the truth, you're the reason I really watch the show. You're one hell of a musician, bruh. I told Reid he needs to convince you to sing sometime. Your ratings would go through the roof. This white boy can sing his ass off!" EJ nudged his bodyguard with his elbow.

Drew's heart stopped racing, and he was pretty sure it had stopped all together. "Wow, thanks. That's um, uh—"

"I wasn't playin' when I said I'd come back and sit in with y'all... but if that falls through, why don't you come through the studio sometime?"

Suddenly everything went dark, like someone had accidentally shut the lights off. Drew thought for a moment he had passed out until he realized he was still on his feet, and that someone standing very close behind him had covered his eyes. Then a familiar giggle floated into his ears. He looked over his shoulder to see April's mischievous grin.

"Hey, babe." She kissed his cheek. "Hello," she said to EJ then shot a bug-eyed look at Drew.

"Oh, um, yeah, EJ, this is my, um, my... April."

She smiled. "Hi. I'm Drew's ex-wife," she said, pushing Drew out of her way to offer EJ her hand. "I really enjoyed your segment, and I looove your music."

"Thanks. Thank you, Miss April. I really appreciate that," EJ said, shaking her hand.

April blushed. "I'm sorry to intrude on your conversation. Drew, I can wait for you out front," she offered, sticking her thumb out toward the stage. But she didn't take a single step or her eyes off EJ.

"No, no, no, you're not intruding," EJ said. "I gotta bounce anyway." He handed a card to Drew. "Hit me up sometime."

Drew took the plain black card and read it carefully, although there wasn't much to read. It didn't even have a name on it, only a telephone number.

EJ placed a gentle hand on April's upper arm. "It was nice to meet you," he said. Then Terrance led him and his bodyguard to the exit.

"You too," April said as her eyes followed EJ until he disappeared around the corner. "Damn." She whistled out a long breath. "Too bad he put his shirt back on."

That remark pulled Drew's attention away from the business card. "You need a fresh pair of panties, April?" he snarled, looking her up and down.

"No, I do not, Andrew. Do you? Surely, you pooped your pants at some point during that conversation with your man crush," she said with a furrowed brow, but he had already lost interest.

"Have you ever been complimented by an icon?" he asked, staring at the little black card again.

She reached up and caressed his cheek. "I'd like to think so."

"Did you hear him, April? He said I was one hell of a musician and invited me to his studio!" he blurted out, no longer able to contain himself.

"I know! And he gave you his number!" She snatched the card from him and ogled the single line of text. "That means he wasn't blowing smoke up your butt!" she squealed and threw her arms around him.

Drew exhaled, finally. April's hugs always relaxed him. The divorce had changed nothing in that regard; his body responded the same way it always had when she was in his presence.

"I take it you enjoyed the show," Drew said as he escorted April to his dressing room.

"Oh my God, Drew, that was fantastic!" She plopped down on his leather loveseat, paying no attention to the pile of dirty clothes that occupied one cushion. "Thank you so much for getting us tickets. My sister told me to tell you thank you from the bottom of her vagina!" She laughed.

"Egh! Gross," he said, laughing too. "Tell her I said no problem. And thank *you*, April, for letting your sister take her top off. My sax player nearly lost his shit and now he wants to kill himself."

"Oh no!" she gasped. "Poor guy. I'm sorry about that, Drew, but you know I can't control Jennifer."

Drew shook his head. "Where's Crazy now, anyway?"

"Reid offered to give her a private tour. I assume she's off somewhere molesting him right about now."

"Some things never change. So... what'd you really think about the show?" he asked, gnawing on a fingernail. Another thing that hadn't changed since the divorce was how much he valued her opinion.

"It was a good show, Drew. I'm serious. I don't think you missed a single cue. Your timing was spot on. You're really getting the hang of this."

"Thanks, April, I—"

A knock at the door cut him off.

"That's probably Jen. Come in!"

"Ha! Not a chance," April said as Shanice walked in.

"Drew, here're the songs for next week." She handed him a folder. "You want me to go ahead and throw this in the trash?" she said without missing a beat. She pursed her lips tightly, then she glanced over at the couch. "Oh! April! Hey, girl! My bad. I didn't realize you were in here." She went over for a hug. "Did you enjoy the show?"

"You know I did!"

"Hey, Shanice? Sorry about earlier," Drew said, even though he wasn't really sorry for going along with Reid's last-minute changes to the set list. Things like that happened all the time, especially with Reid. He was a born entertainer and while he was a tremendously talented and serious musician, his greatest strength was his instinct. He always played what he felt the audience needed to hear. Shanice was the opposite. She lived for lists, schedules, and predictability. She worked hard to keep things running smoothly around there. Some remorse always crept in when things didn't work out the way she planned, especially if he had something to do with it.

Shanice glared at Drew. He braced himself, fully prepared for her to read him the riot act, but her expression switched to a pleasant smile.

She waved her hand. "Oh, don't worry about it, Drew," she said, flashing a toothy grin. "It all turned out just fine."

Drew's eyebrows flew up, and he looked over his shoulder to see who she was talking to—and smiling at. Someone she actually liked.

"Hey, listen, Drew," she said, still smiling. "Did you think about what I asked you last week? My father called me today to find out if you had given me an answer yet."

"Oh. That's why you're acting weird. Yeah, I thought about it a little, but I haven't decided yet."

"Well, like I told you last week, you can call my dad if you have any questions. I gave you his number, right?"

He nodded.

"So, call him. You can ask him anything you want," she said. "Please promise me you'll seriously consider it, Drew. Everybody who does it says it's a life-changing experience."

Drew said he would think about it. Then Shanice gave April another hug and left.

"Shanice sounded like me when I tried to get you to try kale," April teased.

Drew chuckled. "Have you seen that genealogy show called *Bloodlines*?"

"Yeah, that's the show where they trace a celebrity's family tree back to Alexander Hamilton or Henry the VIII or something like that. It's interesting when they reveal family secrets or solve family mysteries. It can get kinda dark sometimes, but I like the little history lessons they give."

"Shanice's dad's the host. They want me to do the show."

"And you don't want to?"

"I dunno." He shrugged. "Part of me thinks it'd be cool. But it's not just about what I want. It's one thing to agree to let people dig into my personal business, but it's way more intense when you're talking about digging into my family history. They could find out something really embarrassing for all of us, you know?"

"Possibly, but you've always wanted to know more about your ancestors, especially on your mom's side. And since you can't talk to her and you *won't* talk to your dad, this would be a great way to satisfy that curiosity. I think it'll be good for you—and the kids."

"Psshh. The kids won't care. They're more interested in video games and their friends."

"You're wrong, Drew," she said, shaking her head. "Last week, out of the blue, Paige asked me a bunch of questions about your family. Questions I couldn't answer."

"Why didn't she call me?"

"Because of your son," she said with an eye roll. "Zach was in the kitchen making himself a snack when I told Paige to call you with her questions. He laughed and said, 'Dad doesn't know anything. And even if he did, it's not like he's gonna call her back.'"

Drew frowned. "Why would he say something like that?"

April sighed and looked down at her hands. "Do you really need me to answer that?"

Drew rested his elbows on his knees and hung his head. He didn't need April to answer. He already knew why Zach would say that—too many broken promises. And even though he had been making an effort to be a more active parent, he was afraid that at sixteen it was too little, too late with Zach.

"Hey, I didn't tell you that to make you feel bad," April said. "I just want you to see that being on *Bloodlines* could be a wonderful opportunity for you to connect with your family, past and present. But whether or not you do the show, you still need to talk to your son."

Drew nodded. "Maybe I'll come by this weekend."

"This weekend?" She bit her bottom lip. "We were planning to take the kids down the shore to see Tony's newest property... But I guess we don't have to take the kids."

"No." He waved his hands. "Don't change your plans. I can talk to Zach next week. That's my weekend anyway, right?"

"Are you sure?" she asked. Her lips puckered into a pout.

"Yeah." He cracked his neck. "I know how much the kids love going to see the houses before Tony guts them. Besides, I wouldn't want to interfere with my kids bonding with your fiancé," he said, forcing a smile.

April jumped up and attacked him with a barrage of kisses on his cheeks. "You are the best ex-husband a girl could ask for!" she said, pulling him up from the chair. "Now, let's go rescue Reid from my sister."

Chapter 6

Drew settled into his seat on the train headed uptown, comfortably camouflaged in his hoodie and dark shades between a gorgeous trans woman and "Dracula."

New York City is the perfect place to hide in plain sight. There were plenty of celebrities in the city, but there were even more regular people—many of them wearing distracting costumes. That is, if anyone paid any attention. With the rampant use of cell phones and ear buds, people didn't always notice other humans, unless they were trying to steal that cell phone or on fire—maybe.

"Hey, you wanna see that movie, *Homecoming,* this weekend?" A dark-haired, young millennial woman sitting across from him asked her friend. The friend also had dark hair, but the ends were turquoise.

"Neva heard of it," Turquoise said, without looking up from her phone.

"You haven't seen the trailer yet?" the first woman asked as she scrolled on her phone and shoved it into the Turquoise's line of vision. "Look who's all in it."

Drew watched the first woman try her best to get through an explanation of the plot and highlights from the trailer without laughing. By the end, they were both openly laughing, along with the passengers on either side of them.

"Okay. That sounds hilarious," Turquoise said.

"I know, right! I saw EJ Wallace on *The Latest* talkin' about it the other night."

Turquoise's forehead wrinkled. "*The Latest?*"

The first woman narrowed her eyes, shaking her head slowly. "Oh, my God! Do you do anything on that phone of yours besides read books on your Kindle app? You don't watch *The Latest*?"

"No. What the hell is it, Syd?"

The train wasn't too crowded for mid-morning and, by some stroke of luck, there was no train entertainer performing in that particular car. So, there wasn't anything to distract Drew from these young women's conversation. He listened intently, despite his ears being plugged with ear buds. He only wore them to discourage people from talking to him. But they were always silent when he roamed the streets.

Syd rolled her eyes. "*The Latest* is that new late-night talk show. But it's like, cooler and crazier than the other ones. You've heard of it. Reid Cox is the host. Drew Simon leads the band."

Turquoise's head jerked back. "How cool can it be? Reid Cox is like sixty! And I thought Drew Simon was dead."

Drew groaned silently as every muscle in his body seized up.

"Bitch, Drew Simon is NOT dead! Dudes that hot don't die!" They both giggled as they stood up.

The young women exited the train at the next stop and a young man entered—a young, dirty man. There were plenty of seats, but the man didn't take one. Instead, he stood in the center of the train and cleared his throat as the doors closed.

Okay. Here's the entertainment.

"Good afternoon, everybody," the man said. It was not afternoon. "My name is Grayson. I do not sing. I do not dance. I do not play a musical instrument. And I do not wish to take up too much of your time." Grayson might not have had any musical talent, but he had a deep, raspy voice that any 1920s jazz musician would have envied. It was as if his vocal cords were made of sandpaper.

"I am a straight, white, American male," he continued. Several of the passengers groaned, but no one looked up from their phones.

"Now, I can tell from your lack of enthusiasm that you are not all that interested in what I might have to say. I'm not surprised, me and my fellow white brethren are gettin' treated real bad lately. But I want you fine people to know that I'm just a white man fresh outta white privilege and I'm hungry as fuck!"

Before his big finish, he had already started making his way around the car with his baseball cap in hand. When he reached the trans woman next to Drew, he held out his hat.

"I know you better get that filthy, shit-smellin, nasty ass hat from out my mutha fukin' face before you wish you had. Ain't nobody neva gave me nothin', but I got a job. And I'll be damned if you'll get a dime of my hard-earned coins," she said and rolled her eyes back down to her phone.

The man simply nodded and moved his hat in front of Drew. Most of the people on the train were likely thinking along similar lines as the trans woman, but there was some change and a few dollars in the hat, nevertheless. Drew dropped in a twenty. First, because he thought the man had giant balls to stand up on a train mostly full of non-white people and say what he said. Second, because he didn't have anything smaller.

The man nodded again and started to move on, but he stopped and gazed at Drew, cocking his head. "I know you," he said, reaching for Drew's sunglasses.

Drew wrenched the man's wrist, twisting it upward. The man began blinking rapidly and breathing heavily. Drew dropped the man's wrist, but he didn't move. The train stopped, and a few passengers got on and off, including the trans woman, but the dirty man just stood there staring at Drew.

"What, man?" Drew barked.

"Some storms can go on for years. People talk about the eye of a storm being quiet and still. But when a storm rages for so long, it can have lots of eyes. That's a trick though, man. It's the devil makin' you think the storm is over so you'll drop your guard.

But it ain't over, not even close. It's only takin' a rest so it can start up again even stronger. One day, though, it'll end, and it'll be beautiful," he said, and immediately moved on to Dracula, who stared straight ahead at the condom ad across from him. The man moved down the line.

"What a weirdo," Dracula said under his breath.

Drew gave him a sideways glance and clamped his mouth shut to hold in a chuckle.

"Sorry I'm late." Drew's sister plopped down on the white wingback chair that would have been out of place in any other coffee shop in the world. But they were on the Upper West Side of New York City, and after that train ride with such an eclectic mix of humans, the shop was a different planet as far as Drew was concerned.

"That's okay, Lia." He leaned over the tiny table and kissed her cheek. "I know you're busy. Did your spin class run late or something?" he asked with a smirk.

"Shut up, Drew. It was Pilates, as a matter of fact," she said, returning his smirk.

"Well, whatever it was, it's paying off. You look good, sis."

"Thanks, big bro. I would return the compliment if I could actually see you. Don't you think the hoodie over the baseball cap in addition to the sunglasses is a bit overkill?" She raised her eyebrow. "Do you really think *that* many people in *this* neighborhood are going to recognize you?"

"Lia, Martha Stewart would say this place was too snobby. I'm not taking any chances that anyone will see me here," he said, pulling his baseball cap further down.

"Well, you are doing a fabulous job blending in, Vanilla Ice," she said as she slid her own sunglasses back to the crown of her blond-streaked, auburn head and placed her cell phone on the table in a position perfectly accessible to her eye and hand.

"Here you go!" sang their server, placing their beverages on the table. "Is there anything else I can get for you... Mr. Simon?" he whispered.

Lia snickered.

"No, thanks. We're good," Drew said quickly.

"Just let me know." The server giggled and skirted off.

"What is this?" Lia asked as she picked up her oversized coffee mug and took a sip. "Mmmm, that's good. How did you know what I get?"

Drew shrugged. "I told him to bring whatever organic, skinny, soy, almond milk, 'atte, 'ito, 'acchiato drink all the WASPs in yoga pants around here order." He chuckled and took a sip of his black coffee.

Lia narrowed her eyes. "Why did you want to meet today, Andrew?"

"Do I have to have a reason to see my baby sister?" he asked in an unusually high octave. "I haven't seen you for months."

Lia tilted her head and glared at him as she sipped her waspy hot beverage.

"Okay, fine. I was approached by the show *Bloodlines*. Do you know it?"

She nodded.

"They want me to be on it. And I wanna know what you think."

Lia placed her mug on the table, sat back, and folded her arms. She stared at Drew for several seconds, then she took a deep breath. "What do *you* think about it?"

Drew's eyes rolled up to the ceiling. That was the same thing their mother used to do when he went to her for advice. She always asked what he thought. It annoyed him at the time because he was used to his father issuing directives that were not to be questioned. He didn't realize until after she was gone that she was trying to teach him how to think for himself, not just follow orders.

"Come on, Lia," he said. "I really want to know what *you* think. It's your family too. And you never know what they'll uncover. If I decide to do it, I won't have any say about what information they put on the show or how they present it."

Lia smiled. "You always think about the worst-case scenario." She grazed his chin with the back of her finger. "You worry too much. Our family is chock-full of military going back before the Revolutionary War, from what Dad always told us. That's good stuff."

"Did you forget we know almost nothing about Mom's side of the family?"

"Okay. Maybe there's a tiny chance they find out one of our long-gone ancestors was a terrible person." She shrugged. "You don't really think something like that could overshadow all our family's brave servicemen and women, several who gave their lives for our country?"

"No, I guess not."

"So, to answer your question; I think it's great. You should do it." She gave his hand a squeeze. "But," she wrinkled her nose, "you're gonna have to talk to Dad first."

Drew rubbed his neck. "I know. I'm going to see him next."

Lia stopped mid-sip and put her mug down again. Her mouth hung open like it had become unhinged. "You're going down there? Physically?" she asked, incredulity swirling around her words. "And when was the last time you went home?"

Drew shrugged. "It's been a while."

"A while? If a decade qualifies as a while, then sure."

"It hasn't been that long," he balked.

"Yeah. It's been ten years. Susan threw that surprise party for Dad when he turned sixty. It was right before the 2008 election. Remember?"

Drew shifted in his seat, wishing he could forget arguing with his father halfway through the party about the one thing April had begged him not to discuss with his dad: politics. Neither of them would back down. The party ended quickly after that.

"Okay. It's been ten years, then," he conceded. "So, I'm due for a visit."

"You think?" she scoffed.

"You act like I haven't seen the man in ten years. I see him every Thanksgiving and Christmas at your house!"

She rolled her eyes. "Just don't do anything to piss him off, Drew."

"Since when do I have to *do* anything to piss him off?" he grumbled as Lia's phone vibrated. She picked it up and read the text message.

"Great," she groaned. "They canceled Lawson's tennis lesson today."

"You have to go, then?"

She pursed her lips. "No, of course not," she said as she shot off a text. "The nanny will get him, but she gets mad when she has to take Lawson to Corbin's swimming lessons. She can be a bit passive aggressive when she's mad. It's really annoying."

"Yeah. It's really annoying when nannies have genuine human emotions," he said.

She glared at him.

"How are my nephews anyway? Is Lawson a senator yet?"

"I know you're poking fun at me, Drew, but my Lawson is going to make an excellent senator one day. It's in his blood. Politics goes as far back in Peter's family as military service goes in ours. So, be prepared to cast your ballot for Lawson Billings in 2038." She poked his chest with her finger.

"Ow! Put that thing away!" He raised his hands. "I surrender. You don't have to punish me with an impromptu campaign rally."

They both laughed.

"But seriously, I'm proud of you, sis," he said. "You have a nice family. I admire the way you've been able to keep it all together and how much your boys love you." He looked down, fiddling with his coffee mug.

"Little boys love their mommas. And mommas love their little boys. You know where I learned that?" She lifted his chin with her finger. "From you and Mom."

Drew flashed a crooked smile.

"How are April and the kids? Is she still dating that construction worker, or whatever he is?"

Drew chuckled. "He's actually a contractor with a successful business flipping houses. And they're not dating. They're… engaged," he said, now intensely fiddling with his mug.

"I'm sorry, Drew."

He looked up at her. "There's nothing to be sorry about. She's happy. That's all that matters."

Lia nodded. "When's the big day?" she asked, checking another text message.

"They haven't picked a date yet—as far as I know."

She looked up abruptly. "Really? How long have they been engaged?"

"A couple months, I guess." *Three months, two weeks, and five days.*

"Oh!" She flicked her wrist like his statement was an annoying gnat. "They are not getting married."

Drew let out a long breath. "Lia, I know you consider yourself some kind of relationship guru, but they're definitely getting married. She's got a diamond boulder on her finger to prove it."

"Oh, Drew, my poor, dumb, big brother." She gave his hand a sympathetic pat. "The ring proves he wants to marry her; the date proves she wants to marry him. What reason would she have for not setting a date yet? No one's in college, no one is deployed, they're of age… *You* guys were married within a month after you proposed."

"And we see how that turned out. Maybe that's why she's taking it slow this time around. But, like I said, she's happy. She's happier now than I've seen her in a very long time, and she told the kids. If she wasn't serious about marrying Tony, she wouldn't have told them."

"Alright, Drew, we'll see," she said with a wink.

"How's everything over here?" the server asked as he poured coffee into Drew's empty mug. Drew noticed his name tag for the first time. It read *Tristan,* but it was odd. The letters were vertical instead of horizontal, confirming Drew's initial opinion that this coffee shop was weird.

"Can I get you another one?" Tristan asked, pointing to Lia's mug.

"No, thank you—still working on this one," she said as she replied to another text message.

Drew was reading a text as well when he realized the server hadn't walked away. He looked up into Tristan's nervous eyes. His broad smile hung haphazardly from his ears.

"What's up, dude?" Drew asked to jump-start whatever question Tristan seemed too terrified to ask.

"Um, Mr. Simon, sir," Tristan said. "I'm sure you hate to be bothered while you're enjoying your coffee, but I just wanted to tell you how much I love your music. I love them all, but your first album is my favorite of all time!"

"The first album?" Drew chuckled. "How old are you, kid? You couldn't possibly be old enough to know anything about that."

"I'm eighteen, sir!" he exclaimed. "My mom said *Threshold* was the only thing that calmed me down when I threw a tantrum. I was Wiretap's youngest fan," he said, sticking his chest out slightly.

"That's cool, man," Drew said. *At least one teenager doesn't think I'm a scumbag.*

"Aw," Lia cooed. "Well, I think this calls for a picture. Where's your phone, kid?"

Tristan's jaw dropped. "Really! Are you sure you won't mind?" he asked as he handed Lia his cell phone.

Drew shook his head. "No, I don't mind. That's a great idea, sis," he said through his clenched teeth as Tristan stooped down and put his arm around Drew's shoulder. No one could miss the name of the coffee shop in big block letters on his T-shirt.

"Okay. Say cheeeeessse!" Lia sang. "Uh oh. Hang on." She reached over and removed Drew's sunglasses. "Now we can see that beautiful face." She shot ten pictures in short order, then handed the phone back. "Here you are, young man."

"Thank you so much!" he said and hurried off.

"Make sure you post those pictures as soon as you can!" she yelled out at him over her shoulder. She turned back and met Drew's angry glare.

"You are pure evil," he snarled.

She burst into laughter. "Sorry. I couldn't resist."

Drew slid his shades back on and slumped back in his chair. "I hate you, Lia."

"Oh, you know you love me." She smiled. Then her expression turned serious. "And you know I love you," she said as she grabbed his hand. "I want you to know that I'm proud of you, Drew. I wouldn't have even thought of pulling that ten years ago. Hell, I wouldn't have done it five years ago. You have come a long way from your days of punching fans in the face."

Drew yanked his cap down again and passed his hand over his face. "That happened one time. It was a paparazzo, not a fan. And I punched his chest when he wouldn't stop taking pictures of Paige while she was crying at the airport."

"You fractured the man's sternum, Drew."

Drew turned his head and stared out the window. "You know I didn't mean to do that," he mumbled.

"I know. My point is that all the work you have put in has really paid off. I can see how much you've changed."

"Thanks. But I must credit my more personable disposition to a sweet, tailor-made cocktail of antidepressants and anti-anxiety medication... and access to some high-quality herbal supplements every now and then." He winked.

"Hello! Thank God for the good stuff," she said, lifting her mug up high. "And wine!" she added as she and Drew clanked their mugs together.

53

Chapter 7

It was a long drive from New York City to Beachwood, New Jersey, over two hours during rush hour. But it still wasn't quite long enough. Drew sat in the car, psyching himself up for the visit with his father. He closed his eyes and took a few cleansing breaths. That didn't seem to help, but when he opened his eyes, he noticed his mother's flowers. Beth had always wanted a garden, but there was never a place for one in any of their military housing. Planting those flowers was one of the first things she did when they moved to that house. So, although his stepmother had maintained the flowers for years, they would always be his mother's flowers to him.

Drew glanced over at his mother as they sat in her car in the driveway behind their house. She hadn't said a word since she dragged him out of Chris's garage by his ear in the middle of their rehearsal, handling him as if he was a naughty, seven-year-old little boy instead of the six-foot-three, seventeen-year-old grown man he thought he was.

"I'm sorry, Mom."

Beth stared at the back of the house through the windshield.

"Aren't you gonna say anything?" he asked.

She shook her head slowly. "I don't know what to say. It's like I don't even know my own son. Are you taking drugs too?" She lowered her head as she tucked a rust-colored spiral of hair behind her ear that had escaped from her otherwise neatly groomed ponytail.

"No, Mom. I don't do drugs." His voice cracked. *Shit.*

"You gave me your word you wouldn't get into any more trouble."

He cleared his throat. "I haven't gotten into any more trouble," he said. "Well, not until today, anyway."

"You got caught today. Staying out of trouble and not getting caught are two different things," she said slowly to the steering wheel.

"I haven't gotten in any more trouble," he assured. "You believe me, don't you, Ma?"

She let out a sigh. "I don't know what to believe anymore. I had no idea that my son was in a band. And until this afternoon, I believed he went to school every day," she said and looked at him for the first time since they got in the car. "How long has this been going on, Andrew?"

"Mom, I swear I—"

"Don't swear," she said with her eyes narrowed so tightly, only a sliver of crystal blue showed through the slit.

"Okay, fine... the truth is, I've skipped a couple classes before, but this was the first time I've ever skipped a full day. I swea— promise."

"How long have you been in that band?" she reiterated. "And when, pray tell, did my classical pianist start playing the guitar?"

Drew took a deep breath. "I've been playing guitar for about two years. Mike taught me. And I joined the band a year ago."

"A year!" she shrieked, making him cringe. "How could you keep this from me? You know how much I detest dishonesty. Especially from my children."

"I know, Mom." He shrugged. "I just didn't think you would understand," he said, looking down at his hands.

"But you still have to try... and if I don't understand, you keep trying until I do." She placed her hand on his. "You can tell me anything, son."

He looked at her.

"And don't ever forget that again."

He nodded. "Yes, ma'am." He looked over at his father's police cruiser, then up at the house. A lump formed in his throat. He swallowed hard. "What should I tell Dad?"

"What do *you* think you should tell Dad?"

His heart dropped into his stomach, triggering a tinge of nausea. "The truth."

"And what is the truth?"

He looked at the house again, and then back at her. "I don't wanna be in ROTC anymore. I don't wanna join the army like Dad wants. I don't wanna go to college like you want. I, um, used the money Dad gave me for my applications to buy an amp—"

Beth gasped. "Andrew."

"I'm in a band," he continued. "We're serious. We're good. And that's what I want to focus on."

"Is that all?"

"Yes, ma'am."

She raised her eyebrow.

Drew looked up at the roof of the car. "And I skipped school today," he groaned.

Beth smiled. "That sounds perfect."

"He's gonna kill me." The words came out shakily, despite his certainty.

She nodded as she wiped away a tear rolling down his cheek. "Your father is going to be livid—especially about the money—and he's going to punish you... Probably forbid you from seeing the guys for a while... Definitely make you get a haircut." She smirked and tousled his overgrown hair. "But you will survive. So, be brave and go on in and talk to him."

Drew reached for the door handle.

"Oh, and by the way," Beth said, placing her hand on his shoulder. "I listened to your band play for a little while before I barged in. You guys are better than good. I knew you could carry a tune, son, but I didn't know you could sing like *that*. Your tone is so rich and mature, you sound like all the Michaels in one!"

"All the Michaels?" he asked, fiddling with the door handle.

"Yeah. You know, Michael McDonald, Michael Bolton, and a little Michael Jackson."

Heat rushed to Drew's face. "I'm still tryin' to find my own sound."

"Well, I think the search is over. I was so thoroughly entertained, I listened to two and a half songs before I remembered I was there to drag your butt outta there." She tucked a few of his curls behind his ear. "You remind me so much of my father. When I was little, I used to sit on the floor next to the piano and listen to him play for hours," she said, looking at him through the lens of a distant place and time.

Drew hadn't seen his grandparents since he was nine, and Beth rarely talked about them. He wanted to hear more about how much he was like his grandfather, and therefore how much he wasn't like his father, especially if it would delay him going into the house. But he didn't want to risk upsetting her more than he already had. The one time Drew asked why they couldn't see their grandparents, she went to bed early, and they had to eat their father's cooking. So instead, he gave her one of his goofy grins that always made her laugh and engulfed her in a tight bear hug.

Drew woke from his daydream and smiled, watching the flowers sway in the gentle spring breeze as if they were waving, welcoming him back from his trip down memory lane. He got out of the car and walked across the brick path and up the steps of the tiny back porch. The door was open, like it always was when the weather was nice enough. And his father sat at the kitchen table reading the paper, like he always did, no matter the weather.

Don't piss him off, Drew said to himself as he sucked in a whiff of the fragrant air and knocked on the screen door.

"Oh my goodness!" his stepmother shrieked. "Is that you, Drew? Get yourself in here right this instant, boy!"

"Hi, Susan," Drew said as she threw her arms around his neck, nearly squeezing the life out of him while she peppered his face with kisses in rapid fire succession.

"What a wonderful surprise! Simon, do you see this?"

"How could I miss it with you carrying on like that?" he barked. "You would think the Pope had walked through the door the way you're acting."

"Hi, Dad," Drew greeted his father with a half-hearted smile.

"Andrew," he said, peering over the top of his paper and his glasses with no hint of a smile.

"Well, come on in and sit down. Let me hang up your jacket," Susan said as she pulled his jacket off his shoulders.

Drew shrugged the jacket back up. "That's alright, Susan. I'll keep it on."

"Are ya sure? It gets pretty hot in here. You know your father doesn't like to turn on the air conditioner until it's at least ninety degrees outside."

Drew sighed. She was right. It was hot in there. Sweat beaded on his forehead. He surrendered and handed his jacket over to Susan. As he sat at the table, the hairs on the back of his neck stood up. He looked up and caught his father eyeing him, or more specifically, the mosaic of tattoos spiraling from under his sleeves down both arms ending at his wrists. Drew wished he had worn a long-sleeved shirt. Simon hated Drew's tattoos; they were always a major distraction for him. The last thing Drew wanted was for his father to be thinking about them when he told him about *Bloodlines.*

Simon went back to his paper without saying a word. Unusual behavior for him, but Drew took it as a sign of hope they might make it through this visit without an argument.

"Can I get you something to eat, sweetheart?" Susan asked when she returned from hanging up his jacket.

"No, thanks, Susan, I'm fine."

"How about a cup of coffee, then?" She nudged his arm with the back of her hand.

Drew nodded. "Okay, sure."

Simon glared at him over the paper again.

Drew cleared his throat. "Yes, ma'am. I'd love a coffee, thank you," he said, returning the glare.

"You got it," she said. "Cream and sugar?"

He held up a hand, shaking his head. "Black, please."

"Ah. I should have known that. Just like your dad," she said, already heading to the counter.

Drew looked over at his father as Simon rolled his eyes up to the ceiling. Their love for black coffee wasn't the only thing they had in common. They also shared a loathing for when people suggested their coffee preference was evidence of a familial bond.

"Well, look at that," Susan said, peering out the back door. "Did you get yourself one of those fancy Ferraris, Drew?"

"It's a Porsche. And it's not mine," he said, responding to his father's raised eyebrow. "I borrowed it from Reid. You wanna ride?"

"Oh heck, no!" she laughed. "I might be able to get in it, but you'd need a crane to get me outta there—it's so low to the ground!"

Drew laughed. "Well, let me know if you change your mind." He turned his attention to his father. "What about you, Dad? Wanna go for a spin?"

"I wouldn't be caught dead in that German piece of shit," he grumbled, without looking up from his newspaper. "There was a time when folks were proud to drive good ol' American cars."

Drew expected that response. Simon hated foreign cars as much as excessive tattoos. "It looks like your buddy, Mr. Russo, has turned to the dark side. I saw the new Audi parked in his garage when I drove up," he said, hoping a conversation about his next-door neighbor's foreign car would transfer some of his father's contempt to someone else for a minute.

"Hmph. Russo and his harlot moved to Florida. That car belongs to the Middle Eastern ISIS trash that moved in last year."

"Patrick William Simon!" Susan barked. She only called him by his first name when she was upset with him as a warning. Jumping straight to his full name was like a declaration of war for her. "Don't listen to your father, Drew," she said as she placed a cup of coffee and a slice of apple pie in front of him.

No danger of that. "Thanks, Susan."

"The Saeeds are Egyptian and a very nice family," she continued. "The father is a doctor, and his wife is a librarian, if you can believe that. I didn't even know they still had libraries anymore with everything on computers these days," she said, as she smoothed down one of Drew's curls. "Oh, and they have two beautiful little girls and a new baby boy. I don't think they have any desire to join ISIS."

"That's the problem, Sue. You don't think. You never know what one of them has on their mind until the planes start crashin' and the bombs start explodin'."

"No, the problem is you think too much," she spat back. "And you spend too much time spying on our neighbors. Always writing things down in that stupid notebook of yours." She nodded at a green spiral notebook sitting on the table not too far from Simon.

"We got ISIS right next door and Black Lives Matter down on the corner. Before you know it, those people'll turn this neighborhood into a dump, just like whatever ghetto cesspool they came from." He slid the notebook closer to himself. "Well, not on my watch they won't."

"Sounds like a full-time job, Dad. Good thing you're retired," Drew said as he took a bite of pie.

Susan laughed.

"Laugh all you want. But when the FBI comes around to talk about those terrorists and traitors we've got living among us, and I have my copious notes to refer to, who's gonna be laughing then?"

Susan pursed her lips. "Me still. *And* the FBI... I'll be upstairs," she said over her shoulder on her way out. "Good luck, Drew. He's in a mood."

Drew snickered. He always liked Susan. To describe Simon as a difficult man would be a gross understatement. In a room full of ex-military, retired cops, and any other alpha male types, he was in charge. But his ultra-macho persona didn't intimidate her at all. She had a way of putting Simon in his place like nobody else.

Simon glowered at Drew until the pressure of his discontent squelched his amusement. "Are you ever gonna get around to tellin' me why you're here?" He folded his newspaper and moved it to the side. "I'm sure you didn't drive all the way down here in rush hour traffic, after all this time, to talk about my neighbor's new car."

Drew took a deep breath and pushed his dessert plate away. "You're right, Dad." He nodded. "I came to tell you I'm gonna be on a show."

"I already know you're on a show—if you can call it that. Are you on drugs too?" he asked, as he slid his reading glasses farther down his nose and studied Drew's face. "I know how much you like pot, and God knows what else."

"What are you talking about?"

"You're a musician, right?"

Drew was about to inform his father that "musician" wasn't a synonym for "drug addict," when a breeze blew in. The smell of his mother's flowers rode in on the wind, cutting through the tension.

"Dad, I'm talking about a different show," he said, ignoring his pot comment. "I've been asked to be on that show, *Bloodlines*."

"No," Simon said flatly.

"What do you mean 'no?' You haven't heard of the show?"

"I've heard of it. You're not going to be on it," he declared and slid his glasses just behind his hairline. The thin wire frames all but disappeared in his salt and still mostly pepper hair, even at seventy.

Drew threw his head back, laughing. "I'm not asking for your permission. I'm only here to tell you I'm going to be on the show… as a courtesy. I've already signed the contract," he lied.

Simon shook his head. "Most people get wiser as they get older. You're the only person I know that gets dumber with age."

Drew narrowed his eyes. "I'm dumb because I think it'd be cool to find out more about my family history?"

"You're dumb because you plan to do it on national TV. You could do whatever research you wanna do on your own; I would even help you if you weren't too stubborn to ask. But letting complete strangers dig up the bones of your dead relatives, then display them for the world to see in whatever light they want is plain stupid."

Drew took his napkin and wiped the sweat forming over his brow. It suddenly felt about ten degrees hotter in that kitchen.

"Look, Dad. With us moving around so much, I never had the chance to know any relatives outside of you, Mom, and Lia. I wanna learn more about my family."

"I've told you about your family, Drew. You just never listened to me."

"No, Dad, you told me about *your* family. I had a mother too. I'd also like to know more about Mom's side."

Simon furrowed his brow. "Beth died when you were, what, twenty-three, twenty-four? Did it ever occur to you that your mother told you everything she wanted you to know about her family!"

Simon's elevated volume triggered Drew to pause and survey his father's face and body language. Simon sat ramrod straight close to the edge of his seat. The black pupils in the center of Simon's brown irises had constricted to the size of a tiny pinprick, and the tips of his ears resembled the color of vine-ripened tomatoes. All familiar signs that his father was speeding toward the point of no return. And despite the heat, a familiar chill rippled down Drew's spine.

"You never even thought about that, did you?" Simon said with a huff. "Look at ya. Nearly forty years old and still the same selfish brat you were as a teenager."

Drew sighed and took a sip of his coffee. "No, Dad, you're the selfish one. It's selfish of you to try and block this opportunity for me. What?" He smirked. "You afraid the Black vets you get drunk with every week might find out you're a 'Make America Great Again' supporter?"

"I'm not afraid of anything, son. My army buddies, Black, white or whatever, know where I stand. They know with me what you see is what you get. I have never pretended to be anything other than exactly what I am." Simon chuckled. "So, you have fun on your family history show. Let me know when it airs. I can't wait to see it blow up in your face."

Drew lowered his head. Simon's words were hard enough to take without having to look at the self-satisfied grin on his face. "Would it kill you to support me for once?"

"Support you?" Simon huffed. "I worked my ass off supporting you, your sister, and your mother. You never went without a damn thing! And I guess all those years I had to send you money while you played starving artist don't count for anything either. Look at me when I'm talking to you, DAMMIT!" He slammed his fist on the table, rattling the fork resting on Drew's dessert plate.

Drew looked up without lifting his head, refusing to show any sign that Simon's outburst had rattled him too. "That's not the kind of support I'm talkin' about, Dad."

"Oh. You must mean being at every baseball, basketball, and football game you ever played in, then? Or sitting through every boring piano recital you ever had? Or being home every single night for dinner? Is that the kind of support you mean, son? Because I thought that's what good fathers do. But I guess you wouldn't know anything about what being a good father is like," he said, looking Drew up and down.

Drew's lip curled into a snarl. "Go to hell!" he barked as he jumped up and rushed over to the front closet. He ripped his jacket off the hanger, stormed back through the kitchen without a glance in his father's direction, and slammed out the back door.

As he hurried to the Porsche, a breeze kicked up again and the fragrance of his mother's flowers swirled around him. He ignored it as he got in the car and revved the engine, making as much noise as possible while he searched his playlist for the perfect song to punctuate his exit in case his father wasn't clear about how much he hated him. He set the volume to its highest level and tapped PLAY. The intro to NWA's "Fuck the Police" blasted from Reid's premium sound system as a gust of wind blew across the yard, causing the flowers to whip around violently like they were trying to get his attention. He groaned as he started a text while he backed out of the driveway.

"HEY!!!!!" a woman shrieked, and then a loud thud made Drew slam on the brake so hard that his head flew back and bounced off the headrest, sending his body flying into the steering wheel.

"FUCK!" he yelled out, despite the fact his heart had taken up residence in his throat, pounding out of control. He looked up into the rearview mirror and let out a sigh of relief as a woman with a jogging stroller landed several more kicks to the bumper, and then trotted down the sidewalk, flipping him off.

As he sat waiting for his hands to stop trembling and his heart rate to come down, Drew looked at the house. His father stood, stiff as ever with his hands on his hips, in the big picture window over his mother's flowers. Simon shook his head as the flowers seemed to sway in agreement with his disappointment.

Drew turned off the music and resumed his text message to Shanice.

Tell your dad I'll do Bloodlines. He hit send, tossed the phone into the back seat, put his seatbelt on, and drove slowly and carefully back to the city.

Chapter 8

"Drew, you don't mind if I record this, do you?" asked Kelvin Pierce, head producer/genealogical researcher from *Bloodlines*. His long dreadlocks hung down on either side of the video camera while he adjusted the focus. "I try to record as many of my interviews as I can," he said as he bent over and twisted his hair around itself into a giant nest on top of his head. "It'll help me keep track of what we talk about, and it'll help you get more comfortable talking about things on camera. By the time we tape the show, you won't even notice the cameras anymore. It comes off way more natural."

Drew shrugged. "It's cool with me, but don't you guys only deal with celebrities? Aren't they used to being on camera?"

Kelvin pursed his lips. "You'd be surprised how tongue-tied celebrities get. I'm talkin' politicians, talk show hosts, performers, they all have problems just being themselves a lot of the time. Athletes are usually worse, but people don't expect them to be particularly articulate." He chuckled.

Drew laughed too.

"So, what do you think happens to you when you die?" Kelvin asked as he lowered himself onto a chair next to the tripod he had set up in Drew's dressing room.

"Wow. Is that your warm-up question?" Drew feigned a shudder. "I'm scared."

"My warmup question was 'do you mind if I tape this?'" He smiled. "Look, Drew, there are no right or wrong answers. If you don't know the answer or you really haven't thought about it before, just say that."

Drew nodded. "I'm not sure what happens when you die. I was raised by a religious mother. She wasn't what I would call a fanatic, but church on Sundays, grace before meals, prayer before bed, was the norm for us. No matter where my dad was stationed, she always first found out where the chapel was located and, second, where the food was. Always those two things, always in that order. So, I'd like to think there's a heaven; especially since she's gone. It's nice to think that she went somewhere and that I might have a chance to see her again."

"So, you think you'll see her again in heaven?"

Drew laughed. "Well, that would be my first choice. But if I don't make it up there, I might know a couple dudes in the other place. Ha! It'll be good to see them again too."

"That's great, man. You're funny!" Kelvin said. "I'm sorry you lost your mom. Sounds like you were close to her."

"Yeah. I was. I could talk to her about anything."

Kelvin arched an eyebrow. "Oh yeah? You told her everything?"

"Well, maybe not everything... at least not automatically. But she had a way of getting me to share. Even some of my deepest teenage secrets. After all these years, she's still the first person I think about calling when something big happens."

"Her death certificate said that she died in a car accident?"

Drew stared at him with his mouth opened slightly. He wasn't prepared to talk about his mother's death.

"Drew," Kelvin said. "Some of the information we find out might not be pleasant to talk about. Someone will always be there to walk you through it, but you have to get used to talking about difficult subjects."

Drew inhaled and blew it out slowly. "Yes, my mother died in a car accident. She got T-boned by a Hummer. It was a distracted driving situation," he said, lowering his head.

"I'm sorry, man. Was anyone prosecuted?"

"They didn't have too many laws restricting cell phone use back then. Besides, she was the distracted driver. She was leaving a voicemail and ran a red light."

"That's tough, man. Do you know who she was calling?" Kelvin asked.

Drew closed his eyes, nodding slowly. *"Drew, honey, it's Mommy. I just put the money you asked for in your account. Now, I could only finagle two hundred from Dad—Lia needed help with some car repairs. Sorry. You and April will have to stretch it. I know you hate the idea, but maybe you two should reconsider moving in with us. I mean, with the baby coming and you on the road with the band so much, April's going to need help. Okay. Call me when you can. I lov—"*

"She was calling me," Drew said and took a drink of water.

"Oh wow, Drew," Kelvin sighed. "I know that was hard, but you did a good job with it. If you can survive talking about something as tragic as losing a parent suddenly like that, then the rest of this will be a breeze by comparison. Alright?" he said, patting him on the shoulder.

"Is it alright if I ask *you* a question?"

"Sure," Kelvin said. "Feel free to ask any questions. I'm not saying that I can answer all of them, but I'll do my best."

"Why did you ask what I think about the afterlife? What does that have to do with my family history?"

Kelvin smiled. "Real talk?"

"Of course."

"Over the next several weeks and months, we're gonna be goin' back in time. There will be nothing but discussions of once upon a time and what once was and who once was. I ask all my clients that question to find out where their head is at—if they ever think about what becomes of their relatives when they die. If a person is open to the concept that a human being's existence can transcend death, it makes this process easier. I think it makes the lives that your ancestors lived, no matter how long ago or how brief, that much more important because you believe they could still be out there somewhere maybe caring about how their story is told."

"That's kinda deep."

A smile spread across Kelvin's face. "Aw, man, you didn't think you was dealin' with a shallow brutha, did you now?"

"Not at all!" Drew laughed.

"Well, like I said earlier, I don't wanna monopolize your time. I know you're in between taping, but I wanted to show you what I've been able to put together so far," he said as he reached into his bag and pulled out a folder. "So, this is a rough outline of your family tree. Now, I haven't done anything with your mother's side of the tree, because there's so much foliage, for lack of a better word, on your dad's side. The information is also easier to compile because of all the servicemen on that side. You were right about that, by the way. It's almost like military service in your dad's family was compulsory."

"Until I came along and blew that family tradition outta the water!"

"Yeah, man, you are squarely in the minority with your career choice. We're definitely gonna have to talk about how you broke out on your own one of these days. But anyway, I have gotten as far back as the French and Indian War."

"That's cool, Kelvin. You've done a lot of work," Drew said as he surveyed the paperwork. He tried to offer a grateful smile, but he couldn't completely mask his disappointment.

"I know it looks crazy, Drew," Kelvin said, his shoulders slumped over ever so slightly. "I promise it'll start coming together."

"I'm sorry, Kelvin. What you've done here in only a couple of weeks is impressive. I was just hoping to get a little more information about my mother's side," he said. "I already knew about the military stuff on my dad's side of the family. He used to talk about it all the time. I found it interesting, but I could never really relate to it, being a more artistic personality type. I always wondered if there were more people like me on my mom's side, but she never talked much about her family."

"Don't even worry about that. We *will* get to your mom's side and hopefully answer some of those questions for you. It's just easier to obtain and decipher military records. As soon as we sew up your father's side, we'll get right on your mother's family. Trust me."

"I trust you, man," Drew said, giving Kelvin a firm pat on the back. "Hey, can I have this?" he asked, holding up the folder.

"Yeah, that's your copy," Kelvin said. "But don't get used to this. I'm only giving this to you because it's pretty much just a list of names and dates of birth. When we get into the meat of these people's lives, we won't share that information until we tape the show. It has to look like you're hearing it for the first time."

"I understand," Drew nodded.

There was a tap on the door.

"Come in!" Drew shouted.

"Hey, Drew," Shanice said as she entered his dressing room. She made it halfway into the room before she looked up from her clipboard. "Oh!" she gasped. "I didn't realize you had company."

"Shanice, this is Kelvin Pierce. He's a genealogist for *Bloodlines*."

"We've met," she said, extending her hand with a big smile Drew wasn't sure he had ever seen on her before, nor the hint of burgundy in her brown cheeks. "How have you been, Kelvin?" she asked, using a soft and sultry voice Drew was certain he had never heard her use before.

"Good. I've been pretty good. And you?" Kelvin asked as he shook her hand. His voice changed too. It got a lot deeper, and he was showing a lot of teeth.

"Good," she replied. Then there was a long silence. But Drew seemed to be the only one who was uncomfortable with it. Shanice and Kelvin appeared perfectly content to stare at each other.

"So... Shanice," Drew said, breaking the silence. "Did you want something?"

"Oh! Right!" She looked down at her clipboard. "I wanted to tell you about the change for the next show."

"Hey, I'm gonna get outta y'all's way," Kelvin said, packing up his equipment. "It was a pleasure to see you again, Ms. Stevenson," he said, dipping his head down. "I'll holla at you later, Drew." He gave him a bro hug. "Have a good show!" he called out over his shoulder on his way out the door.

Shanice followed him with her eyes and let them linger on the closed door for several seconds.

"Uh, Shanice?"

"Oh, yeah, Drew," she said, spinning back around to face him. "So, what do you think about that?"

"About what?"

"Uh, hellooooo, about changing the dunk contest with Steph Curry to poker with Jennifer Lawrence," she said. "Like I said, we're going to have to change the music for that segment."

"You never said—never mind." Drew sighed. "Is it strip poker? Because that will affect the music."

"No! Of course not! Are you crazy?"

Drew pinched the bridge of his nose. "Whose idea was it?"

"Reid's."

"Well, then it's strip poker, for sure. He calls strip poker *poker* and regular poker *regular poker*." He chuckled.

Shanice's happy face twisted into a full scowl. "Reid!" she hissed as she rushed to the door and yanked it open. "I'll be back, Drew," she said as she flew out the door.

Drew started after her. Then his cell phone vibrated.

R u busy tonight? April texted.

I don't have to be

Can u come over for dinner @ 6:30/7?

I can probably do 7:30. What's goin on

Too much to text, but I need u to talk to Zach about making better choices ☹

OK

Drew slid his phone back into his pocket. "Sure. I'll talk to him about making better choices, right after someone talks to me about making better choices." He scratched the stubble on his jawline and let out a breath. Then the muffled sounds of a heated discussion grabbed his attention. He got up and hurried out the door to check it out, hoping to get some useful tips from listening to Shanice chew Reid out about making better choices.

Chapter 9

The skeptical eyes of the Uber driver burned a hole into the back of Drew's neck as he walked over to the garage door. Juan Carlos had talked non-stop for an hour and forty-five minutes through rush-hour traffic. The older man had regaled Drew with stories about growing up in Bolivia and emigrating to New York when he was young. They were like old friends by the time they arrived at the North Jersey gated community where Drew's ex-wife and children lived—where he lived once upon a time.

Juan Carlos obviously didn't think his tattoo-covered passenger had any business being anywhere near the elegant neighborhood of multi-million-dollar homes by his increasingly perplexed expression and the way he asked, "Are you in the right place?" Drew had answered with a quick "yes." But a more truthful answer would have been "no" even though he still owned the house and his family lived there. He smiled and waved goodbye to the worried driver as he punched in the security code on the keypad outside the garage door. As it slid open, he ducked under quickly, then pushed the button to close it, giving Juan Carlos an unsatisfying view of the bottom half of April's Mercedes and Zach's Range Rover.

Drew snickered as he entered the kitchen.

"What's funny?" April asked, standing at the stove, stirring one of her concoctions.

"My Uber driver profiled me. I think he might still be out there waiting to hear screams," he said as he leaned in and kissed her cheek.

"What?" she giggled. "Why would anybody take an Uber to commit a crime? You should give him a low rating for being ridiculous."

"He's not ridiculous. People are nuts these days. I'm sure no one knows that better than Uber drivers. I'm giving him five stars. He had some really interesting stories," he said as he closed the app on his phone. When he looked up, his eyes danced with delight at the view of April's shapely, denim-clad butt. Drew always thought her butt looked good in—and out of—everything, even before she became a personal trainer. His eyes drifted up, tracing the curve of her frame in the snug fitting tank top she had on. Then he spotted the tattoo on the back of her right shoulder, a long-stemmed rose with thorns. The bud drooped down like it was dying. It was a cool tattoo, but he liked the one that was there before much better—𝔇rew.

"You should write a song about him," she said as she came over and leaned against the counter across from Drew, snapping him out of his daydream.

"That's a good idea." He made a note to himself on his phone. "Where're the kids?"

She pointed up at the ceiling. "Homework."

Drew nodded. "So, what's goin' on with Zach?"

She sighed. "I found out today that he hasn't been to school for three days."

"What! What's that about?"

"He went to a video game convention in the city."

"Like Comic Con?"

"No, Comic Con's held on weekends. Zach was at a professional video game designers' convention."

"How'd he pull that off?"

She shrugged. "He claims he mostly hung out in the lobby and snuck into sessions when he could."

He laughed. "That's probably the dorkiest thing I've ever heard!"

"Drew! This is serious."

"I'm sorry, but you have to admit he could have been doing worse things."

"He's been lying and sneaking around for three days. We had no idea where he was. The only reason I found out was because his science teacher called to see how he was doing after getting his wisdom teeth removed." She pursed her lips.

"Didn't he get those out last summer?"

"Exactly!" She threw her hands up in the air. "Are you starting to see the web of lies?"

Drew massaged his temple with a finger. "Yeah. You want me to go up and talk to him now?"

She shook her head. "Let's eat first. It's getting late."

"Sounds good to me. What's for dinner? Whatever it is, it smells great."

"I made vegan teriyaki chicken chili with rice and salad with curry chickpeas."

Drew's lip curled, causing his nose to wrinkle. "I don't understand 'vegan chicken,'" he said, trying hard to recalibrate the horrified expression screaming across his face.

"You've never had vegan chicken?" she asked, her mouth partially agape.

Drew shook his head slowly. "You know how I feel about the concept of vegan meat."

Her eyes lit up. "Well, you're going to like this dish. I bet you won't even be able to tell it's not real chicken!"

"Great! I love it when my food pretends to be something it's not," he said, flashing a fake smile, then his eyes darted around the kitchen. "Is Tony around? It wouldn't be fair if he doesn't get to share."

"Tony left a little while ago," she said with an eye roll. "He and Zach got into a shouting match when we were talking to him about his exploits. Then Zach pulled the old 'you're not my father' trick out of his hat. It was obvious he was trying to get out of the lecture, but Tony thought it would be better if he wasn't around when you came to talk to him."

Drew scratched his neck. "Well, he wasn't lying, April. Tony isn't his father."

She narrowed her eyes. "That's not the point. Zach was being rude and disrespectful. He doesn't have the right to speak like that to any adult. Do you disagree?"

"No," he sighed.

"Good," she said and slapped his chest twice. "Let's eat!"

Drew set the table while April called the kids. As soon as she announced it was dinner time, a stampede rumbled over his head and down the stairs. The kids came tearing into the kitchen and all three of them stopped in their tracks when they saw Drew. The youngest two, Paige and Cole, squealed "Daddy!!!!" with delight as they raced over to him at full speed, nearly tackling him to the floor. Zach opted for a flat, "Hey, Dad," as he sat at the table.

"Drew, will you say grace?" April asked after she had plated everyone's food and took her seat.

"Sure," Drew said, reaching for Paige and Cole's hands as they joined hands with April and Zach. They all bowed their heads, and although he hadn't recited it in years, the prayer his mother taught him rolled off his tongue. "Bless us, oh Lord, in these thy gifts, which we are about to receive, from thy bounty, through Christ our Lord. Amen."

"Amen," April repeated. "Thank you, Drew," she said, smiling. "And thank you for joining us for dinner. What a treat, right, kiddos!"

"Yeah!" said Paige and Cole in unison.

"Mph," Zach grunted. "Ow!" he blurted out. "Why'd you kick me, Mom!"

April's normally pleasant face instantly morphed into her infamous "scary mom" look.

"Yeah, it's great you're here for dinner, Dad," he said as he reached down and rubbed his leg. "Not weird at all," he added under his breath.

"So, Drew, anything new and exciting going on in your world?" she asked, overtalking Zach's grumbling.

Drew nodded as he took his first bite of vegan chicken. "Mmmm," he hummed. "That is good, babe. It does not taste like chicken. But it's still good."

"Babe," Paige giggled.

Heat crept up Drew's neck and spread quickly across his face. His facial hair offered some camouflage for his embarrassment, but April was out of luck. Her smooth skin turned bright pink right before their eyes.

"Thank you, *Drew*," she said, crossing her eyes at Paige. "I knew you'd like it." She smiled. "So, you were about to tell us what's been going on with you lately," she prodded. He had told April he signed on to do *Bloodlines*, but he hadn't told the kids yet.

"Oh, yeah!" He jumped up and grabbed the folder from the counter Kelvin had given him earlier. "I heard you were interrogating your mother about my family," he said to Paige as he tapped her on the head with the folder and sat back down. "What's up with the background check? Who you workin' for?" He raised his eyebrow.

"Moooommm! You told him?" she whined, turning beet red as she rubbed the top of her head.

Drew chuckled at her overreaction. She had a thick mane of dark, curly hair like his. There was no way the light tap did anything more than jostle a few of her ringlets.

"I'm just teasin' you, Paige!" He put his arm around her shoulder and pulled her in for a squeeze. He had forgotten how deeply embarrassing everything was for his twelve-year-old daughter. "I'm happy you were asking questions about our family, but I'm even happier that I have some answers for you. I'm going to be on this family history show and they're doing a ton of research about our ancestors. The researcher gave me this today with all kinds of information." He opened the folder and pulled out Kelvin's notes.

"Whoa!" Cole said as he leaned forward, peering at the paper. "That looks like a March Madness bracket!"

"You're right! It does kinda look like a bracket," Drew agreed. "But it's really only a rough outline of our family tree."

"Really?" Paige said, leaning in to get a good look for herself. "There's my name!" she squealed. "And yours, and Mommy, and Cole and Zach, and Grandpa and Grandma," she rattled off. "Grandpa's name is Patrick? And he was born in 1948? That was a really, really, really long time ago!"

"Okay, Paige, I know you're excited, but you need to stop shouting," April said.

Paige slapped her hand over her mouth. "Sorry, Mom." She resumed perusing the family tree quietly. "Grandpa's father's name was George. Was your Grandpa George as grumpy as Grandpa Simon?" she asked, looking up at Drew.

He chuckled. "I don't know. I never met him. You see the year he died?" He pointed to Grandpa George's information. "1952."

Paige scrunched up her face. "So, Grandpa's dad died when he was four years old?"

"Yep," Drew said.

"Oh," Cole said. "Maybe that's why Grandpa is so grumpy."

Drew pulled on his chin. "Hmmm... you might be onto something."

"How'd he die?" Cole asked.

"He died in the Korean War. He was in the army, like Grandpa."

Paige and Cole were quiet for a few more minutes while they ate their dinner and looked over the family tree.

"Zach!" Cole blurted out. "You gotta see this. Our great, great gazillion, great grandfather's name was Zachary too. He was born in 1809." His mouth dropped open, making him look like an amazed jack-o'-lantern with his missing canines and molars.

"So what?" Zach barked. "You're being a dork right now."

The excitement drained from Cole's face as he slowly lowered his head.

"Seriously, dude? He's nine. Lighten up," Drew said.

Zach shrugged. "I don't see what the big deal is. It's only a bunch of names of a bunch of dead people."

"They're your family, Zach," April said.

"I don't care. It's dumb."

"Zachary! I've had it with you. If you're not interested in the topic of conversation, then sit there and finish your dinner in silence," she ordered, pointing her fork at Zach's plate.

He shoved his mostly full plate away. "I'm done. Can I be excused?" he asked his mother.

"No," Drew said, glaring at Zach. "You can sit up straight and eat the rest of your dinner."

Zach returned Drew's glare for several seconds before he backed down. Then he shifted from his slouching position to fully upright and resumed eating his dinner, or more accurately, stabbing his vegan teriyaki chicken chili, and then shoving it into his mouth. Although Drew was the clear victor in their staring contest, he continued to look at his eldest son. Except for his blond hair and the blatant disrespect, Zach was just like Drew at sixteen. He was tall and skinny, with a curtain of thick curly hair covering the smattering of acne on his forehead—and he hated his father.

"So is skipping school to go to conventions your thing now?" Drew asked.

Zach rolled his eyes. "No," he groaned. "It's not a thing. It was one time."

"Nice try, Zach. You missed three days of school. That means you skipped school three times."

"But it was only one convention," he said with a smirk.

Drew slammed his hand down, causing everything on the table and everyone around the table to jump. "Is this a joke to you! You can't just come and go as you please, Zach."

"Psshh. You do," he muttered.

Drew narrowed his eyes. "What did you say?" he asked, but he had heard it. And he felt it like a stab in the heart.

"Nothing," Zach grumbled.

April put on her scary mom face again, her mouth locked and loaded, ready to lay into Zach. Drew put his hand up. "I got it."

"So, you wanna be like me now?" he asked, chuckling a little. "I'm surprised, man. I thought I was the last person you wanted to be like."

"Nah." Zach shook his head. "You're the first person I *don't* wanna be like," he snarled at his dinner.

"Good," Drew said, surprisingly calm after taking another verbal hit. "Then I expect you to be at school every day from now on like all the other children. And if you want to go anywhere else, you will get your mommy's permission first like a good little boy."

Zach looked up. Paige and Cole snickered. April shot her mom look at them, and they both cleared their throats and shoved a forkful of food into their mouths.

"Are we clear?" Drew asked, his voice slightly elevated.

Zach nodded.

"I can't hear you!" All the kids jumped again. April didn't. She seemed to be tuned in to the tough love show he was putting on.

"Yes! I already got this lecture from Mom and Tony when they grounded me," Zach growled.

"Grounded? What exactly does that entail?" Drew asked, trying to sound more interested than irritated by hearing Tony had a hand in disciplining his son for the second time that evening.

Zach shrugged. "Uh, I can't do anything for two weeks—no car, no friends, no phone... And no video games indefinitely. You don't know what it means to be grounded?" The disbelief in his tone gave voice to his siblings' doubtful expressions.

Drew raised an eyebrow. "Well, since you asked, it's been some time since I was groundable and, to be honest, I didn't get grounded all that often."

Zach groaned. "Awesome. I guess now you're gonna tell me how you never got in any trouble when you were my age and that you were the most obedient, well-behaved kid in the world."

Drew exchanged an amused glance with April. "Not by a long shot. I got in plenty of trouble when I was a kid. But your grandfather preferred a more hands-on approach."

His turn of phrase seemed to confuse Paige and Cole, if their scrunched faces were any indication. But Zach understood. He looked at Drew with a fleeting glimmer of sympathy before his scowl returned.

"April, you don't mind if I try this grounding thing, do you?" he asked, without taking his eyes off Zach. "I think each missed day of school equals one week of grounding. So, let's make it three weeks."

"What! That's not fair!" Zach spat, almost choking on his vegan chicken. "I already—"

"Sounds like a great idea," April said, cutting off his tirade. "And if that doesn't get through to him, maybe we'll try Grandpa's disciplinary technique." She looked Zach squarely in the eyes. "It's been a long time since you've seen that kind of action."

Drew blinked several times. April's statement pulled him out of bad cop mode. Like Drew, she had grown up in a house where "spare the rod, spoil the child" was the prevailing parenting philosophy. But April was never much of a spanker, opting for a gentler parenting style more often than not. He searched her face for a hint of jest. There was none. He looked around the table. April's threat had an effect on all the kids. Paige and Cole stared at her slack jawed, but Zach's eyes grew as big as saucers. He opened his mouth to speak, but April's lips pursed into an even thinner line as her jaw tightened; a sigh came out instead of the protest dancing on the tip of his tongue, and his shoulders slumped.

"I finished my food. May I be excused?" Zach asked through his clenched teeth.

"Are you done with him?" April asked Drew.

"For now," he said, giving Zach a hard look.

"You're excused," April said.

Zach jumped up, dumped his plate in the sink, and raced up the stairs two at a time. Then a door slammed, but opened again quickly. "Sorry!" Zach yelled. "It slipped! I don't need Grandpa's discipline!"

Drew and April snickered.

"Hey, guys," Drew said to Paige and Cole, who had been sitting quietly through their brother's reprimand, their expressions vacillating between giddy and horrified. "Let's give Mom a break and do the dishes." He went over to the fridge and fished out the bottle of wine April always kept way in the back behind a bag of romaine lettuce—her way of child-proofing her alcohol. He poured a glass then handed it and the bottle to April. "Go on out and relax while me and the kids clean up," he said, jerking his head toward the deck.

She smiled. "Thanks, Drew," she said as she took the glass and bottle and headed outside.

While Drew, Paige, and Cole cleaned the kitchen, they talked about the family tree. They asked if they could be on *Bloodlines* with him. He told them he wasn't sure, but he promised to tell them every time he got new information.

After they finished the kitchen, Drew sent Paige and Cole to get ready for bed and finish their homework. He kissed them goodbye on their way up the stairs and yelled goodnight to Zach. A muffled "later" came from behind his closed door. *At least he responded*, he thought, and he went out to say goodnight to April.

"Thanks for cleaning up," April said as he stepped out onto the deck.

"Thanks for dinner," he said and sat on the deck chair across from her. "It was actually pretty good."

"Do you want me to pack some up for you to take home?"

"Uh, no, I, uh, you're not allowed to have food in Ubers."

"They literally have Ubers that only carry food, Drew," she laughed. "Now we know where your son gets his propensity for inventing facts. Maybe you need some of Grandpa's old-fashioned discipline too," she said, raising her eyebrow.

"Ooooh noooo," he shuddered. "I've seen enough of 'that action,' as you called it. But did you see Zach's face when you threatened him? Priceless," he chuckled. "You know that means if he screws up again, you better be prepared to make good on your promise."

"Me? Have you seen your son lately? He's six feet tall. I'm five, five," she reminded him.

"So what?" He shrugged. "Height didn't deter *my* mom the last time she roasted my ass. I was fifteen and as tall as Zach is now, but she had me bawlin' like a five-year-old." He rubbed the back of his neck as he recalled the embarrassing incident sparked by his neglected chores and his backtalk when his mother confronted him about said chores.

"But she had never stopped spanking you. I haven't spanked Zach since he was younger than Cole. So, all things considered, you'd be better suited for that task than me," she said and drained the last bit of wine in her glass.

"Well, let's pray it doesn't come to that. Zach's a good kid. He tries to hide it behind all that attitude because he's confused.

Sixteen is a tough age for a guy. But I think he'll get it together," he said as he tapped the app to order a car.

"Sweet! There's a Lyft right down the street. I'll call you in a few days to see how things are going, but I plan to call Zach tomorrow and every day after that. That'll make his punishment that much more enjoyable." He winked.

"Don't forget I have his phone," she said. "You'll have to call the house."

"Hmmmmm, no. Let him have the phone when I call, and then make him hand it over after we talk. He'll hate that!"

April nodded. "He sure will," she agreed. Then she gave him a strange look. "You're good at this, Drew. I must say, this has been a pleasant co-parenting experience. You really stepped up today," she said, extending her hand.

He slapped it away and bent down and kissed her cheek. "Have a good night, April."

"You too," she said as he trotted down the steps and around the side of the house.

The Lyft was idling in the driveway. He opened the back door and remembered his folder. "Hang on a minute. I forgot something," he told the driver and jogged around to the back of the house.

April had already gone inside. Drew looked inside through the glass door and saw Zach sitting by himself at the kitchen table with an intense expression on his face. Thinking the boy was still angry about his punishment, Drew raised his hand to knock but stopped short when he noticed the family tree folder opened on the table in front of him. Deep in study, Zach didn't look up as Drew backed away slowly.

He settled into the back of the car, smiling ear to ear. He pulled out his phone and texted April.

When does school let out

About 3 wks. On the 6th

The show goes on hiatus on the 1st. Do u mind if I take the kids for a few weeks

Not at all! They will loooooove that... Even Zach ☺

Chapter 10

"Your table is right over here," the party promoter, Les, shouted over the noise as she escorted Drew and Reid through the crowded bar to the VIP section.

They slid into the small booth, and Les scooted in next to Reid.

"I think you're gonna like this showcase," she said as she ran her fingers through her short, electric blue hair, and then rested her crossed arms on the table.

"I told you I was interested in seeing the one girl, and you round up four for me?" Reid asked. "Wow, Les, you spoil me."

She shrugged. "It's what I do, man. I'm an entertainment hustler. It's my job to give you what you want."

"So, what's the lineup?"

"I'm not sure. I think your girl is second, but like I said, all the girls are tight. You will not be disappointed," she said as she shot a quick head nod across the room and stood up.

"You don't have to rush off, Les," Reid said. "Why don't you chill with me and Drew for a little while?"

"Aw, man, Reid, I'd love to, but my wife just sashayed in here with a bunch of our friends," she said, pointing at the entrance, where a sexy redhead stood with six other women of varying degrees of hotness. "It's her birthday and she's lookin' too good tonight to be left alone for too long." Les slapped Reid's hand and leaned in for a bro hug. She repeated the action with Drew, and then floated across the club in her elbow-patched sports jacket like she was on a conveyor belt.

Drew and Reid watched as she reached her wife and planted a passionate kiss on her lips. That triggered a chain reaction among their friends, and suddenly four female couples stood tongue kissing and fondling each other in the middle of the bar.

"Whoa!" Reid blurted out.

Drew's eyebrows jumped to his hairline. "I know, dude, holy shit!"

Drew and Reid looked around, acknowledging people they knew, or who knew them, with head nods or waves when appropriate. After a few minutes of that, Reid shot a scowl at Drew.

"Is it me, or does it feel like we're on a date or something in this little booth?" Reid asked.

"I was thinkin' the same thing."

"Let's go sit at the bar, man."

"Are you sure?" Drew asked. "I don't want you to be uncomfortable so close to the booze."

"Don't worry about me, dude. I've been sober for over a decade now—takin' it one day at a time, one moment at a time, whatever it takes. I got this," he said and headed to the bar.

Drew followed the path Reid wove through the thick crowd. Lucky for them, a couple on the end got up to dance as they approached. Drew ordered a beer for himself and a club soda for Reid, and they plopped down on their poached bar stools.

"Thanks for comin' with me tonight. I know you have the kids. Where are they anyway? You shoulda brought 'em," he chuckled and nudged Drew.

Drew laughed. "I was gonna, but Cole left his fake I.D. at home."

Reid shook his head. "Kids are so freakin' stupid." He smiled. "But seriously, how's that going?"

"It's been alright. Cole cried for April the first two nights, but after that he came around and he seems to be having a good time—Paige too."

"What about Zach?"

Drew took a deep breath and let it out slowly. "As long as he can play video games and use his cell phone he's fine. But if I ask him to turn it off or put his phone away, he looks at me like I sentenced him to death. Being around a sulky teenager kinda sucks."

Reid gave him a firm pat on the shoulder. "Hang in there. You just gotta keep trying. He'll come around. My kids are nineteen and twenty-two. It took a lot of work, but they don't completely hate me anymore. Unfortunately, I can't say the same for their mothers," he said. "You wouldn't know anything about that, though."

"What are you talkin' about, man?" Drew asked, looking Reid up and down. "I know what it's like for your ex to hate your guts."

Reid coughed out a laugh, almost choking on his drink. "Are you messin' with me right now?"

Drew frowned.

"Dude, let me explain something to you because you obviously have no clue how good you have it. I have two ex-wives. I pay alimony out the wazoo on top of the child support for Kiera—got another two years of that. I have been hauled into court for contempt more than once for being ten minutes late dropping off after a weekend visit. I have shown up to get my kid for the weekend to find a note saying, *You were twenty minutes late, so we decided to go to Florida*—fucking Florida!" he shouted. "Has even one of those things happened in all the time you and April have been divorced?"

Drew searched his mental Rolodex for a remotely relatable example, but April had never done anything close to what Reid described. Despite his chronic lateness and occasional no-shows, the worst he'd gotten from her was an earful of choice words. "I can't say that it has," he admitted.

"So what could possibly make you think April hates your guts?"

"She got rid of my tat," Drew sighed.

"Huh?"

"She used to have my name tattooed on her shoulder." He tapped the back of his right shoulder with the opposite hand. "It's a rose now—a dead rose."

"Well, can you blame her?"

"I *don't* blame her," he said, cutting his eyes at Reid as he took a sip of his beer. "That doesn't make it easier."

"Look, man, I know that was hard to see. But I'm sure that had more to do with the fiancé than her," he said. "I mean, how would you feel if every time you smashed your girl from behind her ex's name was staring you in the face?"

Drew's face twisted with disgust. "Thanks, Reid. Thank you very much for that image."

"No sweat, man. That's what friends are for," he said, laughing hysterically while Drew glared at him.

"My man! What's goin' on, Reid!" shouted a young guy as he stumbled to the bar with four other young guys. They looked like frat boys—drunk frat boys. "Drew, man, what's up!" He held up his hand for a slap.

Drew obliged, reminding himself to appear moderately gracious. "Not much, man."

"I had to come over and tell you how much I'm diggin' the show. I'm up half the night anyway and TV usually sucks. Most of the time I'm watching Netflix, but I don't miss *The Latest* unless I'm otherwise occupied, if you know what I'm sayin'!" He let out an obnoxious guffaw as he nudged Reid with his elbow.

You're sayin' you haven't missed one episode, Drew thought, stifling a laugh.

"Wow, thanks, dude. I'm glad you like the show," Reid said with a huge smile. It wasn't his normal smile, Drew noticed. It was the TV one. He admired the way he could turn it on and off so easily.

"Aw, no, thank *you,* man—for being fuckin' awesome—Hey! Do a shot with us!" he said with wild-eyed excitement. "Can we get one, two, five, seven tequila shots?" he shouted at the bartender as he did a headcount.

Before Reid could respond, the bartender slid shot glasses to their new frat buddy, and he passed the drinks out to his friends. Then the bartender placed two shots in front of Drew and Reid.

Drew looked at Reid's glass and then at him. "What are you doing?" he mouthed as the frat guys counted down from five.

"Like I said, dude, moment by moment." Reid winked and downed the shot as the frats yelled, "One!"

Dumbfounded, Drew snatched his shot glass off the bar and threw it back. Then he lurched forward, coughing as the frat boys took to the dance floor. "What the hell?" he said, sniffing the glass. "That was apple juice."

"My fault, man," the bartender said. "I didn't know if you were like Reid or not. I can get you some real Cuervo if you want. I gave those dipshits the cheap stuff, but I got a nice Reserva for VIPs." He grabbed Drew's glass.

Drew held his hand up. "I'm good for right now, thanks."

Reid covered his mouth, doing a poor job concealing his amusement.

"Are you gonna tell me what's up with that?"

Reid shrugged. "I wasn't the rocker who had a DUI or some other catastrophic event and headed off to rehab after a press release. One day I decided I had enough of myself and started going to meetings. Only my close friends and family know I officially stopped drinking or that I consider myself an alcoholic. I figured out how to maintain my sobriety and my image by having a conversation with the bartender when I get to a place. I didn't have to talk to Jason, though." He nodded at the bartender. "We go way back. He knows what to do if somebody wants to buy me a drink," he explained as he slid Jason a twenty.

Jason slipped the tip into his pocket. Then he set a beer in front of Drew and nodded toward the other end of the bar in response to Drew's puzzled expression.

"Hey, is that the caterer from the wrap party?" Reid asked.

Drew looked casually toward the other end of the bar. "Yep," he said as he lifted the beer up and forced a smile at the woman he had loud, drunk sex with in one of the studio's bathrooms a week and a half ago. "Shit," he groaned, turning back to Reid. "She's comin' over, isn't she?" he asked without moving his lips.

"Sure is," Reid said as he hopped up. "What's goin' on, Monica?" He gestured at his stool. "Take my seat! I'm gonna hit the john." He turned to walk away but turned back abruptly. "Unless you two need it." The right side of his mouth and eyebrow twitched upward.

Drew gave him the finger as Reid chuckled his way to the restroom. Monica didn't seem to notice the exchange.

"Well, hey you!" Monica said, wrapping her arms around Drew and smashing her face against his. "You're busted, mister." She giggled, poking him playfully in the side. "You said you had your kids tonight."

"Oh, yeah, I mean no, I mean yeah," Drew stammered, like he did in all awkward social interactions. And he found interacting with his one-night stand well beyond the moment of completion extremely awkward. Unfortunately, Monica felt the opposite, evidenced by her daily calls and/or texts to "check on him."

He took a breath. "I mean, my kids are staying with me, but my sister took them and her kids to the movies, since Reid's makin' me work tonight," he said. And it was mostly true. They were there to scope out new acts for the show, but he wasn't being forced.

"Oh, that's cool," Monica said. And just when he thought things couldn't get more awkward, she gazed lovingly into his eyes.

Drew looked away in the direction she had come from. "So, who are you here with?"

"A couple of girlfriends." She shrugged. "But we're not that close. I can totally ditch them... if you wanna hang out." She rubbed his knee.

Drew winced. "That would be cool, but you know, like I said, I'm working tonight." He shrugged.

"Maybe after, then?" she asked as her hand worked its way up his thigh and swiftly into his pants.

He wrinkled his nose and shook his head. "The kids'll be back by the time I'm done here," he said, matching her persistence with resistance.

"Okay," she said, slowly licking her lips. "Maybe some other time when you're not so busy."

They continued to exchange innocuous small talk for a few minutes, while Drew tried to pretend he wasn't getting a hand job. Then Reid came back.

"You guys enjoy the showcase," Monica said as she grabbed a few napkins, gave one to Drew, and casually wiped her hand. Then she stood and hugged Drew, then Reid. "I better get back to my girls."

"Uh... okay... uh, thanks. Have a good time," Drew said as he quickly tucked and zipped.

"Stay outta trouble, Monica," Reid called out as she walked away.

"Too late!" she yelled over her shoulder.

Drew glanced at Reid from the corner of his eye. "What are you staring at me for, man?"

"I don't get it. That was like free money walking away," Reid said.

"Pssh. That's anything but free. She's been calling me and texting every day for a week and a half."

Reid raised both hands. "Say no more." He laughed. "You must have really laid it down, man! Or maybe she loves you." He fluttered his eyelids.

Drew growled as he took a swig of his beer and turned around to face the stage. The house band had stopped playing and the MC, Big Jake Matlin, jumped up onto the stage. Drew and Reid clapped and whistled right along with everyone else. Even if the acts were terrible, Big Jake would make it worth everyone's while.

"Okay! Okay! Okay! Do we have a show for you dirty club rats tonight!" he shouted and the whole place roared again.

"I'm gonna try to keep it as clean as I can tonight, because we have some really talented young girls for you to enjoy!" he announced, then immediately looked askance, pursing his lips. "Hmmmm, maybe I should choose different words. Nowadays you gotta be careful what you say about young ladies—old ones too," he snickered. The crowd laughed too. "But, seriously, you guys are in for a treat, because all these girls you get the pleasure to hear tonight can sing and play their fine asses off! So, without further ado, let's give it up for our first performer! London Torrence!!!"

The crowd cheered as a petite Black girl with a guitar took the stage. She was light skinned with a big curly 'fro piled on top of her head. The small hairs on Drew's arms stood up from the first note. Her smooth and sultry voice had a gravelly quality that is rare for someone so young. She couldn't have been more than nineteen, but she had a natural ability to punctuate her lyrics in a way that made her audience feel the song, not just hear it. Drew was impressed with how much control she had of her voice and the audience.

Drew nudged Reid. "Is this the girl you wanna put on the show?"

He shook his head. "Uh-uh."

"Well, you should. She's impressive. You can't even keep your eyes off her."

"Yeah, but she's like a combination of folk rock and neo soul. Our audience won't go for it. But she is pretty hot. She looks like Shanice, don't you think?"

"Maybe," he said, tilting his head and squinting. "If I look at her like this."

"You need to get your eyes checked. She looks exactly like Shanice!"

"Sure, man. Whatever you say," Drew agreed to get Reid to shut up so he could enjoy London's performance.

"So, what do you think about that?" Reid asked after a couple of minutes of silence.

"I told you. She's fantastic. I think the second song is better than the first and it's got a pretty alternative vibe. It could work for our audience. Plus, like you said, she's hot. So, even if they don't love her music, they'll love lookin' at her, for sure," Drew prattled on with a hard sell on the young artist's behalf.

"Fine. Okay. I'll talk to her after the showcase. But I was asking what you think about Shanice."

Drew furrowed his brow. "Huh?"

"What do you think about Shanice... and me, man!" he asked, rolling his eyes.

Drew burst into laughter. And he continued to laugh until he realized Reid wasn't.

"You're not joking?"

Reid glared at him.

"Oh! Uh, I dunno, Reid. I've never thought about you and Shanice as a 'you and Shanice,'" Drew said, throwing up air quotes. "Have you ever dated a Black girl before?" he asked as he racked his brain thinking of Reid's lengthy list of conquests.

"Dated?" Reid smirked, moving his eyebrows up and down. "No. So what?" He gave Drew the once over. "You better be careful, man. You're starting to sound like your pops."

"You know I'm not like that. I don't care if you date a Black girl, or any girl, for that matter. But you and Shanice butt heads about everything. I had no clue you thought of her as anything other than a thorn in your side."

"She pisses me off every day," he said. "But she's pretty amazing, don't you think? She keeps me in line—well, as much as anyone can. And she's always saying, 'Reid, you're so much better than silly and sensational. You need to start seeing yourself as a serious contender.' Do you think she means it?" He bit his bottom lip.

Ordinarily, Drew would have taken advantage of the rare opportunity to mess with his normally overconfident friend, but that seemed cruel. Reid looked and sounded like a high school kid trying to work out whether a girl he likes, likes him too. "Yeah, Reid, Shanice is pretty amazing. And I think she meant what she said because it's the truth." He didn't have the heart to tell him that Shanice was crushing on Kelvin. And it wasn't totally out of the realm of possibility that she was madly in love with Reid and was just doing a really, really good job of hiding it.

A sheepish grin spread across Reid's face as London belted out the final note of her song. The crowd went wild, proving that a room of hardcore rock music fans could be entertained by London's folk rock-neo soul style.

"Give it up again for London Torrence!" Jake bellowed. The audience responded with another rowdy round of applause. "Since I know that pretty young thing already knocked your socks off with that performance, you better hold on to your drawers for this next one. And for those of you going commando, well, you're in trouble." He laughed. "Put your hands together for Mickey Snow!"

A tall, thin girl with long purple hair and a matching purple guitar trotted up to the stage. She plugged in and got right down to business with a guitar solo so intense it grabbed the audience by the throat. Drew knew immediately that this was the girl Reid wanted to check out.

"Where'd you find this girl?" Drew asked.

Reid shrugged. "YouTube or something. Wait 'til you hear her sing. She's sick, man," he said. Then they both got comfortable, leaning back against the bar.

Reid was right. Mickey's guitar skills were out of this world. Her fingers danced across the strings and high on the fretboard at the speed of light it seemed. But her singing was in another galaxy. She played her vocal cords with even more precision. Her range was extraordinary, to say the least. Drew was sure he had never seen her before, but there was something awfully familiar about her. His face twisted with confusion.

"What's wrong, dude?" Reid asked.

Drew scratched at the stubble on his face. "I can't figure out where I know this girl from."

Reid's eyes popped as he grabbed his top lip with his bottom teeth, and then he quickly narrowed his eyes and licked his lips with an odd intensity.

Drew tilted his head at his friend's strange reaction. He considered the possibility that Reid might have had a ministroke. Just as he was about to ask him if he needed an ambulance, Mickey's song ended. The crowd cheered as she bowed, graciously receiving the well-deserved accolades.

"I was wondering if you guys would mind if I got a little help with my next song?" Mickey asked with a startlingly soft and sweet voice compared to the rough and powerful songstress they just heard. "My dad, who is also my manager, wrote the song, so I think it sounds better when he's up here with me."

The crowd applauded and whistled their approval.

Mickey clapped excitedly as she leaned back, looking backstage. "Come on out, Dad! Michael Bryant, everybody!" she said, and Drew's old bandmate, Mike, trotted out from stage right.

Drew's jaw dropped. He had been completely right and completely wrong about Mickey. He had never seen her before, not in person anyway, but he knew her. He knew when she was born, how much she weighed, that her real name was Michelle Snowden, why she played the guitar the way she did and could sing so well. He also knew that he owed his life to her—his life as a rock star, at least.

Drew stared at the father/daughter duo playing their hearts out as his cerebral cortex flooded with memories from a lifetime ago, when Wiretap was Joystick, the lead singer was a girl named Lainey Snowden, and Drew was nothing more than the band's biggest fan and occasional co-songwriter. Lainey had been friends with Mike, Travis, Chris, and Randy since middle school. But sometime during sophomore year, while seeing her safely home after band rehearsal, Mike and Lainey became more than friends. Mickey was on the way not long after that, and Drew became the lead singer of the newly christened Wiretap.

That was the abridged version. The details of how Drew became the lead singer of the band were much more complicated than that. Lainey's very Catholic parents didn't take kindly to their sixteen-year-old daughter getting knocked-up. They shipped her off to live with relatives in Virginia within days of finding out. Mike was devastated. They all were devastated. So, the five of them piled into Travis's mom's Honda Civic and headed down to Virginia on a recon mission to get Mike's girl and his kid. Devastated lovesick teen dads and their buddies have never been known for their good decision-making skills. By noon the next day, they were all headed back to Jersey in their parents' custody after being released from jail.

In the months after their trip down south, Mike would cry at random times. The guys would be laughing one minute; the next he'd be bawling. They gave him the time and space he needed to have his breakdown, but they never talked about Lainey and the baby. Seeing Mike performing with the daughter he never got the chance to raise, or barely even meet, brought it all back. Especially that night they went from wannabe heroes to juvenile delinquents.

"Park right here. It's the house on the corner with the white awning and the tire swing," Mike had said to Travis as he pulled to a stop four houses up from Lainey's uncle's house.

Mike sighed, staring at the house.

"You want us to go with you, man?" Chris said, shifting in the middle seat between Drew and Randy. Five hours riding on the hump from Jersey to Virginia had taken its toll on his long legs.

Mike shook his shaggy blond hair out of his face, revealing the deep creases in his forehead and dark circles under his eyes from weeks of worry and sleepless nights. "That's okay. Lainey said her aunt and uncle go play bingo every Saturday night. They leave her home alone with the baby." He jumped out of the car and jogged down the street. The guys had talked and laughed all the way down the highway, but as Mike went up to the door and rang the bell, no one made a sound.

"What's taking her so long?" Randy groaned.

"Chill, dude, he rang the doorbell like five seconds ago," Drew said as he hopped into the passenger seat.

Travis slid down low in the driver's seat. "This was a bad idea, Chris, man. We shouldn't have come. They told him not to come," he said, yanking his baseball cap down over his forehead.

"Look. We all agreed it ain't right for them not to let Mike see his kid," Chris said. "So, calm down. It's gonna be fine—see." He pointed at the house. There was Lainey in the open door, holding a bundle wrapped in a white blanket and wearing the broadest, brightest smile. Mike hugged her and the bundle, and then nodded at the car. Lainey placed the baby in Mike's arms and blew a dozen kisses at the car, bouncing up and down. Travis flashed his lights, and the young family went inside together.

They all exhaled in unison. "We might as well get comfortable," Travis said as he turned off the car and rolled down his window. "We're gonna be here for a while." He glanced at his watch. "There's no way we're gettin' home anywhere near curfew. I'm gonna be so grounded."

"I'm already grounded!" Randy said. "I'll be surprised if I get off lockdown before Halloween."

A robust debate ensued about their impending fate and who would be in the most and least trouble for their impromptu road trip, complete with several shoulder jabs and head smacks. Chris took the last place spot. His mother probably wouldn't even know he was gone. And by unanimous decision, Drew won first place. After congratulating him with a few more sucker punches, they settled down and nodded off, lulled by the sounds of a hot summer evening as insects buzzed, chirped, and hissed just beyond the nearby wood line. A few minutes or hours later, a pickup truck rumbled down the street, shaking the Honda and waking its occupants.

"Who's that?" Travis asked as the truck pulled into the driveway of the house. A huge, bearded man jumped out of the truck and stormed inside the house. A woman followed behind him.

The guys looked at each other with wide eyes and wider mouths. In seconds, they were out of the car and flying down the street. As they got closer, angry voices blared from the house, then a crash. Lainey yelled, "Let him go!" while the baby wailed like an alarm.

Drew made it to the door a fraction of a second before the others. They barreled into the house and found the bearded man holding Mike by his throat against a wall of shattered mirror. Mike clawed at the beefy fingers, squeezing the life out of him as his face went from red to purple. Drew, Chris, Travis, and Randy jumped on the man and took him down.

"Call 911, Linda!" he shouted as the boys kicked and stomped him like a giant cockroach until he stopped moving.

"We gotta get outta here!" somebody shouted.

Drew and Chris picked Mike up off the floor and dragged him out of the house as sirens screamed in the distance.

Drew stared at Mike and Mickey on stage. "You knew about them, didn't you?" he asked Reid.

"Yeah. I'm sorry. I would have told you, but I thought you'd flake on me."

Drew inhaled and exhaled slowly, nodding his head. He couldn't deny the truth of what Reid said. If he thought Mike might be there, let alone there was a possibility he would perform, he wouldn't have come. He would have been too afraid he couldn't handle it. As he watched Mike and Mickey, his muscles twitched, confirming his fear. His body wanted nothing more than to jump on stage and join them. An involuntary reaction to the visceral connection he and Mike shared.

The friendship between them, all five of them, had formed quickly over their passion for music. But it was the experience of supporting Mike through the confusion and resulting chaos of becoming a teenage father that forged their bond. From that moment forward, their lives became so intertwined, so deeply woven together, that the rift between them was injurious. Losing Chris and Randy felt like being ripped apart, and even though they hadn't died, losing Mike and Travis felt the same. They were just as gone.

All the therapy Drew had gone through over the years had helped him with the healing process. But no one truly recovers from that kind of loss.

Chapter 11

"Wow! Just wow!" Big Jake shouted. "I don't even know what to say. And you guys know me, I always got somethin' to say. That was a badass performance—period! Everybody, give it up for Mickey Snow and her pops, Mike Bryant! Where the hell you been at, dude!"

Mike shrugged sheepishly and stepped back while Mickey bowed and blew kisses at the cheering audience. Drew and Mike smiled. Lainey had always done that at the end of a good show and any other time she was extremely happy.

Jake told the crowd that there would be a ten-minute break before the next performer as Mickey and Mike dismounted the stage. Les was waiting at the bottom of the steps. She motioned for them to follow her and led them through the crowd over to Drew and Reid at the bar.

"Mickey, I want you to meet Reid Cox, host of *The Latest Late Show*," Les said, fulfilling her duties as Reid's freelance talent scout. "I'm assuming I don't have to introduce you guys." She glanced between Drew, Mike, and Reid. Then she took off.

Mike gave Reid a bro hug, then Drew.

"You still got it, man," Reid said and gave him a fist bump.

Drew nodded.

"Thanks, man," Mike said and looked over at Mickey. She was doing her best to look normal and calm while the performance adrenaline continued to surge through her veins, making her bounce and fidget a little.

Mike smirked as he put his arm around her and rubbed her back. "Drew, this is Michelle." He smiled from ear to ear.

Drew couldn't help but match Mike's dorky grin. "It's good to finally meet you." He extended his hand.

Mickey ignored Drew's hand and threw her arms around him. "Hi, Uncle Drew." She greeted him like she had known him her whole life. He didn't even know she knew of him before that moment. Either way, her hug felt nice—natural.

"I don't think I have the vocabulary to tell you how much I enjoyed your performance, Mickey," Drew said as she let him go. "You have so much of your parents in you, but you totally have your own thing goin' on... I don't know what I'm saying... I was really impressed."

"I was too, Mickey," Reid jumped in. "The stuff you have online got my attention, but that performance blew me away—all the way away. Can we talk for a few minutes?" He nodded toward the booth he and Drew had abandoned earlier that evening.

Mickey looked at Mike.

"Go on, sweetheart. I wanna talk to Drew for a minute."

"Okay!" Mickey said, and she and Reid went over to the booth.

Mike gestured at Jason, the bartender. "Can I get a beer?"

"You know Reid wants Mickey on *The Latest*, right?" Drew asked as they sat.

Mike nodded, taking a swig of his beer.

"I thought you were her manager."

Mike gave Drew a sideways glance. "You don't have to talk to me, man. I just wanted to give Michelle some space to do her thing."

Drew shook his head. "Aw, dude, I didn't mean it like that. I was only thinkin' you'd wanna be in on the discussion."

"I've already talked to Reid about the show," he said. "I'm fine with all the terms and conditions, but Michelle is the artist and a grown woman. It's her decision if she wants to do it. She's got a good head on her shoulders, a real feel for the business. She likes to call me her manager, but I'm really only here to support her and help her however I can. I think I owe her at least that, you know?"

"Yeah, I get it," Drew said. "How did all that come about, anyway? If you don't mind me asking. When did you try to contact her again?"

Mike shook his head. "I didn't. When they terminated my parental rights, I never tried to contact her again. Lainey would send me a picture and a letter every year on Michelle's birthday, but I never initiated any contact on my own. The judge made it clear that if I bothered them anymore, he would put me in jail for a very long time. I was just a dumb kid, with uneducated parents and a public defender fresh out of law school. Michelle was twelve before I found out my rights had been violated."

Drew nodded. "I remember."

"By then, she was having a nice life without me." He looked over at Mickey, who was talking a mile a minute. "I didn't want to mess that up for her."

"So, how'd you guys get together?"

"When she turned eighteen, she came to find me. Showed up at my door with a suitcase." He chuckled. "She said, 'Hi, Dad. Mom gave me your address and a plane ticket. She said her family got the first eighteen years, you can have the next, and there's nothing anybody can do to stop it.'" He cleared his throat and wiped his eyes. "That was, hands down, the best day of my life. Scary. But really the best thing that has ever happened to me."

"That's great, man. I'm happy for you," Drew said. "She's super talented and she seems like a nice kid."

"Thanks. But you have no idea. I haven't known anyone as positive and as optimistic as Michelle, since, well... since Chris."

Drew flashed an incredulous look. Chris's positivity was supernatural. Positive people get lemons and make lemonade. Chris never had to make anything out of the lemons. He'd take a big bite and say, "Lemons are fuckin' delicious!" He was incapable of being sad or discouraged.

"That's hard to believe, Mike. I've never met anybody anywhere near Chris's level."

"Yeah, I know. It kinda messes with my head. Sometimes she'll say something, and I do a double take. It's like Chris's whispering in her ear."

"Maybe he is," Drew said with a shrug. "Maybe he's been lookin' out for her."

Mike nodded. "Hmph, maybe. But I'm not gonna lie. I got a little suspicious. If she didn't look so much like me, I might have had to ask for a DNA test."

Drew laughed. "The purple hair threw me off somewhat, but she looks exactly like you, dude. Well, she looks exactly how you used to look," he clarified. "I hardly recognized you, man. All the hair you had on your head is now on your face!"

"Right?" Mike ran his fingers through his long, thick beard. "When I started goin' bald, I shaved it off. I'm never doin' the comb over thing like my dad. Had to grow the beard so I wouldn't look like a dick!"

They laughed.

"So, how're April and the kids?" Mike asked as his laughing tapered off.

"Everybody's good." Drew nodded. "The kids are staying with me now for a few weeks. We're havin' a great time," he said as his eyes involuntarily darted over to the booth where Reid was. "April's doin' good. She's got a bunch of clients she's training, and she keeps talking about writing a vegan cookbook. And she's... engaged. So yeah, she's doing real well... real well."

"I heard about that," Mike said. "Travis told me she and the guy came to his restaurant a few months ago."

Drew cracked his neck. "Oh, really? Have you been to his place yet? I hear it's the place to be. Every time I pass it, people are lined up down the block," he said, shifting the conversation to a slightly less uncomfortable topic.

"Yeah, of course. I've been a few times. He's got a nice setup, good food, live music, huge flat screen TVs, pool tables, and some classic arcade games. It's a playground for adult children. It's like he opened a restaurant just for us! You should come out sometime. Travis'd be stoked to see you."

"Sure. I bet he'd give me his best table right out by the dumpster."

Mike reared back on his stool. "Are you serious, man? You really think that?" He looked mad, but he sounded disappointed.

Drew glared at Mike for several seconds. "Let's say I don't expect to be welcomed with open arms." He rolled his beer bottle between his hands. "I'm not under any delusion that you guys don't hate my guts," he said and chugged the rest of his beer.

Mike sighed and shook his head. "We don't hate you, Drew."

"Well, you should. I ruined your lives... and I'm sorry."

Mike rubbed his bald head vigorously like he might be trying to massage his thoughts. "First of all, my life isn't ruined. It's good. I've been workin' steady as a session musician for years—albums, TV shows, movies. I've even had to turn jobs down sometimes. And Trav's life is definitely not ruined. You know he always wanted to own a restaurant like his granddad and he's makin' money hand over fist," he said. "Second, even if our lives were ruined, it wouldn't be your fault, man. Something really shitty happened that changed our lives—all our lives. You didn't cause it, so you don't have anything to apologize for. I think we should apologize to *you*."

"For what?" Drew huffed.

"For forcing you back into the studio before you were ready. I was so wrapped up in healing my own pain and getting back on my feet, I didn't pay attention to how much you were suffering until it was too late. If we had given you the time and space you needed to heal, things wouldn't have turned into such a disaster.

And you wouldn't have felt the need to pull so far away from us—and from April and the kids," he said, concentrating extra hard on peeling the label off his beer bottle. "I apologize for that. I know Travis feels the same way."

"Not your fault, man." Drew shook his head vigorously. "That's all on me. I knew I wasn't ready. I knew my head and my heart weren't in the right place and that I needed help. I just didn't get it soon enough." He waved two fingers at Jason. "We'll take that Cuervo you were talking about earlier."

Jason nodded as he set up the shot glasses in front of Drew and Mike. He grabbed the Reserva from the top shelf and poured. They clinked glasses and immediately threw back the tequila. A toast wasn't necessary. It had always been the same and always would be: "To everything." It went without saying. As did any further declarations of amends.

Reid and Mickey made their way back to the bar, giggling like old friends.

"Looks like you guys had a good talk," Mike said as Mickey attacked him with a hug, nodding her head with so much excitement her whole body shook.

"Sure did!" Reid said, obviously excited too. "Mickey agreed to do the show. She'll be on the season premiere when we come back in a few weeks."

Mike pulled Mickey in and planted a kiss on the side of her head. "That's great, sweetheart. And thanks, Reid. It's real cool how you put unknown artists on your show to give 'em more exposure."

"I know what it's like starting out. Getting attention and building a fan base is tough. I like to give talented artists, like Mickey here, a boost whenever I can," he said, sounding very much like that serious contender Shanice was talking about.

"Well, I think this calls for a celebration," Drew said as he threw four fingers up.

Jason nodded and prepared the shots with his back to them this time. Then he slid the glasses over to the four of them. As Big Jake took to the stage again to introduce the next performer in the showcase, they all clinked their shot glasses and downed their drinks simultaneously—three tequilas and one apple juice.

Chapter 12

Drew cut out of the bar one song into the house band's midnight set. He had noticed the drunk frat boys trying to form a mosh pit even though it wasn't a heavy metal band, and the bar was small. He immediately felt old and annoyed. It was well before most people were even thinking about leaving, but the wait time for a car had been ridiculous.

The elevator door slid open, and Drew jumped a little, not expecting to see a young girl waiting. There were only three apartments on his floor, and although she looked familiar, she wasn't one of his neighbors. The older couple living across from him were out of town, and it was unlikely the gay architect down the hall would be entertaining a teenage girl of Asian descent at that time of night. He was more into Scandinavian-looking bodybuilders from what Drew could tell. So, he found the girl's presence on his floor startling and suspicious; especially since he lived in a secure building requiring keycard access to all the floors.

He decided not to question her. She was too busy texting to notice him, let alone recognize him, and he didn't want to initiate an interaction that could lead to an unwanted selfie and delay him getting to the bathroom. Besides, he was about ninety-nine percent sure why she was there and the person he needed to talk to about it was inside his apartment where the bathroom was anyway.

Drew entered his apartment from the quiet, warmly lit hallway and suddenly his senses were under attack. All the lights were on, the volume of the television was at full blast, and a thick cloud of Lysol lingered, threatening to choke him to death.

I'm gonna kill him, Drew resolved as he stepped inside the small powder room off the entryway. He knew exactly what it smelled like when an amateur tried to cover up the odor of weed.

After Drew took care of his business in the bathroom, he went directly to the living room where Zach sat sunk deep into the sofa cushions, playing video games on his laptop. He snatched the headphones off Zach's head and turned off the TV.

"Ugh! Dad!" he said breathlessly as he sat up panting, pressing his hand to his chest. "You scared me," he growled.

"What the hell, Zach! It's two o'clock in the morning."

Zach looked down at the floor. "I didn't think you'd be home this early. I couldn't sleep."

"No shit, dude. This isn't exactly a soothing environment you've set up. Where're Paige and Cole?" he asked, peering down the dark hallway where their room was located.

"They're asleep. Nothing wakes them up," he said. "I checked on them a few minutes ago."

Drew bit down hard, tightening his jaw. "After your company left."

"What company? What are you talking about, Dad?" His voice went up several octaves.

Drew closed his eyes and blew out a long sigh. *Let the games begin.* "Let's go," he said, gesturing for Zach to follow him.

Zach followed Drew over to the kitchen, dragging his feet like he was being led to the slaughter.

Drew pulled out a stool from under the peninsula. "Sit!" he barked and stood across from him on the other side. Having a buffer between them was in the boy's best interest.

Drew glared at Zach for several minutes, watching his son attempt to suppress a cannabis-induced giggle fit while he organized his thoughts. Zach shifted his weight hopelessly, trying to get comfortable on the metal kitchen stool as Drew desperately tried to reconcile his conflicting emotions. His anger was palpable, but there were also significant hints of pride, guilt, and amusement. With all those emotions swirling around, he reminded himself to be careful in the unfamiliar territory of primary disciplinarian.

"If you need to use the bathroom, I suggest you go now. I don't want any unnecessary interruptions—or accidents—while I'm dealing with you," Drew said, giving Zach a foreboding once over. "And make sure you splash cold water on your face for a few minutes before you come back."

Zach's fidgets and giggles came to a halt. "Okay," he said with wide, bloodshot eyes and scurried off to the bathroom, almost tripping over the stool. He almost tripped again when he returned.

"Why would you bring that girl into the house with your little brother and sister sleeping down the hall?" Drew asked, looking straight into Zach's eyes, more pink now than red.

Zach shook his head. "I didn't—"

Drew held up his hand. "Before you lie, let me show you this," he said, opening the text message Lia had sent him earlier that evening. He showed Zach the picture of himself talking to a waitress at the pizza place Lia had taken them to. Her message read: *Somebody has a crush. LOL!!!!*

"This same girl got on the elevator when I got off," Drew said.

Zach hung his head. "She was nice, Dad," he said slightly above a whisper.

"Are you allowed to bring random girls to your mom's house when she's out? Are you allowed to bring any girls into the house when your mom is out?" he asked, but he knew the answer.

"No."

"Then why the hell would you do it here?"

Zach shrugged. "You never said I couldn't have company, so I didn't think you would care."

"You know what, Zach? If you had some of your buddies or even a girlfriend over, I probably wouldn't have minded that. I'd be irritated if you didn't ask, but I wouldn't get bent out of shape about it," he conceded. "But you brought a stranger into my house. Did you happen to notice I have a few Grammys and some other awards, as well as some gold and platinum records lying around here?"

He nodded. "Yeah."

"What if she took something? What if she had brought a friend and they came in and took something, while you and the girl were gettin' busy? Or worse, what if they hurt you or your brother and sister? People may seem nice, but you never know what they're capable of these days."

He looked down and sighed. "I didn't think about that."

Drew shook his head. "Did you at least use one of the rubbers I gave you?"

Zach looked askance and cracked his neck.

"Are you kidding me, Zach! I gave you a box of a hundred condoms!" In the blink of an eye, he had circled the island buffer and yanked Zach off his stool. "You can't be that irresponsible!" He was two inches from Zach's face with a death grip on his upper arms. "Are you ready to be a father? Or maybe you wanna know what it feels like to shoot fire outta your dick!"

"No! Ow, Dad! Wait!" Zach shrieked. "I did use a condom! I used one of yours! The ones you gave me are gone!"

Drew released him and stepped back, scratching his head while he worked out the most improbable math problem in the universe. "You used a hundred condoms in six months?"

"No! I gave a bunch to my friends," Zach said, rubbing his arms. "And, um, well, this one time we, um, we didn't have enough balloons for the water balloon fight and, um—"

"I got it," Drew said as he closed his eyes and took a long, cleansing breath. Then he slowly returned to the other side of the peninsula, massaging his temples.

"Um... Dad?"

Drew looked up.

"Are you... gonna tell Mom?"

"I'm not gonna tell Mom."

Relief washed over Zach's face. "Thanks, Dad. Cool. Can I go to bed now?" He hopped off the stool and turned toward the living room.

"Sit your ass down! I'm not done with you yet. Just because I'm not telling your mother about what you pulled tonight doesn't mean you're off the hook," he said. "You *are* going to be punished."

Zach's relieved expression withered away as he slumped back onto the stool. "Are... are you... gonna hit me?"

Drew looked into his son's face and saw himself. He had been in Zach's position many times, staring into the angry eyes of a pissed off father, wondering how bad the punishment would be. The difference was Drew never had to ask if his father was going to hit him.

Drew shook his head. "I'm not gonna hit you, Zach. But I am taking your phone and your laptop and any other devices you brought with you." He held out his hand. "And no video games for the rest of the time you're here."

Zach groaned as he fished his cell phone out of his pocket and handed it over. Then he went to gather his laptop and other electronics as Drew shot off a text to April. *I took Zach's phone because of his attitude. In case you text him and he doesn't respond.*

"Is there anything else? You want my clothes? My toothbrush?" Zach asked with an eye roll as he stacked the devices on the island.

"Keep the clothes and the toothbrush. But you can drop the attitude and show some respect before I reconsider my decision not to tell your mom."

A huge fake smile spread across Zach's face. "May I please go to bed now, Daddy, sir?"

Drew chuckled. "Sure, go ahead."

Zach turned to leave the kitchen. "Oh! I almost forgot," Drew said. Zach turned back around slowly. The fake smile was significantly weaker, but still there. "When you smoke up a man's stash, it only adds insult to injury using his entire can of Lysol to cover it up," he said with his own fake smile as Zach's turned into a gaping hole.

Zach shook his head adamantly. "Dad, I didn't—"

"Don't waste your breath, Zach. It was in the same drawer as the condoms. So, sleep well, my son. We're gonna have a long talk tomorrow about stealing my weed after you clean this whole apartment. Starting with organizing my closet," he said as Zach trudged off to bed.

Drew grabbed Zach's electronics and went to his bedroom, ready to collapse into bed, but stopped short at the door. Not only had Zach helped himself to Drew's condoms and marijuana, but he had also made sloppy use of his bed. He seriously contemplated going to sleep anyway. It wasn't like he had never slept in a bed after a guy had used it. Things like that happened with five guys on the road. But he wasn't twenty anymore—or thirty—and there was something disgustingly incestuous about sleeping anywhere near his own son's wet spot.

Right as he finished changing the sheets, someone tapped his lower back.

"Ugh!" he yelled and spun around to find Cole standing there. "Oh, Cole, you scared me, kid. What're you doin' up? Did me and Zach wake you?"

"I don't feel good, Dad," he whimpered with tears in his eyes.

Drew's heart sank a little. He thought Cole had gotten over his homesickness. "You're okay, buddy?" He gave him a gentle pat on his shoulder. "You wanna sleep with me?"

Cole nodded as Drew rubbed his head. "You feel kinda warm, Cole. Are you really sick?"

Cole looked up at him. While all the kids bore a resemblance to Drew, Cole was his twin. Looking at him was like looking at his nine-year-old self—his unwell nine-year-old self.

Cole opened his quivering mouth to respond, and it turned into a scene from *The Exorcist*. Drew watched in horror as chunks of pizza, popcorn, and French fries spewed from Cole's mouth on a river of chocolate milkshake all over the fresh sheets he had just put on his bed with "bounce a quarter off 'em" military perfection.

Drew stood paralyzed for a minute, in shock, trying to suppress the gag reflex pulling at his throat, while Cole cried hysterically.

"I'm sorry, Daddy!" he wailed.

Snapping out of his paralysis, Drew scooped Cole up and carried him to the bathroom. He cleaned him up and took his temperature with the thermometer April had sent along with all their other "just in case" paraphernalia. It wasn't too bad—only ninety-nine. He put one of his smaller T-shirts on him and stuffed his pajamas and the sheets in a garbage bag. Then he threw a few big towels on the bed and laid Cole on top of them.

As he lay there with his youngest son's knee in his back, his little hand on the side of his face, and the smell of his vomit lingering in his nose, Drew thought about how easy April made parenting look and sighed.

Thank God Paige doesn't give me any trouble, he thought. *I think she's my favorite.* He chuckled, drifting off to sleep.

"Daddy..." Paige whispered, tapping his shoulder. "Something's wrong."

Chapter 13

Drew sat on the rooftop deck of his apartment building, holding a cup of coffee in one hand and his head in the other. It was early, a little after nine, usually the perfect time to sit quietly by himself to decompress and gather his thoughts. There was something sobering about the 360-degree view of the city his rooftop perch provided. He always felt equally connected and detached up there, which was ironically centering. But not today.

"Is this seat taken?" April asked as she sat on the deck chair next to him.

Drew jumped. He hadn't heard her coming. "How'd you find me?" he asked with a sheepish smirk.

"I've known you for twenty-two years, Drew. You seek solitude when there's chaos. And with all that went on last night, I figured it was either the roof or a flight to Antarctica," she said with a hardy laugh laced with a hint of vindication.

Drew scowled. "You're eating this up, aren't you? Having to come rescue me from my own kids."

April continued to snicker.

"For your information, I was doing fine until Paige started her period in the middle of the night. The only thing she would let me do is go buy her, um, girl things from the drugstore. When I came back, she had locked herself in the bathroom. She said she didn't want anybody to look at her and she was staying in there until you came to get her."

April rolled her eyes. "You know she gets her flair for drama from you, right?"

"I don't know what you're talking about," Drew muttered, staring out across the city.

April smirked as she grabbed his coffee mug and took a sip. "Mmmm, that's good," she said, peering into the cup.

"It's vegan."

April nodded with an impressed expression as she settled back into her seat and continued to drink her newly acquired hot beverage.

"So, how is she? Did you get her out of the bathroom?"

"Of course I got her out of the bathroom. And she's fine. She's cleaned up and all set with her two-year supply of feminine products courtesy of her overdramatic daddy." She snickered again.

"Good," he said, ignoring the dig. "You guys headed out soon?"

"You guys?"

"Aren't you taking the kids home?" he asked as he rubbed the back of his neck.

"I hadn't planned to. Do you want me to take them home?" She tilted her head slightly.

"No, but I'm sure they wanna go after last night."

April's face pinched in contemplation. "They didn't tell me they want to go home. I talked to Paige. She's fine. I promise. I've been talking to her about her period for years. She just didn't expect to get it here with you for the first time. She was embarrassed that she messed up her jammies and that you know she's 'a woman' now." She chuckled.

Drew chuckled too, but not from amusement. The reminder that his little girl was officially growing up made him nervous in a way it never had with Zach. Part of him would always see Paige as the three-year-old in footed pajamas who sat on his lap sucking her thumb and enjoyed twirling his curls around her finger more than her own.

"And Cole remembers nothing about throwing up last night," April continued. "But I reminded him he can't eat processed meats like pepperoni. He gets sick every time."

"What about Zach? I'm sure he wants to get outta here."

"If he does, he didn't mention it to me. He didn't seem happy to see me at all. He actually looked like he had seen a ghost when he came into the living room and saw me talking to Paige."

"Oh yeah?" he asked, adding a higher pitch at the end to sound surprised.

"Yep. He said, 'Hi, Mom,' did a one-eighty, and hurried back down the hall. When I was done with Paige, I went to look for him and I found him pulling everything out of your closet. I told him you wouldn't like him messing around with your stuff, but he assured me he was helping you out and you knew all about it."

"Hmph," Drew nodded.

April raised her eyebrow. "Hmph," she mimicked him. "It must have been a doozy," she said as she took a sip of her coffee.

"What?"

"Whatever Zach did to lose all his electronics *and* get sentenced to housework."

Drew sighed. "April, I can't—"

She put her hand up. "It's fine. You don't have to tell me. I get the sense that it's probably something I don't wanna know. And it looks like you have everything under control."

"Psshh. You don't have to do that. I know I suck at this."

April narrowed her eyes. "What are you talking about?"

"I don't know what I'm doing, April!"

She wrinkled her nose. "Oh, Drew. I know that," she teased.

"I'm serious. You make this parenting thing look like a piece of cake, and it isn't. I haven't slept all night, and they're not even babies!" He threw his hands up. "I don't know how you've managed to do this so well for so long all on your own. You're amazing. I don't tell you that enough."

The apples of April's cheeks turned bright pink. "Thank you, Drew, but I did have some help. My parents, my sister, my friends... you."

"Me?" he huffed. "That's nice of you to add me to the list, but we both know I don't make the cut. When I wasn't on the road with the band, I was in the studio with the band. During the brief periods I was home, I was too exhausted, too preoccupied, or too depressed to be of any use to you or the kids. I know, most of the time, I was like another kid for you to take care of. And I'm sorry for that," he said, rubbing her knee.

April stared at Drew for a few seconds. "The minute I looked up and saw that wild, curly-haired eighteen-year-old kid on stage with a voice that reaches in and grabs hold of your soul, that was it," she said. "I knew you'd always be a part of my life. I didn't know if that meant as a crazy groupie following you from gig to gig or what, but I knew I was in for the long haul. I jumped into this situation, feet first, with my eyes wide open. And whether or not you believe it, I don't have any regrets. You're not perfect, but you're a good man with a good heart, Andrew Simon. And you're a good dad." She grabbed his hand and gave it a squeeze.

"Thanks," he said with a chuckle. He never understood how April always knew the right thing to say to help him feel better. He was still exhausted, but her pep talk gave him a confidence boost. He just might make it through the next couple of weeks without messing the kids up too badly.

"Well, I'm gonna get out of here," April said as she stood. He grabbed her hand.

"You don't have to leave. I'm gonna make breakfast. You should join us," he said as he stood up with her. "I might have an apple you could eat, and there's plenty more coffee where that came from." He nodded at the coffee mug.

April glanced at her watch. "Can't. I gotta get back. Tony and I have a meeting with a caterer and then I have a client. Rain check?"

Drew nodded. "Sure," he said flatly to disguise his disappointment.

"Great!" she said as she wrapped her arms around his midsection. Then she leaned back a little and grinned, still holding him securely around his waist.

Drew didn't return her smile. He gazed into her hazel-green eyes, taking advantage of the rare opportunity to be so close to her beautiful face. Then he gently pinched a fallen eyelash off her cheek.

"Make a wish," he said, bringing the tiny halfmoon-shaped hair on the tip of his index finger close to her lips.

April closed her eyes and blew softly on his finger. As the lash sailed through the air, she looked up into Drew's eyes, smiling again, but with a heavy-lidded seductiveness he hadn't seen in a long time. He angled his head down and hovered about a half inch from her lips, waiting for any sign of opposition. There was none. He pressed his lips against hers. And for a solid minute, they kissed each other as their hands reacquainted themselves with their bodies. Then Drew slid his cold hand under April's shirt. She gasped the moment it made contact with her warm skin and pulled away abruptly. In seconds, she was gone, disappearing behind the thud of the heavy roof door.

Drew stood still for a few minutes, feeling partially deflated. And as he waited for another part of him to fully deflate, his phone vibrated. His first thought was that April was calling to tell him off, but it wasn't her.

"Hey, Kelvin."

"Drew! Yo, what's up, man?"

"Not too much. I was wondering if you had forgotten about me, man. I haven't heard from you in weeks. You got good news for me? Am I related to Jesus?" he joked.

"Ha! Yes, sir! He's your father and your brother, but not in a West Virginia kinda way," he said, letting out such a sharp bark of a laugh at his own joke that Drew had to move the phone away from his ear. "But seriously, we found a British royal in your line. Can't tell you who, but I think you'll be pleasantly surprised when it's revealed."

"Oh yeah? That's cool. Is that on my mom's side?" Drew asked eagerly.

"I'm sorry, man. That's still on your dad's side. I'm afraid we hit a, um, roadblock with your mother's side."

"Really? How far have you gotten?"

"Your grandparents," he admitted.

"That's the information I gave *you*," Drew said, making no effort to conceal his disappointment. "Are you trying to tell me you're not going to be able to go back any further than that!?"

"Noooo, nah, man, I'm not saying that at all. It's just... some of the information you gave us was kinda misleading. I mean, I'm not saying you deliberately gave us misinformation," he said quickly over Drew's low grumble. "But it sent us in a direction that turned out to be a dead end."

"Sorry, dude," Drew apologized, trying to manage his irritation. "I told you everything I was told."

"Don't even worry about it, man. It happens all the time with this stuff. A lot of what we think we know about our family history is mostly based on the retelling of assumptions and misunderstandings," he said. "Hey, you went down and let the lab get a sample of your DNA, right?"

"Yeah, I did that a few weeks ago."

"Good, good, that should be back soon then..." he trailed off.

"So, is that it, then?" Drew asked curtly, ready to end the call. After so many weeks with no new information about his mother's family, he was already frustrated. Kelvin suggesting the little bit of information his mother had shared with him about her family could be false was going to make him say something he would regret.

"Are you busy today? I have some more interesting discoveries about your dad's side of the family I can show you," he offered.

"Did you know that you have family members that fought on opposite sides of the Civil War *and* the Revolutionary War?"

"I did not know that. But I thought you said you weren't gonna give me any details like that."

"You're right. I did say that. I would normally wait 'til the show, but I feel bad about not having anything to tell you about your mother's family. So, can we meet somewhere?"

"I'm taking my kids to that bowling place at Chelsea Piers around three," Drew said.

"Cool! That place is tight. You mind if I meet you there?"

"Sure, but I should warn you. My younger two have been askin' about bein' on the show with me. They will hound you about that until they wear you down."

Kelvin laughed. "If your family is anywhere near as persuasive as my wife and kids, they're as good as on the show."

Chapter 14

Drew tried to ignore the pulsating pain behind his right eye. But each time the Lyft jerked forward through rush hour traffic, the pain intensified, making it impossible to concentrate on Cole's animated blow-by-blow account of their time at Chelsea Piers. Good thing their driver was engaged, offering a "whoa, that's so cool!" and an "is that right?" at regular intervals because Drew was drifting in and out while Paige sat in the middle seat, pretending she didn't know Cole at all. Zach sat in the front, pretending he didn't know any of them.

"What's wrong, Daddy?" Paige asked as Drew massaged his temples.

"Nothing, sweetheart. I'm getting a headache, that's all."

"It's Cole's fault, isn't it? You want me to tell him to shut up?"

Drew managed a chuckle. "Leave your brother alone. I just need to get some sleep."

"Oh." She grimaced. "I guess that's my fault, then. Sorry I kept you up all night."

He gave her knee a pat. "It's not *all* your fault. Your brothers had a hand in it too, but don't worry about me. I'll be fine... How are you feeling, by the way? Your tummy okay?" he whispered.

Her cheeks flushed bright red. "Yeah. I'm good," she said quietly.

Drew laid his head back against the headrest.

"You better go straight to bed when we get home."

Drew smiled. She said, "when we get home," and not "when we get to your house."

"Yes, ma'am. Did you have fun today?"

"Yeah! Well, not as much as him, apparently," she said, flinging her thumb to her left at Cole, still chattering away about his rock wall climbing prowess. "But that place was so much fun!"

"What was your favorite part—wait, let me guess, basketball? I think I'm gonna start calling you Stephanie Curry. You didn't miss one shot."

She giggled. "I love basketball, but my favorite part was talking to Mr. Kelvin."

"Oh," Drew grunted and resumed massaging his temples.

"You don't like him much, do you?"

"What makes you say that?"

"You made your mean face the whole time he was telling us about Grandpa's ancestors."

Drew stopped massaging and looked at Paige. "What's my mean face?"

She pinched her brows together and curled up the right corner of her lip slightly.

"Ha. Wow. I guess I better apologize to Kelvin if I looked like that."

"Yeah," she said, wrinkling her nose. "But why were you so mad at him?"

"I wasn't mad at him, Paige. I actually like Kelvin. A lot. And I think the stuff about our ancestors on your grandfather's side is cool. I was just a little disappointed."

She nodded. "You wanted him to tell us more about your mom?"

He nodded. "Yeah. She's really the only reason I agreed to do this."

"I get it," she said, placing her hand on his shoulder. "But he seems like a real smart guy, Daddy. It must be hard to find out all that stuff about dead people. I'm sure he'll get to the bottom of things, though. Maybe grandma was a spy or something. Wouldn't that be cool!"

Drew smiled at his daughter. She was a beautiful little girl, or rather "young woman" as she had reminded him at least three times that day, but he always felt bad that she came out looking more like him than April. But Paige was so much like her mother in all the ways that mattered most. She had inherited all the best parts of April, including the ability to be honest with him about his shortcomings without making him feel small. Pulling her into a side hug, he buried his face into Paige's cascade of unruly curls and planted a kiss on the crown of her head. "And you're a real smart young woman."

As soon as they got home, Paige handed Drew his migraine medication and a glass of water, then shoved him down the hall toward his bedroom. He was fast asleep as soon as his head hit the pillow. And in no time, the seed planted by Paige had taken root in his dreams and flourished like a weed.

"Calm down, Drew," Lia said, surprisingly relaxed in the seedy bar. She stood out like a sore thumb in a white lace dress surrounded by grungy bikers. "Why are you so upset?"

"Those assholes want me to believe that Mom was a Russian spy. That she made up her entire identity. And that the people we thought were our grandparents were also spies," he said with his brow pinched so tightly it formed a wrinkled unibrow over his eyes.

Lia nodded, taking it all in, but she remained expressionless. "What's the big deal?" She shrugged without looking up from her phone.

"What's the big deal!" His voice shot up to its highest octave. "They duped me. It's a scam! They fabricated a bunch of research to make the show more interesting. FUUUUCK!!!" he howled.

"So, what now? You're gonna drop out?" she asked as she tapped out a text message fast and furious. "Dad will love that. You know what he thinks about quitters. I can hear him now. 'Andrew! Simons honor our commitments.'"

"Disappointing Dad and breaking my contract are the least of my problems." He rubbed the back of his neck. "I need your help to get outta town, Lia."

She rolled her eyes. "Oh my God, Drew, you are so dramatic. You wanna leave town because you don't like what they're telling you about Mommy?"

"No, I *need* to leave because I don't wanna go to jail." He leaned in close to her ear. "I just kicked Kelvin's ass for the lies he told me about Mom."

She finally put her phone down and looked him in the eyes. "Is he okay?"

He shrugged. "Don't know, don't care. Last I saw, he was sprawled at the bottom of the stairs I tossed him down."

"Drew!" Lia gasped. "We gotta get you outta here. The police will be after you!" Her wide, wild eyes darted around the suddenly empty room. All the bikers had vanished, and they were now alone in their father's kitchen. "We need to get you to Mommy right away," she whispered.

Drew narrowed his eyes. "What are you talkin' about?"

"You have to go stay with Mom, Drew. She'll keep you safe."

He cocked his head like a confused puppy.

"What?" she asked with a sly grin. "You know Mommy's alive, right? Kelvin told you the truth. She *was* a Russian spy and had to disappear when Putin took office."

Drew grabbed Lia's hand. "Mom is dead. You remember the car accident, don't you?" he said slowly, like she was a mental patient. "You alright, sis?"

Lia snatched her hand back, threw her head back, and cackled at the ceiling. "Oh, *I'm* fine," she said as one side of her mouth curled up. "But I'm not so sure about you, bro. You're definitely gonna get it when Mommy finds out you fell for the death hoax."

Drew stared at Lia in disbelief. She didn't even sound like herself, at least not her adult self.

"Look, Drew. If you don't believe me, ask her yourself." She glanced over her shoulder.

Drew looked past his sister right as their mother strolled into the kitchen with a basket of flowers from her garden. The frown she wore, along with a deeply furrowed brow, said loud and clear how disappointed she was in him. He froze, rendered speechless and breathless. And everything around him went silent and still as well until his phone vibrated. He glanced down at it out of habit, but looked back up right away to see Kelvin, covered in blood, running his way at full speed. Then Drew's phone started vibrating violently, and the whole house shook.

"Ugh!" Drew bellowed, nearly jumping out of the bed. He was fully awake from his nightmare, but he didn't want to open his eyes. After his heart rate stabilized, he forced his lids open slowly, one at a time, and looked over at his alarm clock. It was only 11:00 p.m.

His bedroom was quiet except for the intermittent buzzing from the phone and Cole's snoring. In true Cole form, the screaming and all the back-to-back text messages coming in didn't wake him. He lifted his phone off the nightstand to see what the commotion was about.

I just left this event and I got a bunch of bomb ass musicians comin thru the studio tonight. Y'all down? (From EJ to Drew and Reid)

Reid: Aw man!! I'm outta town

EJ: Nice. Where u at? Rio? Fiji? Tahiti?

Reid: I wish. I'm in Phoenix visiting my grandma. LOL

EJ: That's hot

Reid: FU

EJ: Ha! No judgment. I just got back from home a couple days ago. My dad guilted me into helping my brothers clean out the garage. LOL

Reid: That's funny as hell. I gotta go to church tomorrow. I hope the building doesn't spontaneously combust

EJ: Yea, you might wanna give the fire dept a heads-up. Where u at Drew?

Reid: Probably changing a diaper or something

EJ: He got a baby

Nope

EJ: There he is! U comin thru?

Wish I could, but I got my kids. They're not babies, but I can't leave my son in charge after what he did last night

Reid: What he do?

A random waitress and my weed

Reid: Whoa

EJ: How old is he

16

EJ: Dayuuuumn! Where he get all that game

Reid: From his Mom. LOL

LOL Sad, but tru

EJ: Well holla at me when u can come thru. I'm serious. I got some ideas I wanna run by you

Drew stared at the last text for five minutes, trying to think of a response. His heart pounded with excitement, and his mind reeled with questions. But he had to be careful. He didn't want to come off as a dork, but he didn't want to look like a dick either. He had to craft a careful response to strike an elegant balance between the two.

Cool

He tapped send, set the phone back on the nightstand, and fell into a peaceful sleep with a goofy grin on his face.

Chapter 15

Drew and the kids spent the next two weeks enjoying family-friendly fun in and around New York City. They went to museums, parks, the Bronx Zoo, the Statue of Liberty, and the Empire State Building like they were tourists. He even let Paige convince him to get up at four a.m. to take her and Cole to the *Today Show*. They couldn't convince Zach to go, however, especially after he saw them making their "HI MOMMY!" sign. But they got Al Roker's attention and their five seconds of fame as Drew stood off to the side, successfully avoiding detection in his trusty long sleeved T-shirt, baseball cap, and shades.

Except for the *Today Show*, the kids had already been to most of the places they visited, either with April or on field trips, but they had never been to any of the places with Drew. Being together for such an extended period of time was a novel experience for all of them. But after the first rocky week, Drew started to relax and enjoy the time with his children. So much so that when the day arrived for April to pick them up, he couldn't shake the sadness gnawing at him.

"Here she comes!" Cole squealed, bouncing up and down in the booth.

"Daddiieeee," Paige whined. "Make him stop. He's gonna ruin the surprise," she snapped at Cole.

"Chill. Both of you," Drew ordered as he waved April over from the hostess stand.

She waved back and glided across the restaurant in her normal graceful stride.

"My babies!" She stretched her arms out.

Paige and Cole jumped up and barreled into her, almost knocking her off balance. Drew and Zach rose like civilized gentlemen and hugged her gently. Then Cole escorted April to her specially designated seat in the center and plopped down next to her as everyone else took their seats.

"I'm so happy to see you guys!" April said. "I feel like I haven't seen you in months. You've all grown at least two inches, I think."

"Daddy, too?" Paige asked with a giggle.

"Sure. Daddy too." She tapped Paige's nose. "I'm also excited to try this restaurant. I've been wanting to come here forever. What made you pick this place?" she asked Drew.

"It's vegan and it got good reviews," he said with a smile.

"Oh, so you knew it was a totally vegan restaurant and you picked it anyway?"

"Yeah. You seem surprised."

"I am surprised—and impressed," she said as she perused the lunch options.

"We have more surprises for you, Mommy!" Cole blurted out and resumed bouncing in his seat. "Can I give it to her, Daddy? Please, please, please!"

Paige and Zach rolled their eyes.

"Sure, bud. Go 'head."

"Yes!" Cole punched the air, then pulled a light blue bag with a dozen white, long stem roses sticking out the top from its hiding spot under the table.

"Surprise!" yelled Drew and the kids.

April gasped as Cole placed the bag on the table. "What are you guys doing?"

"Happy birthday!" they all screamed, triggering annoyed looks from some of the other patrons.

"My birthday is a week away, guys," she said as she pulled the roses out of the bag. "These are beautiful!"

"That's not all there is, Mom," Paige said. "Look inside!"

April peeked in the bag, then immediately shot Drew a *"what did you do"* look.

He put his hands up. "Don't look at me. It's from the kids," he said as she pulled two silver picture frames from the bag. One had a picture of Paige, Cole, and Al Roker with their "HI MOMMY" sign. The other contained a picture of Zach, Paige, and Cole on the observatory level of the Empire State Building, the view of New York behind them.

April wiped a tear away. "Well, we might want to think about adjusting their allowances then." She giggled. "These are Tiffany picture frames, Drew."

He shrugged. "Tiffany, Target, what's the difference, really?"

"About a thousand dollars! But thank you. This is the best gift." She got up and worked her way around the table, hugging and kissing everyone.

"Were you really surprised, Mommy?" Cole asked eagerly.

"Totally surprised!" she said, caressing his cheek. "And I thought I was the only one with a surprise."

The kids looked at each other quizzically. Drew was curious as well. He and the kids leaned forward as April reeled them in with her intriguing opening.

"You have a surprise for us?" Cole asked and started bouncing again.

"What is it, Mommy!" Paige asked, bouncing too.

April grinned. "Okay. I won't torture you with suspense." She laced her fingers together and rested her chin on top of them. "Tony is taking us on a ten-day Disney Cruise!" she announced, spreading her hands out like she had just performed a magic trick. "We're going to Miami tomorrow night and the ship leaves the following afternoon!"

Cole and Paige squealed with delight. Then Cole jumped up, shouting, "Yes! Yes! Yes!" as he did a touchdown celebration dance next to his seat. Everyone near their table laughed at the spectacle he made.

"Alright, Cole, that's enough," Drew said as the laughter settled down.

Cole sat down and threw his arms around April. "Thank you, thank you, thank you!"

"You're welcome, but it was really all Tony's idea. I wish I had recorded your little dance for him to see. You are a nutcase, kiddo!"

As April, Paige, and Cole continued to chatter about the details of the cruise, Drew pulled all the tools out from his arsenal of coping skills to construct a pleasant demeanor around the deep resentment welling up inside. He took a sip of lemonade, hoping to dilute the bitterness.

"What's wrong, Zach?" April asked.

Zach hadn't said anything in response to the announcement. Drew looked over at him. He sat slouched as far down in his seat as humanly possible with a scowl ten times more intense than the one he had worn for three days after Drew confiscated his devices.

"Nothing," Zach said, folding his arms across his torso.

"Obviously something's wrong. It's written all over your face. You're not excited about the cruise?"

"I said nothing's wrong, Mom, damn!"

"Hey! Don't talk to your mother like that," Drew warned as he swiftly reached over and plucked the back of Zach's neck with enough force to induce a full body flinch. "Be grateful. And sit up straight."

"Be grateful for what, Dad?" He jerked himself into an upright position as he angrily rubbed his neck. "I spent three weeks stuck at your place and now I have to spend another week and a half stuck on a ship for little kids. Nobody asked me what I wanted to do for the summer. I haven't got to hang out with my friends or anybody my age. Everything we do has to be appropriate for Cole and I'm tired of doing little kid activities."

"Humph, I'm not a little kid," Cole said with a pout.

"Come on, Zach," Drew said. "You're exaggerating. We did plenty of stuff you like." He snapped his fingers. "We went to the phone store that time."

Zach looked up at the ceiling and sighed. "That was only because we had a few minutes to kill before the Disney movie Paige and Cole wanted to see. We were only there for like twenty minutes," he said. "But, whatever. I don't even know why you asked me what's wrong. You don't care about me or what I like, so it doesn't make a fucking difference anyway."

Paige and Cole both gasped as their eyes darted back and forth between Drew and April. Zach didn't look at them. He squirmed in his chair as he slowly eased himself out of his father's reach.

Drew didn't know what to say. He looked over at April for guidance, but she was too busy staring at Zach with her mouth partially opened to offer any help.

"So, what do you wanna do, Zach? Play video games all day?" Drew asked. "You don't even go anywhere with your friends. All you do is meet up online and play games or text or Snapchat or whatever."

April nodded in agreement. "You and your friends even text each other when you're in a room together. It's the strangest thing. They don't even talk to each other," she said to Drew with a shrug.

Zach shook his head slowly. "See? You guys don't know anything about me. And you don't want to."

"That's not true, Zach," Drew said. "Why do you keep sayin' that?"

"You and Mom never even asked me why I went to that video game designers' convention. I don't just like playing video games. I want to design them too. I have my real-life friends, but I also have real friends from different parts of the world I met online. We're designing a video game together that's gonna blow everybody away. Or at least I was. They've probably kicked me off the team by now. I keep losing my devices for weeks at a time. I'm sure they think I'm some immature jerk who can't keep from getting grounded all the time," he said, as tears welled up in his eyes, but he snapped them shut before any fell.

"Why didn't you ever say any of this before now?" Drew asked.

"Because you wouldn't understand. You'd think I was trying to get out of my punishment so I could goof off online." He hopped up and stormed off to the bathroom.

Drew wanted to kick himself for being clueless about what Zach was going through, especially since he had lived through a similar situation with his own parents when he was the same age. But this was only one more line item on his long list of parenting fails. April, on the other hand, was supermom. He glanced over at her. She was on the verge of tears herself.

After a few minutes, Zach came back to his seat. "I'm sorry for my bad attitude and language," he said slowly to April. His eyes were noticeably redder and puffier than they were when he left, but they were earnest.

"Thank you for the apology, sweetheart," April said with a smile. She made no mention of him crying.

No one else mentioned it either. While they waited quietly for their lunch orders, Drew handed Zach his cell phone. He perked up instantly and looked at April with hopeful eyes. She nodded, agreeing to temporarily lifting her strict policy prohibiting phones during meals. And with that, Zach turned on his phone and happily disconnected from the family lunch to catch up with his friends.

After they cleaned their plates, Drew paid the check, and then helped Zach put their bags in April's car. He wasn't ready to see them go, so he suggested they round off their healthy vegan lunch with a walk in the park. And to guarantee an affirmative response from April, he made his proposal in front of the kids, hoping their excited pleas would weaken any resistance she might have.

Although it was a weekday, the park was moderately populated, as it was a sunny and warm summer afternoon. Paige and Cole found a friendly dog to play with and Zach found a shady spot to use his phone, oblivious to the couples canoodling on either side of him. With the kids occupied, Drew and April took a quiet stroll by the lake.

"You look nice today, April," Drew said, as he dropped back a step to get a view of April in her cut-offs from a different angle.

"That's fine," she said, obviously spacing out.

"What're you thinkin' about?" he asked.

"Zach." She sat on an empty bench. "I'm a terrible mother." She covered her face with her hands.

"You're kidding, right?"

"I'm serious, Drew. How could I have missed something so simple as what my kid wants to be when he grows up? That's Parenting 101, isn't it?"

"I guess. But you can't know what he doesn't tell you." He sat next to her.

April gazed out across the lake. "We used to be so close. He was my little buddy. When you were on the road, he would crawl into our bed on Saturday mornings, and we'd cuddle and talk. He would tell me everything. And now he's got this whole secret life I had no clue about."

"You underestimate a teenager's ability to keep secrets— especially about what they've been up to. You must have forgotten I was lead singer of a band, sneaking out to do gigs for a year before my parents found out."

"Well, we are going to have some serious mommy/son time for sure during this cruise. Paige and Cole can do activities in the kid's club or with Tony, while Zach and I have some long overdue one-on-one time."

"How will Tony feel about that? I'm sure he's gonna want some attention too." He blew out a rumbling breath through his pursed lips. "I can keep the kids longer if you want so you guys can have a grown-up vacation for your birthday."

"Aw, Drew. That's thoughtful. But, no, Tony planned this last-minute trip to celebrate more than my birthday. He wants to tell the kids about the wedding."

"Huh? They already know you guys are getting married."

"Yeah, but they don't know that we settled on a date."

"Oh? You picked a date?" he asked, surprised that he was able to maintain an even tone after the plunge his heart had just taken. His sister's theory about wedding dates sounded off like an annoying car alarm in his head.

"Yes, finally," she groaned. "It's gonna be May 11th, next year!"

Drew gazed out at the water. "Perfect. I'm sure it'll be the big, fancy wedding we never got to have."

"Yeah," she said, staring out at the water too. "Tony's family is enormous, so it'll be big. And he wants to impress the business community, so it'll be fancy too."

"You okay with all that?"

She shrugged. "It's what Tony wants. I've already had the wedding of my dreams. So, it doesn't really matter to me."

Drew gnawed on the corner of his bottom lip. "Unless you've been married more times than I thought, you're lying big time right now," he said. "You and I got married at the courthouse, then went to a bar to hang out with our friends."

"Is that how you remember our wedding, Drew?" She looked at him through narrowed eyes. "Because I remember cramming into the chambers of the oldest and funniest judge on the planet with our parents, sisters, and friends. Then going over to Pagans to celebrate. I remember eating and drinking and laughing and dancing and being serenaded by my new husband and his band until well after closing time. And I can't remember being happier, either before or after."

Drew sighed. "I remember it that way too."

They sat still and quiet for several minutes.

"So, what are you planning to do with yourself for the rest of your hiatus? Any vacation plans?"

"Not sure about going away yet, but I'm goin' to a jam session later," he said, grateful for the shift in conversation.

April's eyes lit up and she slapped his arm. "Shut up! You're gonna go jam with EJ Wallace, aren't you?"

A smile spread across his face. "Yep."

"And you're just telling me now? You loser!" she screeched, commencing an onslaught of rapid jabs to his bicep.

"Ooow! Okay, April!" He rubbed his arm. "Do I look like your speed bag?"

"Sorry, Drew. But I'm so excited for you, babe!" she squealed, pattering her feet on the ground. "Aren't you excited? You're acting so calm."

"I'm not calm at all. I'm nervous as hell," he said. There was no need to pretend with April. She was well acquainted with all of his insecurities.

"What do you have to be nervous about? You've been to tons of jam sessions, and you practice every day."

"I know, but this feels different. This is EJ Wallace we're talkin' about. Everybody knows his sessions are intense, like a boot camp or something. And on top of that, he keeps mentioning that he has these ideas he wants to talk about."

"Like a project?"

"Yeah. A collaboration. He said, 'think *We are the World* on a more intimate level.'"

"Oh, that sounds interesting!" she sang as she poked him in his side. "Who all's gonna be there?"

"Reid's coming. Other than him, I dunno. All EJ said was that it's gonna be a small group of bangin' old heads."

April's nose wrinkled. "Huh? Bangin' heads? Does he mean metal heads?"

"No, bangin' meaning awesome or talented. And old heads meaning, like old musicians."

"Ohhhhh! I get it." She winced. "Ouch. Has it come to that already? Are we old enough to be old heads?"

Drew chuckled. Slang always sounded funny when April used it. "At least he didn't say has-been." He cracked his neck.

April put her hand on his thigh. "Hey, watch your mouth. That's my baby daddy you're talkin' about," she teased, rubbing his hand. "You are far from a has-been, Andrew Simon."

Drew looked over at her and smiled. "Thanks, babe."

"There's no need to thank me. It's the truth." She ran her fingers through his hair like she always had. He was sporting a much shorter curly quiff than his normal length, but he found her touch just as soothing.

Drew slid closer and wrapped his arms around her, engulfing her in a bear hug. He held her tightly for several seconds. She gave him a few pats on the back, then pulled away, and a wave of desire and desperation surged through his body. He kissed her, not gently. She grunted, pushing against his chest, and the wave turned into a flood. He tightened his grasp, kissing her harder.

April yanked herself out of his grip and slid as far away from him as she could on the bench. He grabbed hold of her arm, pulling her back to him. She leaned back, resisting being dragged across the bench. Her left arm slipped out of his tight hold. He reached for her right arm, as she wound up, bringing her hand up and back down so quickly, his ear recognized the sound of the slap before his cheek registered the sting.

"What the hell are you doing, Drew?" she snarled, jumping to her feet. "You feelin' rapey today?"

"April, I'm sorry. That was a dick move," he said, resisting the urge to rub his burning face. "But I miss you. I—"

"No! I'm not doing this!" She shook her head vigorously as she pivoted and started speed walking away, but she stopped short and whipped back around. She stormed over to the bench, reminding him that her scary mom face was nothing compared to her scary ex-wife face. He rose from the bench and braced himself. If he was going to get slapped again, he would take it like a man. On his feet.

"You have to stop this, Drew!" she said. "I'm with Tony now. We are getting married. Do you get that?"

"Yeah, I get it. But you don't have to do that. You don't have to marry him."

April looked at him like he had ten heads. "Oh, yeah? And what do you suggest I do instead?"

"Be with me again," he said with pleading eyes.

She threw her hands up in the air. "You're unbelievable. You left *me!* Did you forget that?"

"I didn't leave you, April. I just went away for a little while to clear my head, and you filed for divorce."

"After two years, Drew!" she shrieked. "I didn't even know where you were for three months until I finally got Reid to admit you were living with him! And we didn't hear a word from you for seven and a half months! Not a single word! That's not 'going to clear your head.' That's abandoning your family."

Drew closed his eyes. He preferred the sting of her powerful slap over the swift kick below the belt. He sat back down on the bench, his body heavy with shame and regret.

"I didn't know what else to do, April." He rested his elbows on his knees and stared at the ground. "All I ever did was sleep, cry, or yell. There was no other state of being for me and I didn't want you and the kids to see me like that anymore. Leaving was the hardest thing I have ever had to do—I told you that—but I came too close to hitting you too many times. I had to go," he looked up at her, "and I knew you were never gonna ask me to leave."

"I wanted us to work on our problems together, Drew."

"They weren't our problems. They were my problems. And I got the help I needed. Now I can be the husband and father I'm supposed to be—that you deserve for me to be. I love you, April. Let me come home. Please."

She shook her head. "I can't do that."

"Because you don't love me?"

"Of course I love you. I don't seem to have much control over that."

"Then why not? Why can't I come home?"

"Because you broke my heart!" She grabbed two fists full of his T-shirt at his collarbone and shoved him against the back of the bench. "I loved you so much I couldn't see straight. You were my whole world—No. You were the sun, and everything revolved around you. I didn't even realize how much of me was tied up in you until you pulled the cord, and I went free-falling. Without your crazy schedule to work around or your eggshells to walk on, I didn't know who I was. It felt like I was flailing aimlessly through the air. Then Tony caught me and helped me find my footing. He showed me, for the first time, what it was like to be a priority."

Drew clenched his jaw. "You don't think you were a priority to me, April?" he asked, looking out at the water.

She closed her eyes and inhaled slowly. "Drew, I always knew the music came first. And I was happy to take my place behind everything related to the music and the band, because I believed your talent was too big to keep to yourself—I still believe that. I was proud of the role I played in helping you share it with the world. But I've had a taste of what it's like to be first in someone's life. I can't go back to the way things were before. I'm not the same person."

"I'm not the same person either. Can't you see that?" He looked up at her.

"Yes, I can see that." She sat next to him. "When I see how well you're doing now and how you've reconnected with the kids, it brings tears to my eyes... happy tears. I know how hard you've worked to pull yourself out of that pit of despair you were wallowing in for so long. You have no idea how long and hard I prayed for that, because the kids need you and you need them. But I'm moving on, Drew," she said with tears in her eyes. "And it's time for you to do the same."

April leaned in and kissed his cheek. Then she got up and walked slowly across the grass, beckoning the kids as she quickly wiped her face. Zach, Paige, and Cole hurried to her, and she pointed over to the park bench where Drew sat. They raced to him.

"Thanks, Dad," Zach said, winning the race by a mile.

Paige came in second. "Bye, Daddy!" she squealed as she jumped onto his lap.

Cole plowed into them a few seconds later, panting like he had given his all to the race with his siblings, but he didn't seem remotely disappointed by his crushing defeat. "Dad... can we... come back... next week?" he asked as he tried to catch his breath.

Drew smiled. "I'd love that, buddy. But you're goin' on a cruise, remember?"

"Oh yeah!" he said and did his touchdown dance again.

"We can talk about a time for you guys to come back over after your trip. Maybe we could go on a quick camping trip or something," Drew suggested. "Is that cool?"

Cole pumped his fist in the air. "Yes! This is the best summer ever!"

Paige and Drew laughed. "What about you, man?" He flashed a hopeful glance at Zach. "Is that cool?"

"Sure, Dad. That's cool," Zach said. Then he did something with his face that might qualify as a smile in some cultures.

Chapter 16

Drew stood awestruck in the center of Paragon Studios' live room. He had been in plenty of well-appointed and well-equipped studios. But EJ's place put the other ones to shame. All five of Paragon's studios had state-of-the-art equipment and instruments, but at the end of a long hallway covered in gold and platinum records was the giant live room. It was big enough to hold an orchestra if needed, but it was more like a musical history museum with vintage guitars, pictures of all the musicians that had come through the studio, and the most frantically colorful paintings on the walls. Drew's eyes darted from one eye-catching item to another, unable to focus on any one thing, until they landed on a wall of mugshots. He scanned the familiar faces: Johnny Cash, Tupac, Steven Tyler, James Brown, Mick Jagger, Prince, Amy Winehouse and dozens of other musical greats on their not-so-great days, in wide-ranging states of dishevelment and disorientation.

At first glance, the collage was all at once humbling and humorous. But with a closer look, humbleness overtook humor when Drew noticed the two idiots in the top right corner of the lineup, none other than him and Chris.

Rubbing the back of his head, Drew recalled the time he flew off the stage in a rage to confront a group of guys that kept throwing bottle caps and insults at him during their set. Chris jumped into the brawl that ensued seconds before a pack of bouncers intervened. Unfortunately, the bouncers were also off-duty cops. They made quick work of quashing the melee and getting everyone involved into handcuffs. Thinking about the commotion of that night made Drew oblivious to the commotion building among the other musicians in the room.

EJ shouted and clapped to get their attention. "Alright, fam! Since we have reached the portion of the evening where everybody clowns Kwayk about his reality show, it seems we're all comfortable enough with each other to move on to the business at hand."

"Yeah, yeah, E, I think that's a good idea," said Kwayk, better known as Earf Kwayk the Rapper to his fans. "I thought we was supposed to be makin' music. Ain't nobody got time for this bullshit," he grumbled.

"Aw, Kwayk, you mad?" laughed Rick Dyson, drummer of On the Agenda, an R&B group popular in the '80s and '90s. "We just messin' with you, man," he said, laughing harder.

"Well, hee hee haw, fuck all y'all jealous mutha fuckas," Kwayk blustered.

"Ha!" blurted out Vondell Morris, saxophone player, best known for his acid jazz albums in the '90s. "Ain't nobody jealous of you and all that hood rat, baby mama drama you got goin' on with that damn show, man."

"You think you better than me?" Kwayk snarled as he jumped up from his seat and moved quickly toward Vondell with the agility and speed of a much smaller man.

Vondell sneered as he slipped his sax strap over his head and handed the instrument and his glasses to Drew. His tall, slender frame took several steps forward. Despite the considerable size difference between the two men, Vondell didn't appear to be fazed as he stood tall facing his opponent: a wolf ready to go toe to toe with a grizzly bear.

"Yo, chill!" EJ yelled as he jumped between them, placing his hands on their chests. "Go sit your ass back down, Kwayk. Von's right, ain't nobody trippin' off you doin' your thing and gettin' your hustle on. We're all tryin' to keep a roof over our heads and stay relevant just like you."

Kwayk continued to glare at Von with his jaw clenched so tightly the veins in his neck bulged and pulsated.

"Seriously, man, no judgment," EJ added and nudged Von with his elbow. "Right, Von?"

"Yeah, no judgment," Von said. "I mean, I was on *Dancing with the Stars* a few years back, so I ain't got no business judgin' anybody."

"I didn't know you were on that," Rick said.

"Because he got voted off the first week!" Reid announced, gently placing his Fender guitar in a nearby stand.

"Really, man? It's like that?" Von asked.

"Well, am I wrong?"

Von hung his head. "No."

"Aw, Von. I voted for you," said Kimmie Logan, a pop singer who rose to superstardom in the early 2000s before a series of bad professional and personal decisions caused her to crash and burn.

"Well, I didn't vote for you. I couldn't do it," EJ admitted, shaking his head as he studied Von's face. "I love you, man, but you are one hundred percent rhythm and zero percent coordination. It's messed up you got voted off so quick, but you should be grateful they put you outta your misery."

"Yeah, we're all grateful for that," chimed in Bret Hughes, blues musician out of New Orleans.

Everybody burst into laughter, even Kwayk.

"Whatever, man," Von said to EJ, looking him up and down. "We good?" he asked Kwayk, offering his hand.

Kwayk glared at Von's hand for a few seconds and then flashed a crooked smile. He grabbed his hand, leaned in for a man hug and they separated with a loud snap, signaling the end of their conflict.

"Well, now that's outta the way, y'all ready to light this joint up?" EJ asked.

Everybody clapped and cheered.

"Good. Sounds like y'all ready to get to work. Let's warm up with some Beatles shit—'Come Together'," he said. "Everybody knows it, and we can stretch it out as long as we want to give everybody a chance to solo."

Everyone except Kwayk nodded in agreement.

"What about me?" Kwayk asked.

"Just be ready to freestyle."

"To *that*? What the hell am I supposed to do with them lyrics?"

"Don't do anything with the lyrics, feel the music and flow with the moment. Like you always do." EJ turned his attention to Drew. "You been real quiet. You didn't lose your voice, did you?"

Drew shook his head. "Nope."

"Great! You got lead then. Kimmie, you back him up. Aiight?"

"Sure thing!" Kimmie said as she claimed the microphone closest to her.

"Alright," Drew agreed casually, trying to conceal his surprise. While the room was full of hugely talented musicians from different musical genres, and most of them could sing well, Kimmie was by far the best singer in that group. He didn't understand why EJ wanted him to sing first, but he chalked it up to random selection and stepped up to his mic as the music started. Besides, it was EJ's session and his studio. He called the shots.

Drew sang the first verse with no problem. He knew the song well. "Come Together" was one of Wiretap's go-to songs when they first started out. It was a real crowd pleaser, and he had sung the nonsensical lyrics John Lennon characterized as "gobbledygook" more times than he could count, but he never tired of it. It was still one of his favorite songs. It was like a quick trip back to the good old days.

By the time he reached the second verse, Drew was feeling good in his comfort zone. He mindlessly strummed his guitar as his fingers easily recalled the chords. And Kimmie harmonized beautifully with him. But when he finished the second verse, EJ raised his hand in the air and the music came to a halt.

"That was good, Drew. You too, Reid—real polite," he said with a smirk. "Y'all scared or somethin'?" He raised an eyebrow.

"Huh?" Drew said. It was unusual for anyone to interrupt a jam session mid-song. He shot an inquisitive glance at Reid. Since he and EJ were friends, Drew hoped he could explain the unorthodox behavior. But Reid didn't look at him, he was busy glaring at EJ.

"Get the fuck outta here, man!" Reid said.

"No disrespect, man, but I didn't invite y'all here because of your manners," EJ chuckled. "Kwayk's sittin' over there with his best serial killer face, waitin' for some inspiration for his freestyle. And he ain't gon' get it from y'all just goin' through the motions. So, if you gonna play, then play. If you gonna sing, then sing." He looked around the room at all the suddenly very quiet musicians. "You feel me?" he said, looking at Reid.

"Yeah," Reid snarled.

"Drew?"

"Got it," Drew replied with a thumbs up.

"Okay, let's take it from the top. Drew, this time I want less John Lennon and more Drew Simon. Von, you're too loud. Reid, don't be scared to break some strings on that axe. We got plenty of replacements if you need 'em. Aiight? Let's do this."

Reid grumbled something incoherent as Drew cleared his throat and took a sip of water. He wasn't miffed like Reid was by EJ's flagrant use of the "s" word, only a little embarrassed to be called out. But EJ was right. He had been phoning it in. That could make any musician appear timid or afraid. But he wasn't scared, just rusty, and he didn't know what was expected of him. Now that the challenge had been issued, he was more than ready, because it was simple—be yourself. He knew exactly who he was as an artist.

Drew stepped up to the mic again. He gave a head nod to signal he was ready, and the nerves disappeared. He crushed the first and second verses, emphasizing certain notes with a raspy vibrato or exaggerated staccato to increase the dramatic effect—putting his typical hardcore yet soulful style on full display for the audience of seasoned musicians surrounding him.

"Yes! There he is!" EJ said, putting everyone's impressed expressions into words.

Drew realized his guitar was redundant as he started the third verse. He swung the instrument around to his back and grabbed hold of the mic stand. Then he pulled it in like it needed to be reminded who was in charge. He slowly and firmly wrapped both hands around the shaft of the microphone and leaned in, a visual manifestation of the controlled intensity heard in his vocal performance.

"Give it to me now..." Drew said at the end of the chorus, signaling the guitarists and bassist to commence the riffing portion of the song. Then he looked over at Kwayk. His deep-set eyes were dark, and his nostrils flared wide, intensifying his serial killer expression. He swayed back and forth, chomping at the bit for his shot on the mic. Drew pointed to Kwayk as he snatched his microphone off the stand and tossed it to him.

Unh, Yeah, Come Togetha'
Drew, where you been
Got me feelin' this shit like original sin
People be like, they knew you when
Now you out here dancin' and prancin,'
Takin' stances, hopin' for glances and second chances
But niggas be trippin', forgettin'
Out there sleepin' on champions

Thinkin' we chasin' complacence
Bankin' on royalties, coastin' on loyalties
Niggas be blind to reality
The only thing we sellin' out is localities
Still out here breakin' records in totality

But we ain't even scratched the surface
When you gon' learn this?
Got you back on your feet, just to bring you to your knees
Got no mercy for your pleas,
Just like it was back then
Fuck that shit they said 'bout a has-been
Burnin' up this track
Comin' togetha' with that old school comeback

"Oooohhh shhhiit!" EJ blurted out, rushing over to Kwayk to give him dap as the instrument solos began. Reid started off, bringing his signature saturated shred. He didn't break any strings. But as fast and loud as he played, he definitely broke a sweat and nearly broke the sound barrier. Von, Rick, EJ, and Bret followed with awe-inspiring sax, drums, guitar, and electric harmonica solos of their own. By the time everyone had a turn, the normally three-minute-long song had quadrupled in length, and it wasn't over yet. Drew stepped back up to the mic drenched in sweat and satisfaction to sing the final verse.

When he belted out the last note, all playing ceased simultaneously and everything was quiet for exactly one second before the room erupted in celebration. Everyone clapped, stomped, and cheered as they came over to Drew, slapping him on the back and rubbing his sweaty head like his team had been down by two at the end of double overtime and he had hit a three pointer at the buzzer from clear on the other side of the court. Rick even emerged from behind his drum kit to shake Drew's hand. All the direct and aggressive attention made Drew red in the face as he humbly accepted their praise.

"What I tell y'all?" EJ shouted over the boisterous chatter in the room. "That boy can sing his ASS off! Okay, who's next?"

"DREW!" everyone replied in unison.

EJ smirked and gestured to the mic. "The tribe has spoken," he said as he set his guitar down and stepped behind the keyboard. "What's the next song?"

"What about 'Force Field'?" Reid said.

Drew's head snapped toward Reid. The menacing scowl accompanied by a subtle head shake was an unequivocal, *absolutely fucking not*. He hadn't sung that song since they performed it live at the Grammys over eight years before. Most people considered that his best performance, praising it for its raw honesty. Drew considered it his worst. He sang the entire song with his eyes closed and tears streaming down his face, nearly choking on his grief. That song reminded him of one of the worst times in his life, but that wasn't the only reason he didn't want to sing it. "Force Field" was about April. It was the first in a trilogy of songs about the story of their relationship on Wiretap's *To Scale* album. There were too many feelings associated with the song, the whole album, really. It was a memoir about their lives and loves up to that point—the end point.

Reid gripped Drew's shoulder. "There's never going to be a better place."

Drew closed his eyes and took a deep breath. Reid was right. Other than in the privacy of his own shower, what would be a safer space than a room of weather-worn musicians, bruised and travel weary from the pitfalls of their own musical journeys?

"Okay," he agreed with a sigh and opened his eyes as EJ started the intro. Everyone else followed suit. Drew swung his guitar back in front of his torso and joined them.

Another show to play
Another crowd to sway
Plugged in and shreddin' and jammin' just like the other day
Can hear the people, but it's too dark to see
Can only feel their energy surrounding me
Sometimes they like it, they love it, say they want more of it
Sometimes they hate it, berate it, and tell us to shove it
But either way's the same
Know how to play this game
Got some tricks to take the licks and keep my feelings at bay

No oh, whoa oh, whoa oh, put up the force field
People can get me 'cause I keep it real
But they can't get to me, won't get to me through this force field,
   through this force field

But then I broke the rule
Looked out at the crowd
A pretty girl was in the front, singin' along out loud
The shield, it took a hit
And I can admit
Never knew a simple smile could penetrate it.
A shot from the dark, straight to my heart

Uh oh, whoa oh, uh oh, there goes the force field
She got to me, shit just got real
But I can't show, can't let her know she got through the force field

Suddenly defenseless
This is senseless
She got in the fortress
Her smile enough to rival supernatural forces
The walls are breakin' down
Like I was lost, then found

No oh, uh oh, whoa oh, there goes my force field, now
My walls are comin' down
Whoa oh, uh oh uh oh, there goes my force field, now...

To his surprise, Drew finished "Force Field" in its entirety without shedding a tear. He was relieved that he had controlled his emotions and grateful that no one made a big deal about it. They all quickly offered a positive comment, or a smile, and then they moved on to the next song. Eventually, Kimmie took over lead vocals and dominated the rest of the session that lasted for over five hours.

Chapter 17

"I need another woman," EJ said to Drew and Reid. The other musicians had left after they demolished the subs EJ ordered after the jam session.

"I think we have a good group here, but we need to balance out all the testosterone," he said as he put the studio back in order. "Y'all saw how Kwayk and Von were about to get into it and jack up my studio over some stupid shit."

"Who'd you have in mind?" Drew asked, getting up to help.

"I've been tryna get Lady Lovely in here for a minute, but she won't come."

"Why not?" Reid chimed in from his resting place stretched out on the burgundy leather sofa. "Because she and Kwayk used to be together?"

"Nah. That was a rumor. They're good friends, but they didn't go out. People just liked the idea of them together, so any time they were spotted anywhere near each other got the rumor mill churning."

"I hope you can get her to change her mind. Her smooth, feminine style would be a great contrast to Kwayk's bold aggression," Reid said.

"I know, right!" EJ said. "But she said she gained too much weight with her last kid and doesn't want people talkin' about how she ain't hot no more."

"Is it that bad? Have you seen her?" Drew asked. "Cuz she was really hot."

EJ shrugged. "I don't think she's bad at all. I like my women with some cushion. And I'm sure she's killin' it with the carpool set, but when you go from being that fine to looking like a normal person, people can be brutal. I think she's just lost some of her confidence. She said she was gonna get with a personal trainer and get back to me."

"Maybe she should call April," Reid suggested as he sat up and reached for his guitar case.

EJ looked at Drew with a confused expression.

"My ex is a personal trainer. Where does Lovely live?"

"She's a Jersey girl. Hoboken, if you can believe that."

Drew grimaced. "That's about an hour from us—I mean her. But I can get you her contact info. It wouldn't hurt to call."

"Yeah, that's what's up. I'll pass it on. I'm hoping the idea of gettin' back out there will be motivation for her to get herself together."

"Speaking of workin' out, I'm gonna get outta here," Reid said as he hauled himself off the sofa.

"Since when do you go to the gym this time of night?" Drew asked as he checked his watch to verify that it was midnight.

"I don't. I'm meeting somebody at the gym in the morning," he said with a sly grin. "It's a woman. I have a date," he added with a satisfied nod.

"You're takin' a girl to the gym for a date?" EJ asked. "That doesn't sound like you."

"It's not. She invited me, so—"

"Wait a minute. Who is this girl?" Drew asked.

Reid's sly grin broadened. "Shanice."

"Shanice asked you to meet her at the gym in the morning so you two can go on a date?" Drew asked. "She actually said those words to you?"

"Maybe not those exact words."

"Ha! Well, what words did she use, man?" EJ asked. He had stopped straightening up and took a seat on the piano bench.

"She told me where she goes to the gym, what time she goes, and that I should check it out some time." He counted off each point on his fingers.

Drew and EJ looked at each other and burst out laughing.

"What the hell's so funny?" Reid asked.

"It sounds more like you're stalking her than dating her!" EJ said through his laughter.

"You say tomato, I say tom*ah*to," Reid sang cheerfully as he placed his guitar in its case and snapped it closed.

"Dude, you realize she's said the same thing to me and the rest of the band," Drew said. "I think they waive her membership fee if she gets people to join."

"Whatever, dude," Reid grumbled, hooking his backpack on his shoulder. "Thanks for the invite, E. Let me know what I need to do to help you make something real out of this." He extended his hand. EJ stood, grabbed his hand, and leaned in for a bro hug. As Reid brought his arm around EJ's back, he gave Drew the finger.

EJ shook his head after Reid walked out the door. "You need to talk to your boy," he said, moving a microphone stand back to its place against the wall with the others.

"Pssshh. When Reid has a girl in his crosshairs, he's like a dog with a bone—literally. You could lose a limb interfering with that."

"You're right about that! That dude is persistent as hell. It's a necessary ingredient for success, but it can get you in trouble if you don't know when to pull back. The last thing I wanna see is Reid's face all over the news behind some ol' harassment scandal. It's been enough guys goin' down for that lately."

"You're right, there has been a lot of that goin' around," Drew conceded. "But he's a good guy. I've never heard anything about him crossing the line." He chuckled. "He'd be too afraid of his grandmother finding out."

"Ha! I'm with him on that one. I let a cuss word slip out when I was visiting my grandma down in Virginia a couple of months ago.

She gave me that look, and said, 'Eric, I would hate to interrupt our nice visit by having to wash your mouth out with soap.'"

"Heh, heh. What did you say?"

"I said, 'I would hate that too, Gran.' Then I apologized and promised it wouldn't happen again. I mean, she's like ninety, so I think I could take her, but I wasn't gonna chance it. That sweet old woman still scares the crap outta me," he said with a smirk.

"That's hilarious, man. But I hear you. I don't have too much experience with grandmothers, but I'm more familiar than I'd like to be with the taste of soap. My mom used that technique for lying and backtalk too." Drew grimaced as he started packing up his guitar. "Definitely something you wanna avoid at all costs."

"So, how'd you feel about the session, man? How you think this group vibes?" EJ asked and sat on the sofa.

"Oh, yeah," Drew nodded. "It was like fire in here. I can't even tell you how many times I literally had goosebumps. I admit I was a little apprehensive when I came in and saw so many different genres represented in one room, but it worked. I don't know how, but it did, and it felt good. You're a genius, man."

"Aw, go 'head with all that," EJ said. "Good musicians are good musicians. If you can really play, you can play anything. If you can really sing, you can sing anything. And real musicians—real artists—just love music. Genres and categories and boxes to put people into are for *them* out there." He waved his hand toward the door. "Those folks need you to fit in a neat little box, like with race. But it never made sense to me, especially with contemporary music. Blues and jazz and R&B and rock 'n' roll and all the subgenres are all related. We're all one family, playing the same twelve notes. You know what I mean?"

"Of course. But you could do this with new artists. Why pull us old folks out of our retirement villages?"

"Well, there's a long answer to that and a short answer," he started. "As a producer in this day and age, it's always about finding the next big thing. Some hot young artist that's got a good buzz goin' on social media is what's gonna get you the most bang for your buck. But as a musician who came up pre-social media, I feel like veteran artists are being pushed to the back burner and forgotten. They may not know enough or care enough about social media to keep their names out there. And it's a damn shame because music suffers in general when we experienced artists fade away and let folks forget who paved the way for these new cats. Talent doesn't fade and everybody that was in this room today still has so much to offer. I honestly believe we will add a richness and depth that tends to be missing from today's musical landscape."

Drew nodded. It was a surreal experience to be talking so casually with someone he admired so much. He knew that EJ was talented and passionate, but he was surprised that he seemed genuinely more concerned about the art of making music than the business of making music.

"You've spent some time thinking about this," Drew said. "What's the short answer?"

EJ smiled. "People love collaborations. People love comebacks. A collaboration of comebacks is gonna blow 'em away!"

"So, you really want this group to record a song?"

"A song? Nah, man, you're thinkin' way too small! I'm talkin' about an album—at least an EP of like five songs—and a concert. A live, televised concert, where we'll perform together and with our original groups." He was on his feet now. Then his eyes got wide as both eyebrows shot straight up to the ceiling. "And then we go on tour," he said slowly, placing his hands on Drew's shoulders. "Tell me that's not some epic shit."

Drew shuddered. The goosebumps had returned. "That is some epic shit. What do you need me to do?"

"We need songs."

Drew winced. "Sorry, dude. I'm afraid my songwriting ability falls short of epic."

"What! You got like five Grammys. I know at least three of them are for songwriting."

"Two of them are for songwriting. The second one being for the song I wrote for a *Real Housewife* who wanted to know what it was like to be a pop star. I wrote those lyrics on the toilet in thirty minutes. And that's where I keep that Grammy. In my bathroom, over my toilet. So, if you're looking for something deeper than a party anthem, you are barking up the wrong tree."

EJ took a step back and looked Drew up and down. "What's wrong with a party anthem? Sometimes people just wanna shake their asses and forget their problems. Songs that move people to dance are equally important as songs that move people to tears." He sat back down. "But regardless of all that, I've heard your music, Drew. I know what you're capable of. I bet you're working on something profound right now in your head as we speak."

"How would you know that? Are you a mind reader?"

"Nah, man, I'm a vibe reader. And I'm gettin' a strong vibe that you have a lot on your mind right now. There's no way that your brain isn't tryin' to make it into a song. So, stop frontin' and let me hear it."

Drew stared at EJ for a few seconds. He wanted to sing. There was no way he would decline a request from EJ Wallace to sing an original song, but there were so many songs and pieces of songs floating around in his head. It was impossible to choose.

"Alright," Drew said as he took a seat on the piano bench. He decided not to decide. He threw himself into Beethoven's "Moonlight Sonata," and the song weighing on his heart eventually flowed from it.

After all this time, it doesn't feel real
Each day I wake up and you're gone
I wonder when the pain will heal
When I'll be okay with you movin' on

They say it gets better with time and space
It should be easier by now
I should be in a better place
Be happy you're safe and sound

The day breaks, but the light is dim
My heartaches, 'cause you shine for Him
You don't get the last time again
To say what you should have said then
But I'll. . . keep. . . tryin'. . .

Drew moved through the rest of the song with ease, like he had been performing it for years. The last note hung briefly in the air like it didn't want to leave, and then it was silent. He looked over at EJ, making no effort to conceal his approval-seeking expression.

EJ stared at Drew with a furrowed brow. "Damn," he said, looking away. Then he jumped to his feet and rubbed his head and face several times as he paced back and forth a little.

"I'm sorry, man," Drew said. "I told you I wasn't that great a songwriter."

EJ spun around to face Drew. "What? Nah, man. That was great. I just, it just, the song made me think of my mom. I mean the lyrics, and you started with 'Moonlight Sonata.' That was her—she played that all the time before she got sick." He took a deep breath. "I'm sorry, bruh. It's been almost a year since she died. I still get all discombobulated sometimes. Fuck cancer."

"Don't apologize, E. It's been over sixteen years since my mom died and it happens to me too sometimes. As you can see, I'm still writing songs about her."

"I didn't know you lost your mother. I'm sorry."

Drew nodded. "Fuck car accidents."

"Right," EJ said with a sigh.

Drew played through "Für Elise" while EJ sat back on the sofa. "I had no idea you played classical piano. That was impressive," EJ said.

"Thanks. My mom taught me."

"Word? So did mine. She taught all six of us, all our cousins, and most of the kids in our neighborhood how to play the piano. She taught voice lessons too. Music was a big part of our lives growing up. That's why I have so many of my family members working for me now!"

"That's cool. My mom only taught me and my sister. But my sister hated it. She and our mom always argued over practice time, which was dumb on my sister's part. She never seemed to learn that practice was so much more excruciating when your butt's on fire."

"Amen to that... Hey, I want you to get with Kimmie and Kwayk to write some songs. Aiight?"

"Sure," Drew agreed as a muffled buzzing sound interrupted their conversation. "That's not me," he said as he felt his pocket.

"It's me," EJ said, pulling out his phone. "Yo! What's up?" he greeted the caller. "Tomorrow? Yeah, that's fine. Nah, man, I wish I could, but Maya's comin' home in the morning. You know she hates baseball. . . Ha! No way in hell I'm gonna pass on a chance to spend the day with my wife to hang out with y'all. I haven't seen her in a week. . . Aiight. Love you too. Bye."

Drew tried to pretend he wasn't listening, but his head snapped up at the "love you too" part.

"That was my brother," EJ said. "He wants to use my box for the Yankees game tomorrow—Hey, you wanna go to the game? You got kids, right? There's plenty of room. It's just gonna be one of my brothers and one of my sisters and their families."

"Aw, thanks, man, but my kids are goin' on a cruise with their mom tomorrow."

"Nice. Well, let me know if you ever wanna go to a game—" His cell phone vibrated again. "Aw, yeah!" A smile stretched across his face. "I must have talked her up," he said, looking at his phone. "I gotta bounce, man. My wife's lookin' for me. She got home early, so that's where I need to be."

Drew smiled knowingly as he hauled himself to his feet and picked up his guitar case.

"You don't have to go if you don't want to. Feel free to stay and use the studio. No one's scheduled to come in until eight. But do me a favor and give the security guard a nod when you leave so he'll know everybody is out of the studio," he said as he darted out the room.

Drew stood in the middle of the quiet studio with his guitar case in hand and yawned. It was well after midnight. He had been there since five, and he was tired, but then he glanced over at the beautiful grand piano. *The Latest* didn't even have a piano that nice.

"I'll just play one song," he said as he put his guitar down.

An hour and a half and five sonatas later, Drew had been transported. He imagined himself in a massive concert hall in nineteenth century Europe as his fingers danced across the keys. Then, in the corner of his eye, he noticed some movement near the door of the live room. He jumped up from the bench and squared off, ready to defend himself.

Chapter 18

"Drew, I'm so sorry!" Kimmie said as he stood wide-eyed, breathing heavily. "I just came back to get my jacket. I didn't mean to scare you."

"That's okay... you just surprised me... that's all," he said as he sat back down, taking several deep breaths. "How long have you been standing there?"

Kimmie shrugged. "Not long, maybe an hour?"

"An hour!"

She smiled sheepishly. "It was so beautiful... I didn't want you to stop. I had no idea you could play like that," she said as she walked over to the piano.

"Thanks," he said, shutting the fallboard with a little too much force.

"Aw, Drew, I didn't mean to interrupt you. Don't stop playing on my account."

"Don't worry about it, Kimmie, really. It's late. I should get outta here." He stood and reached for his guitar case. "So, you came back to get your jacket? Were you at home?"

"Oh, heck no! I was right down the street. I met up with a couple of friends for drinks," she said, grabbing her jacket off the sofa.

Drew stared at Kimmie as his mind flashed back to when she first hit the scene. She was a twenty-year-old, platinum blonde sex symbol that wore more makeup than clothing, it seemed. Every man in the twelve to dead demographic would have jumped at the chance to be with her, and he was no exception. But that evening she was fully clothed in jeans and a plain white T-shirt. Her light brown ponytail swung playfully behind her head. And from what

Drew could tell, she had on no makeup. He was more taken by her beauty than ever before.

Kimmie narrowed her eyes. "Why are you staring at me?"

"I'm sorry," Drew said, as he quickly shifted his attention to his guitar case and fiddled with the closures. "I, um, don't think I ever knew you had freckles." He glanced back at her.

"Oh. Yeah. I used to hate my freckles when I was a kid, but now they're my best friends. Most people don't recognize me without makeup. Turns out looking like myself is the best disguise!"

"Lucky you. I have to wear hoodies and hats and sunglasses. My ex-wife calls me the Unabomber." He chuckled.

"Oh my God, that's so funny. I can totally see that!" she said. "Hey, you probably don't remember, but my ex and I sat next to you and April at the Billboard Awards one year. April is one of the nicest and realist people I have ever met, especially in this business. I think that was the best time I've ever had at an awards show."

"Yeah, I remember that. It was '08, right?"

"It was '09. April and I were supposed to get together, but that was right when everything started falling apart with Rod and me—and everything else, really—so I never got around to it," she said. "I always regretted not calling her. It would have been nice to have her for a friend. I mean, I admired the two of you so much and your relationship. She was so supportive, and you guys seemed to be so in love with each other. I think I may have been more upset about your breakup than my own."

Drew pursed his lips and tilted his head slightly.

"I'm serious! I wasn't remotely surprised when I found out Rod had cheated on me with any and every woman who came anywhere near our house. I was hurt and angry to find out the dirty details, and embarrassed that the entire world knew about it, but not surprised it happened. When I heard that you and April split, it was like, like, finding out there's no Santa Claus or something. I was devastated!" she laughed.

Drew laughed too.

"But now that I know you guys are back together, my faith in relationships has been restored," she declared.

Drew's laughter came to a halt. "Huh? What guys are back together?"

"You and April, of course."

Drew shook his head slowly. "Who told you that?"

"No one told me. It's all over the internet. Don't you get alerts when the internet is buzzing about you?"

"Ugh," he groaned, pulling his phone out of his pocket. "I forgot to turn it back on after the session," he said as he powered on his cell phone. It buzzed urgently, almost immediately. There were dozens of text messages and voicemails from Lia, his publicist, Reid, and Tony. One of the texts from his publicist linked to a video posted by a popular internet tabloid. Drew's jaw dropped to the floor as he watched an artfully edited video of April and him kissing and caressing in Central Park the previous afternoon.

"Holy fucking shit," Drew gasped. He dropped his guitar case and sat back down on the piano bench. "No, no, no, no," he repeated as he rubbed his temples.

Kimmie rushed to his side. "What's wrong, Drew?"

"They, they, they made it look like... that's, that's not the way—" He took a few breaths. "This isn't the way it went down. I kissed April, and she slapped me. We're not back together. She's engaged."

"Oh, Drew, I'm so sorry."

"I don't get it." He shrugged. "Why wouldn't they just put the real video out there? Wouldn't it be more interesting to see my ex-wife slapping the crap outta me?"

"It sucks, but some of these tabloids get off on making people believe made up stuff."

Drew shook his head. Then his phone buzzed again.

*Zach: I can hear Mom crying in her room, but she won't let me
in. IDK what 2 do. I saw you guys on TMI. What's going on?*

"Fuck," Drew hissed.

"Tell me how I can help you, Drew?" Kimmie asked as she sat
on the piano bench next to him.

Drew showed her Zach's text message. "What should I tell him
to do?"

Kimmie winced. "Tell him to leave her alone, go to bed and
that you'll handle it."

"Really?"

"Yes. Kids need to know that, despite all the chaos going on
outside, their parents are in control. My biggest mistake—other
than setting my ex's car and a good amount of his personal items
on fire—was involving the kids in too much of the drama between
me and Rod. Even simply relying on them to be our little liaisons
and sending messages back and forth was a huge mistake. They're
sixteen and thirteen now, and they got really good at using our
lack of communication to their advantage. Last year, the oldest
ended up in Puerto Rico with his girlfriend; neither of us knew
he was there until my cousin sent me a screenshot of one of
her girlfriend's Instagram posts. She had noticed Ace lounging
poolside in the background of her selfie."

"Whoa. That's an unlucky coincidence. What did you do?"

"Hmph! I was on the next plane to Puerto Rico with Rod and
the girl's parents to drag our children back home—what was left
of them anyway."

Drew shook his head. "That was bold of Ace. I'm sure you were
blazing mad by the time you got down there."

"There are no words to describe how angry I was, but it was a
loud and clear wake-up call for both Rod and me. It forced us to
work on our communication for the sake of the kids. They won't
be able to use that weakness against us ever again."

Drew sighed as he reluctantly heeded Kimmie's advice.

Go to bed. I'll take care of it

OK

Drew was partially relieved Zach had agreed so quickly, but he had an uneasy feeling when ellipses appeared. He held his breath, waiting for Zach's follow-up message to come through.

R U and Mom getting back 2gether????????

Drew showed Kimmie the text.
"Be honest with him," she said.

No. Go to bed. We'll talk about TMI in the morning

OK. GN

Drew smiled. "Thanks, Kim."
"You're very welcome. I know how hard it is with teens. How old is Zach now?"
"Same age as Ace."
"Such an adorable age, isn't it?" she asked with a smirk.
"Heh. Yeah, Zach's a good kid. He's gonna be a video game designer—says he's workin' on something that's gonna blow everybody away," Drew said. His chest poked out a little.
"Oh yeah? It's awesome he knows what he wants to do and that he's doin' it!"
"I know. He's pretty awesome."
"Make sure you tell him that sometimes," she said, giving Drew a nudge. "Alright, then. That's enough mushy talk about our knucklehead crumb snatchers. You wanna walk me to my Uber?" She stood and offered Drew a hand.

He took it and escorted Kimmie out of the studio, making sure the door was locked securely before they headed down the hallway. They yawned simultaneously as the elevator doors closed, causing them to giggle. Drew watched Kimmie while she watched the numbers on the elevator panel descend.

"Please don't look at me in this harsh elevator light, Drew," she said without taking her eyes off the numbers.

"Why not? You look pretty under fluorescent light."

"Ha! Says no one to anyone over thirty-five, ever!" she said. "You need sleep. You're delirious. I—"

"You wanna go out sometime?"

She glanced at Drew, then back up at the numbers, smirking. "I thought you'd never ask," she said as the doors slid open.

Chapter 19

1997

Drew tapped his foot against the base of the gas station pay phone stand as he flipped his jacket collar up to protect his neck from the early spring chill. "I met a girl," Drew announced into the receiver.

"Oh, sweetheart, that's wonderful," Beth said. Her voice wavered.

"What's wrong, Mom? Are you sick?"

"No, no, honey, I'm fine. I'm... just a little tired, that's all," she said. "Tell me about this young lady."

Drew wasn't convinced his mother was fine, but his excitement over telling someone new about April overwhelmed his concern. It had only been a week since he met her, and his bandmates had let him know, in no uncertain terms, they were sick of hearing about her. Randy promised him a gut punch every time he mentioned her name, and they had fought three times already that day. Chris and Randy also fought when Randy punched Chris for mentioning a spring band festival scheduled in April.

"She's beautiful, Mom," he said. "She's got long blond hair, and, uh, what do you call brownish, greenish eyes?"

"Hazel?"

"Yeah, big hazel eyes. I met her at our show last week and we talked after the set 'til they kicked us out. Then we sat outside and talked until the sun came up. She's really smart and has a great sense of humor."

"She sounds lovely, Drew. I certainly hope you were the perfect gentleman I taught you to be."

"Always, Mom. Besides, this girl wouldn't put up with anything less. And she definitely wouldn't be comin' all the way out here from Hackensack for our show tonight."

"And where exactly are you?" Beth asked.

"Pittsburgh. Didn't I tell you?"

"I haven't heard from you in two weeks, Andrew," she said sharply, and it finally occurred to him why she sounded weird. She was trying to pretend she wasn't angry.

"I didn't realize it had been that long. We've been really busy these last couple weeks."

"I'm sure. Falling in love is very time consuming. Not to mention playing gigs in New York City. It's a good thing I ran into Chris's mother, or I'd never have known about that exciting news."

"I'm sorry, Mom."

"I know you and your dad had a fight. But just because you're not speaking to him, doesn't mean you can't call me and at least let me know where you are and that you're alright."

"It wasn't a fight, Mom. I never even hit him back, but he still—" Drew's grip on the receiver tightened as he squeezed his eyes shut.

Beth sighed. "I know... I'm sorry," she said somberly, then there was a long pause. "Hang on, Drew. Your father wants to speak to you."

"No, Mom—"

"Andrew!" Simon barked.

"Yes, sir."

"Your mother's been worried sick," he said, sounding like he was on the move. The noise from the TV got further away until it was gone completely, then a door closed. "I couldn't get her out of bed for three days after you left," he whispered, despite being in another room.

Drew's jaw contracted. "Are you blaming me for that?" he said with his teeth clamped tightly. "You're the one who kicked me out."

"I didn't kick you out. You chose to leave rather than follow the rules of this house."

"I chose? I didn't have a choice. Your rules are unreasonable, Dad. I'm eighteen and you gave me a midnight curfew. That's too early, especially when I'm working. Sometimes we don't even start playing until after midnight."

"Hmph, working," he scoffed. "Working means getting paid and supporting yourself. You play in a band. Playing is not working. That's why they call it playing."

Drew didn't respond. Arguing was pointless. All previous attempts to convince his father that music was a viable career option and not just some hobby had failed miserably.

"You need money?"

"No, sir," he lied.

"I'll put three hundred dollars in your account tomorrow."

"Thanks."

"Call your mother at least once a week, okay? She's much happier when she knows you're safe."

"Yes, sir," he said. "Is Lia home?"

* * *

Lia's ringtone and accompanying vibrations matched her personality perfectly. Drew could always tell it was her from the prodding and relentless pattern of the buzz, even when the sound was off.

"Hey sis, what's up?"

"It's about time you answered your phone! I've been trying to get in touch with you since last night."

"The video's a fake."

"How can that be? It's clearly you and April kissing in the park."

"I kissed her. She slapped me. They edited that out."

"Well, that sucks."

"Sorry to disappoint you."

"Drew, stop. I'm not disappointed *in* you; I'm disappointed *for* you. What did April say?"

"Nothing. At least not to me. I called and texted her last night when I was on my way home and again this morning. She won't answer the phone and she won't reply. But Tony won't stop calling and texting me."

"Uh oh. Did you talk to him? What did you say?"

"Yeah, I talked to him. I told him I kissed April, but she didn't kiss me back."

"What did he say?"

"What do you think he said? He wants to kick my ass."

"Oh, Drew, what are you going to do? Why don't you go over there to talk to April?"

"I'm not going over there to serve myself up for an ass whuppin'."

"You could totally take that guy. You go to the gym. You've got muscles. Go over there and fight for your woman!"

Drew held the phone at arm's length and looked at it. "Are you nuts? I have musician muscles. They are for show and maybe fighting another musician. Tony tears down houses with his bare hands. So, yeah, no. Going over there to fight him will only piss April off more, scare the kids, and feed the tabloid beast. It's better I give 'em their space and let things blow over."

"In other words, you're going to do nothing."

"I wouldn't say that. I'm gonna enjoy the rest of my hiatus before the season starts back up."

"I hope that means you're planning a real vacation."

"'Fraid not, but I do have a date."

"Wow. That's a new development. Are you at liberty to tell me who the lucky lady is?"

"You remember Kimmie Logan?"

"What! I love Kimmie Logan! I wanted to be Kimmie Logan! I had a serious girl crush on her! You're going out with her? How did that come about?"

"Let's just say I got a chance to talk to her at an event."

"I'm so excited!" she said. "Do me a favor and make sure you call me as soon as you get home from your date and tell me every detail."

"Why don't I wait until our next slumber party and tell you all about it while you braid my hair?" he chuckled, then another call buzzed in. "Lia, I gotta go."

"Okay, call me when you ca—"

"Hey, Kim," he said, engaging a much lower octave than he had used with his sister.

"Hi, Drew!" she sang. "I hope I didn't wake you."

"Oh, nah. I'm up. What's goin' on?"

"Well, I woke up thinking about you and—"

"You woke up thinkin' about me?" Drew asked. A grin spread across his face.

"Yeaahhh," she said with a smile in her voice. "I was thinking about how cute you were talking about Zach's passion for video game design. It made me remember when I worked on a pop star version of Guitar Hero a few years ago."

"I didn't know you did that."

"Yeah, they never used the stuff I did, but it was a nice paycheck, nevertheless."

"I'm sure it was."

"So, one of the guys over there started his own company. And he's friends with EJ. I asked him to get in touch with the guy—his name is Jordan Bull or Ball or something—and find out if he'd be open to having Zach work there as an intern for a few weeks. Do you think he'd like that?"

"Uh, hell yeah," Drew said. "That's really cool, Kimmie. I mean, it's so cool, I might not even tell Zach about it and take the internship myself!" he laughed.

"Don't you dare!"

"Heh, heh, I'm kidding. Thank you, Kimmie. It may even get a genuine smile outta Zach."

"Ah, the elusive teenager smile. That reminds me of when I walked into the living room a few weeks ago and found Ace lying on the sofa, smiling. Turns out he was wincing because his brother had kicked him in the balls. It's been so long since he's smiled for me, I couldn't tell the difference."

"I'll smile for you. Matter of fact, I'm doing it right now."

"Can't wait to see it. We still on for tonight?"

"Yep, can you be ready by nine?"

"Oooooo, that's cutting it close. It only gives me nine hours to put on my face!"

"Don't go through any major reconstruction for me. I like your face exactly the way it is."

"Aw, Drew. That's so sweet! I was joking anyway. I like my face the way it is too."

They said goodbye and Drew rolled over to go back to sleep. Just as he drifted off, the phone buzzed.

> *EJ: Yo. Kimmie asked me to call my boy Jordan Bale about Zach workin with him. He said that's cool and the end of July/ early Aug would be a good time. I'm sending you his contact info.*
>
> **Thanks, E. Zach will shit himself**
>
> *LOL No problem. I hope he gets a lot outta it. Lata. My wife's givin me the evil eye. LOL*

Jordan had a lot of questions about Zach's interest and experience that Drew couldn't answer, but he was satisfied enough to offer him a week-long internship with GameVision, Inc. He said if the week went well, he would consider extending it another week or two.

Jordan explained that he didn't usually take high school kids, but because EJ had asked him to make an exception, he promised to give Zach a chance. Drew thanked him profusely and immediately called Zach to tell him the good news. He didn't answer, so Drew shot off a text message. He didn't respond. After several minutes, he tried again. Zach still didn't answer. "Maybe he lost his phone privileges again," he said to himself as he dialed April. Then he thought of a quicker way to get to Zach and ended the call before she had a chance to hit decline.

Drew powered up his Xbox and there he found Zach, his avatar anyway, deep into a mission of a futuristic, bio-terrorism game.

"Zakariazz, I need to talk to you," Drew said, using Zach's gamertag. The game chatter ceased immediately.

"Dad?" Zach blurted out. "Uh, okay. I'm out, guys."

His friends burst into laughter, then they ganged up and ragged on Zach for getting pulled out of the game by his dad. But he logged off before the truly brutal insults started flying. Drew's cellphone rang a second later.

"Did you have to do that, Dad?" Zach hissed before Drew could say hello.

"What?"

"You could have messaged me privately."

"What fun would that have been?" Drew asked, laughing.

"You're not funny, Dad."

"You're right! I'm hilarious!"

"Come on, man," Zach groaned.

"Hey, don't be mad at me. It's not like my tag is 'Zachsdaddy.' You're the one who identified me as your dad. And if you had answered your phone or texted me back, I wouldn't have had to go through the game in the first place, right?"

"Right," he conceded. "What's up, Dad?"

"How's your mom?"

"She seems fine. She and Tony talked for a long time behind closed doors this morning. I didn't hear them yelling or anything, and now she's helping Cole pack for the trip. I guess that means it's all good."

"I guess so," Drew agreed. "Do Paige and Cole know anything?"

"No. Mom put us on media restriction last night and took me and Paige's phones. But after Paige and Cole went to bed, I told her I already knew about the video. So, she gave mine back, then she went into her room and started crying."

Drew sighed. "Oh. I see. I'm sorry you had to see that and that Mom took your phone."

"What was that all about, Dad? You know... the stuff in the park?"

"I did a dumb thing," he said. "I kissed your mom when she didn't want me to. I shouldn't have done that. *You* should never do that—"

"Do you still love her?"

Drew took a deep breath. The conversation was getting deep. He had to be careful. Zach was his son, not his buddy. It was important to be honest, like Kimmie said, but he didn't want to lay more on Zach than he could process.

"Yes. I love your mother."

"Then why aren't you together? I know she loves *you*."

"Because it takes more than love to make a marriage work. Things can get complicated and it's easy to lose your way."

Zach let out a couple of heavy sighs. "I wish what they said was true... that you guys were back together."

"That would be nice, but that's not the case."

"I know, Dad. But it's what I want. Don't you want that?"

"I want your mom to be happy. And she's happy with Tony. You guys like him, don't you?"

"Yeah. He's cool. I mean, in a corny dad kinda way—like you!"

"Pssshh. I'm the coolest dad in the world," Drew said. "And I can prove it."

"Go for it," Zach taunted.

"Have you ever thought about doing an internship at a video game company?"

"Uh, yeah. I talked to a few reps at the convention I went to, but they told me they don't hire high school kids."

"So, you'd wanna do that, if you had the chance?"

"Hell, yeah!" he blurted out. "I would definitely wanna do that."

"Good. I set up an internship for you with GameVision. It'll be the last week in July. It's in the city, so you'll have to stay with me."

All signs of life ceased from Zach's end of the call.

"Are you still there?"

"Are you serious or is this a corny dad joke? Because that would be really messed up and seriously *not* cool."

"Yes, I'm serious," Drew chuckled. "Do you want to do the internship?"

"Of course. Yeah. Yes. Absolutely! Thanks, Dad!"

"You're welcome, son. We can talk more about the logistics when you get back from the cruise."

After they said their goodbyes, Drew went back to bed. But thoughts of how happy Zach sounded kept chasing away sleep. Then his phone buzzed.

"Hi," he said.

"So, I hear you are the coolest dad in the world," April said.

"Is that news to you?"

"No, but hearing it come out of Zach's mouth was pretty groundbreaking."

"Ha! I bet... So, how are you?"

"I'm fine. I just freaked out a little—or a lot. It's been a long time since lies about us bounced around the internet. I guess I had lulled myself into a false sense of anonymity, and the whole thing caught me off guard. I hate that Tony had to see that."

"I'm sorry, April. I hope he wasn't mad at you. I tried to tell him it was all on me, but he wasn't too interested in what I had to say."

"I know, but thanks for trying. He's fine now. I mean, you aren't his favorite person by any means, but he gets it. And he's not mad at me. We're good."

"Are *we* good?"

"Yeah, we're good. Just... don't do that again."

"Don't worry, I won't. Have fun on the cruise."

"Thanks, babe. We'll see you when we get back."

Drew ended the call and rolled over. He drifted off to sleep feeling, for the first time in a very long time, content. Hearing the smile in Zach's voice and the forgiveness in April's were the pieces of the puzzle he needed to finally finish putting his life back together.

Chapter 20

"You're kidding," Travis said, sitting next to Mike on Drew's couch in his dressing room after Mickey's debut on *The Latest* season premier.

Drew nodded. "Yeah. EJ wants us to perform with our original groups. His vision is for this to be an epic reunion tour," he said, handing them each a beer.

Both Travis and Mike stared at Drew with their mouths partially opened. Then they looked at each other, and then back at Drew.

"Come on guys, you're makin' me nervous," Drew said. "If you're not cool with it, I understand. Just say something."

"I'm cool with it," Mike said casually, as he took a drink. "But the tour bus has gotta be state-of-the-art. My back's too messed up to travel all crammed together like we did back in the day."

"Ha! Nobody would sign up if that was the case—too many old guys with bad knees and backs. But don't worry. Python has a reputation for taking care of its artists," Drew said. "I wouldn't expect a hot tub on the bus or anything, but I'm sure it'll be comfortable."

Drew looked over at Travis. His assurances had done nothing to alter his bewildered expression. "What do you think, Trav?"

"It's a, uh, cool idea. But you know I got the restaurant and the wife and kids," Travis said, rolling his beer bottle between his hands. "To be honest, I'm not playing as much as you and Mike anymore. I don't have the time."

Drew looked over at Mike and he shrugged. "Well, think about it. EJ said he's only going for select cities and possibly a two weeks on, two weeks off schedule since everybody has other stuff goin' on."

"That sounds totally doable," Mike said. "And who cares if you don't play that much? As many times as we've played and practiced our songs, you could play 'em in your sleep."

Travis responded with a grunt and took a sip of his beer.

"Well, like I said, think about it. We haven't started recording the collaboration album, so a tour is a while off. Maybe you can pull out the old keyboard and start practicing," Drew said. "And we can practice together... if you want."

Travis and Mike raised their eyebrows simultaneously. It had been nearly a decade since Drew looked and sounded like their lead singer. Their doubt in his sincerity was understandable, but the conversation had sparked a twinkle in their eyes that was hard to miss. It outshined the apprehension and gave him hope his friends would learn to trust him again. He just had to be patient— and consistent.

They moved on to the lighter topics of work, women, and sports. And like with any old friends, conversations about the present eventually triggered reminiscing about the good old days.

"Remember that girl in Denver?" Mike asked.

"Which one?" Travis asked with a chuckle.

"The one who snuck in me and Chris's room that time."

"Which time?" Travis and Drew blurted out in unison. All three of them nearly fell off their seats, doubled over in laughter. Then a knock at the door brought them back quickly from memory lane.

"Come in!" Drew shouted.

Shanice stuck her head in. "Hey, Drew, I'm sorry to disturb you guys, but I found these handsome gentlemen wandering around out here looking for you," she said as she stepped inside. Kelvin and her father, Gabe Stevenson, followed.

"Hey!" Drew said as he stood to greet them. Kelvin had mentioned he might stop by, but he was surprised to see Dr. Stevenson. Drew hadn't seen him in person since he signed the contract. "Kelvin, Dr. Stevenson, these are my friends, Travis

McKellar and Mike Bryant." Travis and Mike were already on their feet, prepared to shake hands with the men.

"Is this a bad time?" Kelvin asked.

"Not at all. We were just shootin' the breeze," Drew said. "Why don't you guys go on over to Trav's place and I'll catch up with you later."

Travis and Mike repeated the round of handshakes on their way out.

"Well, I'll be on my way too then," Shanice said.

"Okay, I'll see you over at Travis's in a minute," Drew said. "You and Reid can go on without me. I'll get an Uber."

Shanice narrowed her eyes. "Huh?" She seemed confused, which confused Drew because she was the one who arranged for everyone to go over to Travis's restaurant for drinks to celebrate a successful season premier. She had also suggested he ride with her and Reid.

"Kelvin, it was nice to see you again as always," she said with a smile, giving him a quick hug. "Daddy, I'll talk to you later," she said with an even broader smile, giving him a hug and a kiss on the cheek. "Drew, I need to talk to you for a second," she said with no trace of a smile as she quickly stepped out of the dressing room. Drew followed her to the hallway.

He pulled the door closed behind him. "What did I do now?"

"Don't you dare say one word to my father about Reid and me," she snarled.

Drew shrugged. "What are you talkin' about, Shanice?"

"About us going out a couple of times."

His jaw dropped. "I didn't know you went out."

"I thought Reid told you."

He shook his head slowly. "Nope."

"Wow. I can't believe he actually did what I asked him to do," she said. "Well, don't *you* say anything either—to ANYBODY!"

Drew chuckled. "I'm not that kinda dude, Shanice. I don't go around talkin' about who's dating who, especially with people's parents. But why don't you want him to know?"

Shanice glared at him for several seconds. "I understand you and Kimmie Logan have been out a few times."

Drew's eyebrows shot straight up.

"Reid does not share your viewpoint on talking about who's dating who." She smirked. "Did you tell *your* father about that?"

He shook his head.

"Why not?"

Drew put his hands up. "Okay. I get it. It's none of my damn business," he grumbled and went back into his dressing room.

"Sorry about that, Dr. Stevenson, Kelvin."

Dr. Stevenson smiled. "First of all, please call me Gabe. Second, are you okay to talk right now?"

"Sure. Why do you ask?"

"Well, Drew, my baby girl looks exactly like her mother. I know what that face looks like when somebody's about to get told off."

"Heh, heh. You definitely know your daughter. But, yeah, I'm fine and I'm glad you're both here. Kelvin said he had some important stuff to tell me about the show," Drew said, cracking his knuckles.

"Yes, we do," Gabe said. "Um, do you want to sit?" He removed his black fedora, revealing a head of closely cut gray hair that contrasted strikingly with his deep brown complexion.

"Oh, yeah! I'm sorry. Please, have a seat," Drew said, gesturing toward the couch as he sat on a folding chair. "Can I offer you guys a beer?"

Gabe and Kelvin shook their heads as they sat on the couch. "We don't want to drag this out," Gabe said. "But could you tell us again what you know about your mother's side of the family?"

"Oh. Okay. That's easy. Not much. My mother is from New York—Long Island, but I think my grandparents were born in the

South somewhere. I know my grandfather was in the army and fought in World War II. He and my grandmother were teachers, I think. I remember them having tons of books and always correcting our grammar and stuff like that, but I only saw them a handful of times until I was nine or ten. I never saw them after that. From what I was told, they died before my mother died, but I don't know when. And my mom was an only child. But I think my grandfather had at least one brother, because I remember him telling me they played chess together as kids when he tried to teach me. I don't know if my grandmother had any siblings." He shrugged. "That's about all I know."

Kelvin listened intently while Gabe nodded. Then Gabe closed his eyes and took a deep breath. "Alright, Drew, we're going to need you to keep an open mind."

"Alright," Drew agreed. "You guys are making me nervous. You're not about to tell me that my mother was a Russian spy, are you?"

"What!" Kelvin said.

"Nothing. Just tell me. What is it?"

"Kelvin received your genetic test results a couple of weeks ago and your DNA reveals a percentage of African blood," Gabe said.

"Okay," he said, rubbing the back of his neck. "Is that it? I've seen the show before and I remember a couple of episodes where a white dude finds out he's like two percent African. Did you guys think that was going to upset me? Because it doesn't. I'm not racist."

Kelvin shook his head. "We don't think you're racist, Drew, but—"

"But what?"

"Drew, we're not talking about two percent African blood. Your genetic test results revealed that you are twenty-three-point-nine percent Sub-Saharan African," Gabe said.

Drew cocked his head. "That seems high."

"It is high," Gabe conceded. "So, I had them redo the test—twice."

"So, what does that mean?"

"Anyone with that percentage has a close Black relative, at least one grandparent."

"You're saying that one of my grandparents was Black?"

Gabe and Kelvin looked at each other.

"Both of your grandparents on your mother's side are Black, based on what we found."

Drew furrowed his brow as he pulled at his chin. "I'm sorry, I'm confused. Are you telling me that my mother was Black?"

Gabe nodded. "Yes."

"So, my mom wasn't my mother?"

"What do you mean, Drew?" Kelvin asked.

"I don't have a picture of my mom's parents, but I saw them before. They weren't Black. And my mom wasn't Black. Not that there's anything wrong with that. I'm just saying that the woman who raised me wasn't Black, so you must be telling me she wasn't my biological mother. Because I can show you a picture of her. I've got some in my phone," he rambled on about his mother's complexion and red hair like his sister and blue eyes like him. As he pulled his cell phone out of his pocket, it slipped from his hand and hit the floor with a thud. Kelvin picked it up and handed it to him.

"Whoa, calm down, son," Gabe said, taking the phone from Drew's trembling hand and placing it on the couch. "We don't have any reason to believe Beth wasn't your biological mother. Your birth certificate clearly shows that your mother was Elizabeth J. Simon. There are lots of people who identify as or who are classified as Black or African American that look like white people. Your grandparents are Negro according to the census data from 1930 and '40 or colored, as their birth certificates indicate. But, evidently, at some point, they decided to do what is called *pass*. Do you know what that means?"

Drew nodded. "Yeah— Wait. Why do you keep saying *are* when they're dead?"

"Your grandfather is dead. He died a few years ago. But your grandmother is still alive. As far as we can tell, she still lives in the house on Long Island where your mother was born and raised."

Drew shook his head. "No. My father told me they were dead when my mother died."

"He was mistaken."

"Why wouldn't my mother tell me about... the passing?" Drew asked, cracking his neck. "She never put up with any dishonesty. Me and my sister always got in the most trouble for lying."

"More than likely, she didn't know," Kelvin said. "Your grandparents had decided to pass for white. It wouldn't have made much sense for them to tell their offspring."

"But why? Why would they do that? I knew a kid when we lived out in California. He and his family looked as white as any white people I'd ever met, but he made sure to let everyone know he was Black. And he'd fight anybody who challenged him on it."

"Your grandparents were born in the twenties in the segregated South," Gabe explained. "I imagine they did it for better opportunities. But how people in their situation choose to identify themselves is deeply personal and depends heavily on their individual life experiences. We will never know the specific reasons some Black people who look white chose to pass while others didn't. Mainly because this is the type of family secret that is usually discovered when the relative is long gone. So, we can only piece together speculation based only on what we know about their lives and the time in which they lived."

"What happens now?" Drew asked, looking at the floor. "I'm guessing you plan to put this on the show."

Gabe paused for a long time. "We don't need to talk about that right now because, to tell you the truth, I'm not sure what we want to do with it yet. But I knew I wasn't comfortable springing this on you in front of the camera. And the fact that your grandmother is still alive complicates things somewhat. When I was comin' up, Black folks didn't out folks who were passing. It just wasn't done," he said. "So, I'm going to give you all the information we've collected so far, including your grandmother's address and phone number. You look it over and we'll talk more about what we're going to do after you've had time to think and talk to your family. We've also got more research to do in the meantime. Alright?"

Drew nodded.

Gabe and Kelvin said goodbye and left him alone in his dressing room to look over the documents they gave him in private. It was all right there. His grandparents' birth certificates and census data. But the most compelling evidence were the pictures of his grandparents sitting proudly among other Black high school students in their respective graduating classes at a time and in places where Black kids didn't go to school with white kids, no matter how white they looked.

Drew sat for several minutes, waiting for his mind to stop reeling. It wouldn't. There was nothing in his arsenal to help with this situation. He jumped up and rushed over to the restaurant.

Chapter 21

"What do you call a musician without a girlfriend?" Mike asked the group gathered around the bar at Travis's restaurant.

The group responded with a collective shrug.

"Homeless!" he blurted out with a guffaw. Travis, Reid, and the guys from The Latest House Band joined him, taking no offense.

"Oh my God, Dad," Mickey said. "That joke is so sexist."

"What? How?"

"Because its premise assumes all musicians are male," Kimmie said.

"And heterosexual," Shanice added. "And we all know how far that is from reality." Kimmie and Mickey nodded.

The men groaned. "It's a joke, ladies. Don't get your pants suits all wrinkled," Reid said as Drew pushed his way through the group without acknowledging anyone.

"Reid, I need to borrow your car," he said breathlessly, like he had run there from the studio, which he had.

"Why?"

"I just need it," he said slowly through his clenched teeth.

"Okay, okay. No problem," Reid said as he pulled his valet ticket from his pocket and handed it to him.

"Thanks, man," Drew said and turned to leave. Kimmie grabbed his arm.

"What's wrong, Drew?"

"I'm sorry, Kim," he said as he planted the kiss on her cheek he had forgotten in his haste. "I gotta go. It's... it's a family thing."

"Is it the kids?" Kimmie gasped, her forehead creased with worry.

"No, no, they're fine. I gotta go," he said quickly and turned again to leave.

"Wait, Drew! You sure you can drive? You seem so upset."

"I'll be fine. I'll call you," he said as he hurried out.

An hour later, Drew exited the Porsche and raced to his father's back door. He paused for a second to take a deep breath and then pounded on the door. It was after eleven. The house was dark and quiet. He pounded again, harder this time, causing the dogs in the neighborhood to bark viciously. The porch light flicked on as Simon snatched back the curtain, peering out angrily. His angry expression flipped to concern as he quickly unlocked the door and swung it open.

"You told me they were dead!" Drew shouted as he barreled into the kitchen.

"What the hell are you talking about?" Simon asked, closing the door. "And lower your voice. Susan isn't feeling well."

"When I asked you if you told Grandma and Grandpa that Mom died, you told me they were dead," Drew repeated slowly.

"I didn't say that," he said, shaking his head.

"Yes, you did."

"Well, I meant they were dead to me."

Drew's heart skipped a beat, and he closed his eyes. "They live less than two hours from here, less than an hour from me now. How could you make me think they were dead?"

Simon furrowed his brow. "You didn't need those people in your life."

"Those people?" Drew's eyes popped open as the words his father had spoken in that kitchen a few months before echoed in his mind. *... With me, what you see is what you get. I have never pretended to be anything other than exactly what I am...* "So, you knew."

Simon breathed in slowly as he folded his arms across his chest.

"Did you know Mom was Black, Dad?"

He glared at Drew.

"Dad!"

"I said lower your voice!" Simon barked. "Yes! I knew!"

The truth hit Drew like a ton of bricks. If he knew, she knew. She knew, and she had never told him. His heart raced, triggering quick, shallow breaths. He leaned back against the counter, suddenly lightheaded and queasy. It was only a matter of time before he would start hyperventilating. Simon stepped toward Drew. He grabbed him under his arm and pushed him down on a kitchen chair. Drew leaned forward, resting his elbows on his knees.

"Take slow, deep breaths," Simon said as he shoved Drew's head closer to his knees. "Do you need a bag, or can you stop this on your own?"

Drew put his hand up. "I can… stop it," he said, trying to breathe normally.

Simon sat down and waited quietly for the full ten minutes it took Drew to calm himself down.

"When did you find out?" Drew asked, focusing on the pattern in the kitchen tile.

Simon sighed. "1978."

"Mom told you?"

"No. Your grandmother. It was her desperate attempt to chase me off after your grandfather forbidding Beth to see me didn't work."

"Why didn't Mom ever tell us?"

"I guess she thought you and Lia were better off not knowing."

"You guess? You never talked about it?"

Simon pinched the bridge of his nose. "She never wanted to, and I sure as hell wasn't gonna push her to."

"Why not?"

"You know how your mother was. She didn't handle things that made her sad too well. Talking about all that stuff only would have drummed up all that old resentment she held against her parents. Then she'd go deep into that dark place I tried to keep her out of."

"She resented Grandma and Grandpa? For what?"

Simon shrugged. "For lying? For making her lie? For making her be a lie? Look. All I know is, your mom didn't want you and Lia to be conflicted about who you were, so she didn't tell you."

"And you agreed with that."

"No. But I deferred to your mother. She was the one with first-hand knowledge of what it was like to look white, but not be white, at least by society's standards."

They both stared at the tile for a while.

"So, how do you feel?" Simon asked.

Drew shrugged. "I don't know."

"Well, do you feel different?"

"I always feel different," he said, barely above a whisper. "So, I guess I feel the same."

"Good. Because you *are* the same, son," he said as he placed his hand firmly on Drew's shoulder.

Chapter 22

Long Island, New York
1988

"Drew, Lia, wake up! We're here," Beth sang from the driver's seat of their station wagon.

Drew sat up, rubbing his eyes. "This is California?" he asked. They had left North Carolina the night before to meet his father at Fort Irwin in Barstow, California.

"No, sweetie, we're in New York! I thought we'd take a little detour and visit Grandma and Grandpa for a little while," she said, smiling with her mouth, but there was something other than happiness in her eyes. "We've got the whole summer to get to California."

"For real!" he squealed, startling Lia awake. "Wait, won't Daddy be mad?"

"Mad about us having a little adventure? No way!" she said. "Besides, Daddy's far too busy getting used to his new post to worry about us." She nudged his chin gently with her knuckle.

Her voice was light and giggly. She sounded excited, like she believed what she was saying. But Drew saw through the happy, smiling mask she wore. Simon had mapped out a detailed itinerary for them to follow, including the specific route as well as the location, time, and duration of all stops. She knew, as well as him, that his father would be furious when he found out they had veered off course. But he didn't argue with his mother. He had already gotten a stinging reminder of her zero-tolerance policy for any disobedience during moves when he mouthed off about the unauthorized change in their departure time.

"Where are we?" Lia asked groggily from the backseat.

Beth opened her mouth to answer right as the front door of the big white house opened. She gasped and jumped out of the car, meeting her parents halfway down the path. Drew and Lia watched with wide eyes as she collapsed into their arms. After a long hug, Beth beckoned for them to come. They scooted out of the car.

"Don't be scared. They're our grandparents," Drew whispered to his sister.

She looked up at him and nodded as she reached for his hand. He laced his fingers through hers and led her over to the three teary-eyed adults, two they hadn't seen in over four years.

"Well, who do we have here?" Grandpa asked.

Drew looked at his mother for guidance.

"Did you forget your name, sweetie?" she teased.

Drew smiled sheepishly. "I'm Andrew, sir, and this is my sister, Amelia."

"Andrew?" Grandpa asked, scratching his chin. "I have a grandson named Andrew, but he's only nine. You must be a different Andrew because you're at least fourteen."

Drew giggled. "No, I'm him! I'm nine! I'll be ten in a few months."

"WowWee, Bethy! What in the world are you feedin' this boy?"

"I don't know, Daddy. I think he's sneaking Miracle-Gro or something. Every time I look up, his pants are too short," she chuckled.

"And I do believe this is the prettiest little girl I ever did see," Grandpa gushed. "She must've gotten into that Miracle-Gro herself with all this hair," he said, tugging on one of Lia's long, thick, auburn pigtails. "Lookin' just like your Gran with that red hair and those freckles. You see this pretty little girl lookin' just like you, Cheryl?"

"I do indeed," Grandma Cheryl said. "You all must be starving. How 'bout we get you some eggs, bacon, and biscuits?" she rattled off the breakfast menu as she put her arms around Drew and Lia. "You like grits?"

Their faces lit up. "Yes, ma'am!" they exclaimed, nodding eagerly in unison.

Grandma smiled. "Elizabeth, you've been makin' these babies grits?"

"Of course, Mama, we eat grits all the time. They're not as good as yours, though."

"Oh hush, child," Grandma said, blushing. "John, why don't you get their suitcases and let's all go in and eat."

"Yes, dear," Grandpa said with a wink at Drew. "You wanna give your ol' Gramps a hand?"

"Yes, sir!" Drew said and followed Grandpa John to the station wagon.

* * *

"It looks smaller than I remember," Lia said, standing next to Drew at the end of the driveway of their grandmother's Long Island home.

"Well, you were seven the last time we were here," Drew said.

"You sure you wanna do this?"

"Nope. You?"

"I'm sure I don't wanna do this. But I'm here to support you," she said and looked over at him. "You look nice, by the way. Do you have a job interview after this?" She snickered.

Drew looked down at his clothes. "Hey, can you see my tats?" he asked, noticing his white, long-sleeved shirt was doing a terrible job of concealing the tattoos up and down his arms.

"Yep. I can see all your tattoos. So what?"

"I don't want her to think I'm some kind of tattooed freak."

Lia flashed a sinister smirk. "But you are some kind of tattooed freak."

"Aw. Thanks, sis."

"Anytime. Let's do this," she said and started up the driveway.

They reached the door, and Drew rang the bell. A silhouette appeared in the earth tone stain glass cutout, then the door opened a sliver, and a middle-aged Latina woman peeped through the crack.

"Yes?" the woman said.

"Uh, hi," Drew said. "Is Mrs. Jones here... Mrs. Cheryl Jones?"

The woman nodded and closed the door quickly.

"Oh, well, we tried!" Lia said with a shrug as she turned to leave.

Drew grabbed her arm and turned her back around. After a few seconds, the woman opened the door wide. "Please," she said, gesturing for them to come inside.

Drew stood back and waited like a gentleman for Lia to step inside. She didn't move. He gave her a brotherly shove over the threshold, and she thanked him with an elbow to the ribs so stealthily, the woman looked at Drew like he was crazy when he let out a grunt.

As the woman led them through the foyer into the living room, Drew realized it wasn't only the outside of the house that was different than he remembered. The interior had been completely remodeled. The last time they visited, thirty years before, everything looked old. It was a beautiful home that his grandparents took good care of, but in 1988, all the furniture and fixtures looked like antiques to him. Since then, the old house had been through a serious renovation. Walls had been torn down and rooms expanded. Everything was updated. The only familiar thing about the house was the shiny black baby grand piano, sitting in the corner next to the front window. It was the piano he and Lia practiced on during their visit all those years ago, the same one his grandfather had taught his mother to play.

Drew and Lia stood in the center of the living room, marveling at the new interior of the old house. It took almost a full minute before Drew noticed their grandmother sitting in an armchair, smiling at them. She, like the house, seemed smaller, but unlike the house, she had not been renovated. Thirty years had turned her hair completely white and etched her face with creases and wrinkles, but her smile was the same: warm and beautiful.

"Well, hello there, children," she said, starting to stand. The woman rushed to assist her. "I'm fine, Aida," she said, fanning her away as she rose from her seat under her own power and opened her arms wide.

"Hi, Grandma," Drew said, as he went to her and bent to receive her embrace. Lia followed his lead and took her turn gingerly hugging their grandmother.

"It's so wonderful to see you. I prayed so hard I would get a chance to hold you kids again. Thank you, Jesus," she said with tears in her eyes, raising her clasped hands up in the air. "I wish your grandfather was here with us," she said as she grabbed the arm of the burgundy and cream checkered armchair and lowered herself back into it. "Please, children, sit down."

Drew and Lia sat close together on the caramel-colored chesterfield sofa next to her chair, waiting quietly while she cried into a tissue, then smiled at them, then cried a little more. Aida sat quietly on the arm of the chair and gently stroked her back.

"Thank you, dear," she said, looking up at Aida. "I'll be alright. Will you make us some tea? Would you like some tea?" she asked Drew and Lia.

Lia shook her head. "No, thank—"

"Yes, ma'am, we would," Drew said.

Aida nodded and hurried out of the room.

Grandma smiled. "She's lovely, isn't she? She's been with us for nearly thirty years."

"Wow! That's a long time to be with a family," Drew said, hoping he didn't sound like an idiot trying to do the thing he always failed: small talk.

"Indeed it is," she agreed, nodding her head. "But it's even longer to be with*out* your family," she said. "I can't tell you how overjoyed I was when you called, but why haven't you children come to see me before now?" she asked, not beating around the bush.

Drew rubbed his neck, cracked it, and then started working on his knuckles.

"We heard you were dead," Lia blurted out. She never beat around the bush either, apparently having inherited more than red hair and freckles from their grandmother.

"Oh? Well, that's certainly an exaggeration! I guess I don't have to ask who told you that fake news," she said, shaking her head. "Make sure you give your father my best. How in the devil is the devil doing, anyhow?"

"So, Gran, the house looks really nice. It must have taken a long time to remodel this entire house," Drew said, quickly changing the subject. His father was the last thing he wanted to talk about, especially with Lia there. She always played the role of "daddy's little avenger" anytime she thought he was under attack.

"Thank you, sweetheart. This old house is nearly a hundred years old. It got to a point where something needed fixing or replacing every month, if not every week. We decided to go ahead and gut the thing about fifteen years ago and, well, here you have it."

Drew nodded, looking around. His eye caught a glimpse of his mother's high school graduation picture sitting in a frame among the thousands of books on the huge built-in along the wall. He went over to the picture and reached to take it from the shelf. "Do you mind?" he asked before touching it.

"Go right ahead," Grandma said.

He took the picture off the shelf and sat back down.

"She's beautiful, isn't she?" said Grandma as he and Lia stared at their mother's picture. "Andrew, I want to tell you how much I love that show of yours."

Drew looked up abruptly. "You watch *The Latest?*"

"Of course! I try to keep track of everything you kids do. It comes on too late, but Aida and I watch it on the DVR in the morning and just laugh and laugh. Is that Reid really as crazy as he acts on that show?" She chuckled.

He laughed. "No, Grandma. He's crazier!"

"Drew's gonna be on another show soon, Grandma," Lia said, bringing his laughter to a screeching halt. "Why don't you tell her about it, Drew?" She nudged him in the ribs. He grunted and then made a mental note to find out if his sister's elbows were made of steel.

"Oh, Andrew, I'm so happy you're doing so well. Yes, please tell me all about this new show." Her eyes twinkled as Aida returned with a tray filled with a tea set and a plate of heart-shaped butter cookies that looked exactly like the cookies their mother used to make every Christmas. "Thank you, Aida," Grandma said.

"Thank you," Drew and Lia said, staring longingly at the cookies as Aida quickly left the room.

Drew took a deep breath. "Thanks for reminding me about the show, sis," he said through clenched teeth. "I'm going to be on a show called *Bloodlines.* Have you heard of it?" he asked as he poured a cup of tea and handed it to his grandmother.

"Yes, I've seen it," she replied, taking the cup and saucer. "What would make you want to be on a show like that?" She blew on her tea and stared at the ripples.

"I thought it would be interesting to learn about our family history. Mom never really told us too much about her side of the family."

"Oh. I see," she said as she drank her tea, gazing wistfully at Beth's picture. An awkward quietness fell over the room.

Lia let out a sigh. "They had Drew do a DNA test for the show," she said as she went to nudge Drew again, but he quickly moved his arm to block the blow.

Grandma continued to drink her tea without taking her eyes off the picture.

"Well, do you wanna know what the results were?" Lia asked impatiently. Drew looked at her with wide eyes and shook his head. Their visit was quickly turning into an ambush, and he didn't want to go through with it anymore.

Grandma looked up suddenly. "The results? I imagine his results were as varied as any individual's could be. As would yours be. You are both very special. And I'm confident, if nothing else, your mother told you that repeatedly. You certainly didn't need a DNA test to confirm it," she said, shaking her head slowly. Her lips formed a thin, tight line as she sipped her tea.

The sharpness in her tone sent a slight chill down Drew's spine. "I didn't. It's just part of the show. The host always reveals the celebrity's genetic makeup," he explained.

"I will never understand why people these days need to know every little thing about every little thing all the time," Grandma said.

"Drew found out he's nearly a quarter African. That seems like more than a little thing to me," Lia said.

"Does it?" She shrugged. "Well, Amelia, I suppose that depends on your perspective."

Lia and Grandma glared at each other as the tension swirled around the room. Drew glanced at his mother's picture. It looked like she was glaring at him. She would expect him to diffuse the situation.

"Grandma, we're only trying to figure things out," Drew said as he took hold of Lia's hand. "We didn't come here to make you uncomfortable or force you to talk about things you'd rather not. But you're literally the only person who can help us."

She closed her eyes and took a deep breath. "What would you like to know, dear?" She placed her cup and saucer on the coffee table.

He had questions on top of questions since Gabe and Kelvin's visit. There was so much he wanted to know, but his mind went blank. He looked at Lia, expecting her to be as befuddled as he was, but with her eyebrow slightly raised and her lips pursed together, she looked angry more than anything else.

"I don't know, Gran. I guess I wanna know why Mom never told us. It's not like we were kids when she died," he said, keeping his voice low, so Aida wouldn't hear.

"I'm not altogether certain why she didn't tell you. By the time you kids were of age, we didn't talk too often anymore. She'd only call once or twice a year to chat for a few minutes. I asked her a couple times if she told you or if she was planning to. She always quickly changed the subject."

"Okay. So, why do you *think* she never told us?" Drew asked.

"I suppose she was afraid you would react the way she did when we told her."

"She was upset?" Lia asked.

"No, not at first. She was surprised, but she seemed rather happy about it. We had raised her not to think of people in terms of race. But it was the seventies, and your grandfather and I had been heavily involved in the Civil Rights Movement. We helped with voter registration, went on Freedom Rides, to rallies, not with Beth, but we did take her to the March on Washington when she was an itty-bitty thing. So, race, race relations and racial inequality were topics debated between us and our friends on a regular basis. Beth grew up acutely aware of the atrocities suffered by Black people in this country, but she also had a front row seat to the fight to set things right. And I think she was proud to find out she was Black because she associated being Black with unbelievable strength, resiliency, and a commitment to seeking justice."

"If she started out proud about it, what changed?" Drew asked.

"She was sixteen, just starting to figure out who she was as a young woman, and we threw a curve ball at her. Until then, she was a white girl with a keen sense of fairness, who treated everyone she met with respect. Then suddenly she was a white girl with a big secret, and she became overwhelmed with the weight of it all."

"Did she tell anyone?" Lia asked.

Grandma nodded. "One day I realized that her best friend, Judy, hadn't been around in a while, nor had Beth mentioned her name. This was a girl she had known since fifth grade, and they were inseparable. Either Judy was at our house or Beth was at hers. After some prodding, she finally confessed. In tears, she told me she had disobeyed us and confided in her best friend. Judy promised she would keep her secret, but she said her parents wouldn't allow her to be friends with... a nigger."

"What? No," Lia gasped as she stared at Beth's picture.

"Soon after that, my sweet, precious girl changed," Grandma continued. "She started hanging around with some bad kids and coming home late with no explanation. And she'd talk back. Now, I know that probably doesn't sound too bad compared to what kids are doing these days, but it wasn't like Beth at all. She had been the most angelic child up to that point. On the rare occasions she misbehaved, a stern look was usually enough to set her straight. Then her grades started slipping. Your grandfather was fed up. He told her he would not stand by and watch her squander everything we had sacrificed so much for. He threatened to take the strap to her if she didn't shape up."

"Did she shape up?" Drew asked.

"She certainly did. She did not want that strap," Grandma said, shaking her head. "But she wasn't the same. She kept her grades up and got into college, but she was quiet and withdrawn—sad. She didn't run around with the bad kids anymore, but she also didn't run around with anyone else either anymore."

"Sounds like that's when her depression started," Drew said to Lia.

"I think you're right," Grandma agreed.

Drew and Lia looked at each other, then over at Grandma. "You knew she suffered from depression?" Drew asked.

"I knew something was wrong with my baby. Depression makes sense."

"Why didn't you get her help?" Lia snarled. Drew squeezed her hand.

"We tried, dear, but she met your father and assured us she didn't need it," she said with an eye roll. "She said being in love was the best therapy for her. And let me tell you, that did not sit well with your grandfather at all. From what Beth told us, it was clear Simon wasn't the type of man we had in mind for our daughter. He was uneducated and nearly ten years her senior. But we agreed to meet him anyway."

"I'm guessing that didn't go well," Drew said, remembering what his father had told him and knowing how incompatible Simon's personality was with making a good first impression.

Grandma raised both eyebrows. "That's an understatement. Your father and your grandfather got into a heated debate about Vietnam. John had been against the war and never hesitated to tell anyone exactly why, even Vietnam vets like your father. As I'm sure you can imagine, things didn't end well. Simon was even worse at holding his tongue than your grandfather. He called him a disgrace to the uniform and suggested that John should return his Medal of Honor and Purple Heart because he was a coward and a traitor."

Drew's shirt collar suddenly felt tight. He slipped his finger inside to get some relief while Lia shifted in her seat. "Dad said something about Grandpa forbidding Mom to see him?"

Grandma closed her eyes and sighed. "Yes. He did that night. But Beth was nearly twenty-one. She didn't want to upset her father, so she continued to see Simon secretly. Eventually, Simon asked if he could come over and apologize. John flat out refused, but Beth begged him to reconsider. He could never really say no to her."

Lia's eyes brightened. "Daddy apologized?"

"Unfortunately, no. Before Simon arrived, I walked in on Beth getting dressed, and I noticed marks on her arms—very distinct bruising in the shape of handprints around her upper arms." She paused to take a breath as tears formed in her eyes. "I demanded she tell me how she got the marks. She stammered her way through an implausible excuse, of course. But I knew where they came from. I couldn't believe that man had put his hands on my child. I screamed for John, and he came rushing in. Beth tried to cover up quickly, but he saw. When Simon arrived, John confronted him immediately, threatening to kill him if he ever came near Beth again. Simon said he wouldn't stop seeing her, that he loved her too much. I looked at Beth and I could see she loved him too. Suddenly, I felt an overwhelming desperation. I refused to lose my baby girl. Nothing else mattered anymore. We had already lost so much, given up so much. I couldn't lose her too," she said, looking down at her hands. "So, I blurted out, 'We're colored!' before I could stop myself."

"What did Dad do?" Lia asked.

"He got a strange, smug look on his face. It was quite unsettling." She shuddered. "Then he took Beth's hand and said, 'My wife and I will be leaving now,' and they left the house together. We were devastated. For the next few days, I divided my time between crying my eyes out and talking John out of going after Simon with his shotgun."

Lia gasped. "But why did she marry Daddy without telling you? Why not wait until he apologized to Grandpa and things blew over?"

Grandma looked at Drew.

Drew looked down at the floor as a light bulb went on in his head. "Because she was pregnant," he replied, not looking up. A pang of guilt stabbed at his gut.

Grandma sighed. "She wrote to us occasionally and called once or twice, but we didn't see our girl again for almost two years. You were a year old," she said, patting Drew's knee. "It was right before you all went to Germany." She flashed a reassuring smile, but it did nothing to relieve the irrational feeling of remorse. "We didn't see you again until you were five. Lia, you were three. Then another four years passed, and we got the call we had prayed for every day for ten years. Beth had finally decided to leave your father—"

"Excuse me, Miss Cheryl," Aida said as she entered the room. "You wanted me to tell you when the potatoes were ready."

"Oh, yes! Thank you, Aida," she said. "Will you excuse me for a few minutes, children? I'm gonna whip up some potato salad. You have time to stay for dinner, right?"

"Of course," Drew said as his mouth watered at the mere mention of his grandmother's potato salad. He jumped up to help Grandma to her feet, but she swatted him away and left the living room with Aida.

Lia snatched a butter cookie off the plate and hopped up. "Come on, Drew. Let's get out of here," she said, rushing out of the living room.

"Lia!" he called after her in an emphatic whisper as the front door creaked open. He went after her. "Lia!" he called out again, chasing her down the driveway. "Goddammit, Lia! Stop!" he barked, grabbing her arm right as she reached for her door handle.

"I'm sorry, Drew! I can't do this. I can't sit there and listen to her talk about Daddy like that. I know he's difficult and mean and he spanked us a lot, but—

"No, Lia, he spanked *you*. Do you call what he did to me *spanking*?"

She squeezed her eyes shut tight. "No."

They stared out at the lot across the street, empty except for a giant oak tree and overgrown grass. For several minutes, they watched the grass sway and listened to the leaves rustle in the gentle summer breeze. Then Lia took a deep breath. "Look, Drew. The way Dad beat you is inexcusable. I don't blame you for hating him. I hate him for that too. But he loved Mom more than anything. He could barely function after she died. You weren't around. You didn't see him. I had to feed him to make sure he ate, and force him to bathe. It was really scary."

Drew searched his mind, but his memories from that time were spotty. Zach was born a month after Beth's funeral. The whole experience was a blur. "I'm sorry I wasn't there for you, sis."

"Please don't apologize to me. I wasn't saying that to lay a guilt trip on you. I know how devastating losing Mom was for you. I'm just saying Dad loved Mom with all his heart. He could never have hit her. So what the hell was Grandma talking about Mom leaving him? We were only here for like two weeks. She's either a delusional old woman or an evil, lying bitch. Either way, I'm done!"

Drew rubbed the back of his neck. "Don't call her that. She's not delusional and she's not lying."

Lia took a step back. "You believe her?" she asked, her face twisted with incredulity. "Come on, Drew. You really think Dad hit Mom?"

"I didn't see him hit her, but he did grab her."

"How do you know that?"

"Because I saw him do this!" he exclaimed as he grabbed his sister's upper arms and pushed her against the car door. "Except it was a hard slam against the fridge."

"What?" she asked, shaking her head. "When?"

"Right before he went to California."

"Where was I?"

"We were outside playing, and I went in to use the bathroom. I yelled for him to stop. And he did. But then he came after me.

Mom rushed over, pushed me back outside, and closed the door. Then I heard lots of commotion, like things falling on the floor, and Dad shouting. I didn't know what to do. I was so scared. I just stood there and pissed my pants." He covered his face and hung his head low.

Lia put her arms around him, pulling him down into a hug. "You were only nine. There was nothing you could have done," she whispered, rubbing his back. "Why'd she only leave him for two weeks? Why would she go back?"

"Because Dad called and threatened to tell Grandma and Grandpa's secret... and to take us away from her."

"Mom told you that?"

Drew shook his head. "Of course not. I woke up in the middle of the night and heard Mom and Grandpa arguing about it. I couldn't hear everything they said, but I remember him begging her to stay. He kept saying, 'It doesn't matter, Beth! Let him tell the world. We only want you and the kids to be safe! I don't care how much it costs!' I didn't know what that meant until now."

Lia covered her mouth with her hand.

"We left early the next morning."

They continued to lean against the car in silence, gazing at the lot. "Did you tell April and the kids yet?"

"I told April. We're gonna talk to the kids next weekend."

She sighed. "I haven't told Peter. I don't even know how." She looked up at her big brother with tears in her eyes. "And his mother's gonna flip. This will be another thing she can add to her, *That Amelia is Not Good Enough For Our Family* file."

"Pete loves you, Lia. None of this changes anything." He put his arm around her shoulder. "You're still his same annoying, day-drinking wife." He chuckled, giving her a squeeze. "As for his mom... fuck her."

She laughed a little and put her head on his shoulder. "You still wanna leave, don't you?" he asked after several minutes.

She nodded.

He guided her a few steps away from the car and opened her door. "Are you coming?" she asked as she got in.

He shook his head.

"Will you be okay getting back?"

He nodded.

"Please tell Grandma I'm sorry, but I—"

"I'll tell her." He leaned in and kissed her cheek. "I'll call you later."

She drove off as Drew headed back up the driveway, eager to make up for all the lost time with his grandmother—and for her potato salad.

Chapter 23

"**I** like it," EJ said after Kimmie finished singing a song she and Drew had been working on for the collaboration album. "But the bridge needs to be in a minor key. And it would be more dramatic if you slow it down."

"Like this?" Drew asked, striking the keys with more force in the suggested key.

"Yeah! That's it," he said.

Drew flashed Kimmie an "I told you so" look.

"Okay, you were right," she said with an eye roll.

Drew pointed to himself and looked over his shoulder. "Who, me?" he asked with a smirk.

"Alright, smarty pants. Don't get cocky." She leaned over and gave him a quick peck on the lips. She turned away, but Drew hooked his finger in her back pocket and pulled her back for a full and proper kiss.

"Come on, Kimmie, that was your idea?" EJ asked. "You of all people should know how to write a pop song. If the main part is in a major key, the bridge is minor. That's 101."

"I know, I know," she groaned. "I was trying something different."

"Oh. Well, if you wanna do something different, take the bridge out altogether."

"Really? How will that make it better?"

"It won't! That song will suck without the bridge, but you said you wanted different, not better. Ha!"

"Whatever, E," she huffed.

"Don't get me wrong, 'Back to Me' is a good song," EJ said. "Most songs with that title are about getting a lost love to come back. Yours is about losing someone and finding yourself again. I like the lyrics, they just need some polish. Why don't y'all get with Kwayk? He can help make it pop a little bit more."

Drew and Kimmie looked at each other and snickered.

"What I miss?" EJ asked.

"Kwayk wrote the lyrics," Drew said.

EJ's jaw dropped. "That's a breakup song. A chick breakup song," he said. "Damn. He's really gettin' in touch with his feminine side."

Drew and Kimmie burst into laughter. "Hey, I gotta get outta here. My kids have a half day and I promised them lunch," Kimmie said as she stood up.

Drew tugged on her pocket again and pulled her onto his lap, making her giggle. "Hey!" she said, feigning a protest as she kissed him softly. He kissed her back, slipping his tongue into her mouth. They carried on like no one was there until EJ cleared his throat. Kimmie giggled again and pulled herself away from Drew.

"Bye-bye, boys," she said, laughing her way out of the studio.

Drew chuckled as he wiped his mouth and came down slowly off his make-out high. Then he looked over and met EJ's glare.

"I guess that whole 'we're just friends' BS y'all been sellin' is out the window," he said.

"I don't know what you're talkin' about, man," Drew said, suddenly intensely focused on wiping smudges off the piano keys.

"Yeah, okay. FYI, that box up there always has some condoms in it," he said, pointing to a shiny red box on a high shelf. "In case you and your *friend* find yourselves here alone late one night." He winked.

Drew looked up at the shelf. "Nice," he said. "That must come in handy."

EJ sighed. "Once upon a time, bruh. Once upon a time," he said as a nostalgic grin spread across his face. Then he looked at his watch. "I need to get outta here too, man. Let's meet up later. Me, my cousins, and a few of my boys are gonna ball around two, if you're free."

"Thanks for the invite, man, but I have a meeting at two and I gotta be at work by four."

"Aiight. Holla at me later then," EJ said as he gave Drew dap.

"Thanks for coming, Drew," Gabe said, extending his hand as Drew entered his office.

"No problem," Drew said as he shook his hand and sat on a chair in front of Gabe's mahogany desk. With the piles of files and books on it, he could only see Gabe from the chest up. There were also books and papers stacked in several neat piles on the floor. A filing system born out of necessity, Drew surmised, as he looked around the small office crammed with bookcases crammed with books. "I think you need a bigger office."

"Who you tellin'?" Gabe said with a hearty laugh as he leaned back in his chair, looking surprisingly relaxed among the chaos in a golf shirt and khakis. "But don't worry, I know exactly where everything is."

"Ah." Drew nodded. "Spoken like a true hoarder." He smiled.

"Ha, ha, ha, hilarious," he said. "Anyway, like I said, I'm glad you could come. I've got good news. We have completed the research on your mother's family history."

"Cool," Drew said in an even tone, hoping he didn't look as anxious as he felt. He hadn't talked to Gabe much since he and Kelvin told him that his mother was Black, only a few brief conversations on the phone. However, when Gabe called him in for a meeting, he got nervous. He was afraid there might be more shocking news, and he didn't want to come as close to losing it as he had before.

"You've seen the show before, right?" Gabe asked.

"Yes, sir," Drew said.

"So, you've seen in many of our episodes we've been able to find a common ancestor between our featured celebrities?"

Drew nodded.

"Well, we've linked your DNA to another celebrity we're researching for this season. And because of how closely you two are related, we want to change our format a little and do your episode together, perhaps even make it a two-parter. You have a lot in common even without the genetic link—" His office phone buzzed, and he picked it up. "Yes? Perfect, send him in please," Gabe said as he stood.

"I asked him to meet us here, but I wasn't sure he was going to make it," he said, moving from behind his desk as the door opened.

Drew's confusion multiplied exponentially when EJ walked into the office. He looked just as confused as Drew. And the fact he was dressed in full basketball gear made him look like he had gotten terribly lost on his way to the gym.

"Hey there, EJ!" Gabe said, extending his hand. "Come on in, son."

EJ shook his hand. "Hey, Gabe, man. I told you I would make time for you," he said. Then he looked at Drew and smiled. "You're kiddin' me, right? Is this the celebrity you think I'm related to?" he asked, making air quotes as he said the word "celebrity."

"Ha! Seriously, dude?" Drew said as he stood and gave EJ a bro hug. He didn't understand anything that was happening in that moment, but the subtle dig on his celebrity status made him laugh out loud. That eased his anxiety.

"Have a seat, EJ, Drew," Gabe said, gesturing at his guest chairs as he went back behind his desk. He sat down and blew out a long breath. "Okay, fellas, I know you two know each other, but did you know that both of you had signed on to do *Bloodlines*?"

Drew and EJ both shook their heads.

"Great! It's good to know that people take our non-disclosure agreement seriously." Gabe nodded and took another breath.

"Alright. You're both busy and we've got a lot to unpack. So, I'm gonna start at the end, then explain everything. Bottom line, you two are cousins."

"When you say cousins..." EJ raised his eyebrows and looked over at Drew, "you mean like way, way, down the line, right?" He chuckled as he nudged Drew's arm. Drew smirked a little and shifted in his seat; the uneasy feeling had returned.

EJ's laughter faded away as he noticed Gabe and Drew hadn't joined him. "I'm just joking. Why're you guys so serious?" he asked with a shrug. "Kelvin told me my DNA test results. I'm like twenty percent European or something like that, right?"

"That's about right," Gabe said.

"Okay, so Drew is my white cousin. What? His great-great-grandfather owned my great-great-grandmother and... well... you know..."

"Well, yes, there was certainly a lot of that going on with your mother's ancestors. But as for your theory, it's more like your great-great-grandmother *was* Drew's great-great-grandmother."

"What're you talkin' about, man?" EJ asked.

Drew couldn't help but think that, as different as they looked from each other, there must have been some family resemblance in the puzzled expressions on their faces.

Gabe turned slightly, reaching for a thick binder on the credenza behind him. "You and Drew are very closely related, EJ," he said as he opened the binder in front of him and pulled out some papers. "It's true you are twenty-two-point-four percent European, but Drew is twenty-three-point-nine percent Sub-Saharan African. You are genetically linked through your African blood," he said and handed Drew and EJ each a sheet of paper.

"Word?" EJ said as he took the paper.

Drew took his copy. Although he was fully aware his contract with *Bloodlines* gave him no say in how or with whom they shared any and all information they discovered about his family, he wasn't prepared for this scenario at all. A wave of discomfort hit him when Gabe told EJ about his DNA test results, causing his mind to spin a little. *"How am I gonna do this on national television?"* he thought. He tried to reconcile in his head why it mattered so much, why it mattered at all, but not one rational reason came to mind.

"What the hell is this?" EJ blurted out, startling Drew out of the wrestling match with his emotions. "Do you see this shit?" He waved the paper in Drew's face.

Drew looked at his copy. It was a family tree, his, or rather, a portion of it. His grandparents' names appeared at the top of the page in two boxes, joined by a horizontal line. And like any family tree, a vertical line dropped down from the horizontal line, connecting to their offspring. But instead of a single box with his mother's name below his grandparent's boxes, there were two boxes. One of the boxes contained the name Elizabeth Josephine Jones, Drew's mother. The other box read: Geneva Grace Jones. Those two boxes connected to his grandparents' boxes, like his box and Lia's box connected to his parents' boxes, like Zach, Paige, and Cole's boxes connected to his and April's.

His mother had a sister. And her sister's box connected to six offspring: four boys and two girls. The oldest was EJ.

Gabe put both his hands up. "Calm down, son," he said to EJ. "I can answer any questions you have."

"Okay. Are you fucking crazy?" EJ snarled. "My grandparents are Rocelia and James Jones. Who are Cheryl and John Jones?"

"Those are my grandparents," Drew said.

EJ turned his daggers on Drew. "No shit, man. I can read."

Drew clenched his jaw, glaring at EJ as a powerful impulse to punch him in the mouth surged through him. He looked EJ up and down, assessing the situation. EJ had a similar build, only slightly shorter and thicker. But EJ was a few years older. In Drew's mind, that meant EJ was a few years slower and weaker. He was certain he could take him down, but the voice in his head reminded him of all the thoughts and emotions that came from hearing news like this. EJ was letting his emotions get the best of him, like Drew had. He didn't know how to help him, but a fight would have been counterproductive.

"What is this bullshit you're tryna sell me?" he asked Gabe.

Gabe shook his head slowly. "I understand this is unsettling news, EJ. I know you're upset. But you are going to watch your mouth in my office," he said in a calm but stern voice. "If you can do that, I will be more than happy to go over the information we discovered about your family history. But if not, you are welcome to leave and come back when you can. Are we clear?" He sounded much more like a father to a son than a television host to his guest.

EJ sat on the edge of his chair, staring Gabe down like he wanted to dive over the desk and wrap his hands around his throat. But Gabe was unmoved. He stared EJ down for nearly sixty of the most uncomfortable seconds Drew had ever witnessed. Then EJ's expression softened significantly, and he sat back in his chair.

"Thank you, EJ," Gabe said as he slid two more sheets out of the binder, handing one to each of them. It was a broader family tree, showing their great-grandparents and their offspring.

"EJ, we believe that John Jones, Jr. is your biological grandfather, and the man you knew as your grandfather was his brother, James. It appears your great aunt and uncle raised their niece as their daughter."

"And what makes you believe that?" EJ asked calmly, but through his clenched teeth.

"We stumbled across some employment records from the publishing company where your grandparents worked in the fifties," he said as he pulled another document from the binder and handed it to EJ. "I only have one of those. Please share." With a grumble, EJ held it so that Drew could see it too. "According to that document, the company demoted Cheryl Jones from a junior editor to a freelance editor due to 'pregnancy complications.'"

"They could do that?" Drew asked.

Gabe nodded. "In the fifties? Absolutely. She was lucky she didn't get fired."

"That sucks," Drew said. "But my mom was born in the fifties. She could have been pregnant with her."

"The dates don't match up. The document is dated March 8, 1953. Your mother was born in July of '57."

EJ rubbed his bottom lip with a vacant expression on his face.

"When was your mother born?" Drew asked EJ.

He rolled his eyes. "April 23, 1953, but that doesn't prove anything. This says the Cheryl lady got demoted for pregnancy complications. How do you know she didn't lose that baby? My Grandma Rocelia had seven kids, all pretty close together. They both could have been pregnant at the same time."

"There're no records from that time period for Cheryl."

"What do you mean there are no records for Cheryl?" EJ asked.

"Well, we know she was pregnant, but there are no hospital records saying she was treated for miscarriage or stillbirth. There's no birth certificate. There's no death certificate. It's like the baby just disappeared," Gabe said as he pulled out another document and handed it to EJ. "This is your mother's birth certificate."

"Okay," EJ shrugged. "This says her parents are Rocelia and James Jones."

"Yes, it does!" Gabe exclaimed. "But check this out." He handed them a second birth certificate. "This is your Uncle Jasper's birth certificate. He was born only eight and a half months after your mother, and he was eleven pounds. At that weight, it's very unlikely he was born prematurely. And while Rocelia had babies very close together, all the other siblings are no less than eighteen months apart."

EJ shrugged as he flung the documents back onto Gabe's desk. "I mean, it looks suspicious, but I don't think this is concrete proof."

"Why don't we ask her?" Drew suggested.

"Ask who?" EJ said.

"My grandmo—our grandmother."

EJ turned toward Drew. "So, you buyin' this shit?" he snapped, then glanced over at Gabe. "Sorry. But hell nah. I'm not talkin' to her."

"It's not a bad idea, EJ."

EJ held his hand up. "Whoa. Slow down. Let's say, for argument's sake, what you're saying is true. Why would *his* grandmother want to talk to me? She gave my mother away like a hand-me-down. If she didn't want to have anything to do with my mother, why would she want to have anything to do with me?" he snarled.

Drew shook his head. "She's not like that, man. There's got to be an explanation for why they did that."

EJ narrowed his eyes. "Let me ask you this... Your grandparents look like you? Your mom look like you? They white... like you?"

"More or less, I guess," Drew said with a shrug.

"Right." EJ nodded. "There's the explanation. She gave my mom away because she was Black and kept yours because she was white," he said as he stood and stormed toward the door.

"Wait, EJ, I have more information to share," Gabe said.

EJ stopped and turned back around. "I can't do this anymore, Gabe. I'll have my lawyer work out a settlement or whatever, but I'm not gonna let you tell the world that my mother, my amazing mother, got thrown away like a piece of trash. Family was the most important thing to her. If she wasn't already dead, this would have killed her." He yanked the door open and flew out.

"I'm sorry about that, Drew," Gabe said. "I know this is a lot of information to process and I wish there was an easier way to tell you guys this stuff. Do you have any questions?"

Drew thought for a minute as he looked over the family tree. "Are you sure about this? That my grandparents gave their daughter away?" he asked, staring at the paper.

Gabe nodded. "Yes, we're sure."

"Because of her employment documents saying she was pregnant around the time EJ's mom was born? I don't get how that makes you so sure. Maybe it didn't happen like that at all. Maybe my grandparents lost that baby and there's no record of it. I mean, it was the fifties. That still would make EJ my second cousin. Our grandfathers were brothers."

"That's what we initially thought. But your DNA test results showed a closer genetic relationship. That confused us a bit, so we looked deeper, and that's when Kelvin found the employment records. Then we asked your grandmother for a sample... and she agreed. EJ was a match to her. There's only one explanation for that."

Drew's jaw dropped. "Does my grandmother know you know she gave her baby away?"

"We didn't discuss that, but I think she had a suspicion. She's a smart lady; I really enjoyed talking with her. And it's a good idea you had to ask her about Geneva. I think she's ready to talk about it."

"What makes you think that?"

"I asked her if she'd allow us to interview her for the show, and she said yes with no hesitation."

Drew talked to Gabe a while longer, going over the family tree. For a simple sheet of paper with a bunch of boxes and lines, there was a wealth of information. Geneva's side was cluttered with boxes. Apparently, she had been married twice. Her first husband, Eric Wallace Sr. was EJ's and his brother, Damon's, father. After Eric Sr. died, she married a man named Carl Jeffries. Geneva and Carl had four children together.

The family tree was bursting with color, like a beautiful piece of art. The color of an individual family member's box could tell you if they were alive or dead, divorced or never married, or a biological or an adopted offspring. Drew learned more about his family from a single sheet of paper in an hour than he had learned in his entire life.

He stumbled out of Gabe's office building unsteady and overwhelmed as a tornado of information and emotion whipped around inside of him. He took out his phone and stared at it, not sure whose number to call first. Lia needed to know everything he had learned, but she was just warming to the idea of welcoming their grandmother into her life. Would she be able to accept a slew of black relatives? Would their black relatives accept them? And how was he going to tell Kimmie things were about to get really awkward on the collaboration project? That's if EJ would even want him to stay on the project.

Drew continued to scroll his contacts and noticed the time. He had to be on set in less than an hour. As he picked up his pace toward the subway, his finger hovered over the name at the top of his Favorites list: April. She was the only person who could help him figure out what to say to Lia, Kimmie, the kids, and his grandmother; and also make sense of the big feelings coursing through him that seemed to grow more intense with every step.

As he was about to tap April's name, a man's voice called out from a black Escalade parked near the building. "Yo, Drew!" Normally, he would have ignored it, not wanting to get delayed by a fan, but he recognized the voice. It was the head of Python's A&R Division, EJ's cousin, James—his cousin, James, according to Gabe's detailed family tree.

Drew stopped short. "Hey, what's up, man?" he said over his shoulder. He doubled back to the truck and gave James dap as he nodded at the driver, Andre. Another cousin. They were both dressed to play basketball.

"Get in, man," James said, jerking his head toward the backseat. Drew glanced over James's shoulder and saw EJ behind the driver on his cell phone, still looking very angry.

Drew shook his head. "I gotta get to work. I'm about to hop on the train."

"We'll take you. Get in," James reiterated.

"That's okay, man. I'm good."

EJ covered the speaker with his free hand. "Get in the damn truck!" he barked. "Yes, I'm here," he said into his cell phone. Drew looked over his shoulder. He was only a few steps away from the subway stairs, but he got in the backseat.

"Yes, I know. . . I know . . . I'm about to do that now, Daddy. . . Okay. . . I gotta go," EJ said and ended the call. He looked over at Drew. "I'm sorry for talkin' to you like that just then and before in Gabe's office."

"Cool. Whatever," Drew said flatly as he reached for the door handle. It was locked. He glanced up to see Andre smirking at him in the rearview mirror. Drew looked over at EJ. "I don't have time for this, dude."

"We got stuff to talk about."

"I gotta go to work," Drew said as he tried the handle again and sighed.

"You heard the man," EJ said to Andre. He nodded and pulled the Escalade away from the curb into traffic.

Drew glared at EJ, certain he was about to be fired. He hoped it would be quick, but brevity wasn't EJ's strong suit, especially when he was worked up about something. From the look on his face, Drew feared he'd be trapped forever. The lavish and roomy interior of the truck began to shrink as his heart pounded. He cracked the window, wondering what *TMI* would make of the cell phone footage of Drew Simon climbing out the window of EJ Wallace's Escalade driving through Midtown Manhattan. Drew's eyebrows knitted more tightly at that thought.

"Why you mad?" EJ said.

"Why are *you* mad?" Drew said.

"I'm not mad. I'm pissed."

"At me?"

"No."

Drew shrugged. "I can't tell."

"I'm sittin' here tryin' to apologize to you, man. What else do you want from me?"

"I want you not to look like you wanna punch me in the face."

"Can't do that. All I wanna do is punch somebody in the face."

Drew raised an eyebrow.

"Relax man. I've only punched one of my cousins in the face before, and that didn't turn out so good for me."

"You damn right it didn't," James said, looking EJ up and down over his shoulder.

"So who do you wanna punch, then, E, my grandmother?" Drew asked before EJ could slam James with the retort forming on his lips.

EJ shrugged and gazed out the window.

"Well, that's never gonna happen. So you can forget about that shit."

EJ's head snapped back to face Drew. "You really think I would hit an old woman? You really think I would hit any woman!"

"I don't think so, but there's a lot of unexpected things happening lately. I need you to understand that if you even breathe too hard on my grandmother, I will end you."

James and Andre exchanged glances. Andre was EJ's main security guard and huge. He was built and looked like "The Rock," but he didn't say a word.

EJ narrowed his eyes, shaking his head slowly. "I thought she was *our* grandmother?" He turned his glower back to the city traffic outside his window. "I would never hit a woman. My daddy would kick my ass, and my mom would come back from the dead to help him," he muttered.

They sat in silence for several minutes.

"Did your mother know... that she was Black?" EJ asked.

"Yeah."

"Did you know?"

"No."

"Did she know about my mom?"

"I have no idea. She never talked about her family," Drew said, making no attempt to mask his resentment toward Beth for not telling him the truth, or his guilt for not asking her more questions about herself. "Did your mom know? About my mom? About my grandparents?"

"My dad said no."

"Maybe she kept it a secret. Like my mother."

EJ, James, and Andre chuckled. "My mom was great at just about everything—except keeping secrets. I guarantee you, if she knew she had a little sister out there somewhere, she would have found her, and we wouldn't be going through this right now."

Drew smiled. "I wish somebody would have told her. It would have been nice to have cousins," he said as he turned to gaze out his own window.

"You don't have any cousins!" James asked, turning almost completely around. He and EJ looked at Drew in disbelief.

"Nope. Both my parents were only children—as far as I knew."

"Damn. I have twenty cousins from my mom's brothers and sister alone," EJ said, shaking his head. "I can't imagine what having none would be like. That must be... nice!"

"Man, shut up!" James said as he took off his shoe and threw it at EJ's head, but he caught it right before it hit his forehead and lobbed it back at James. The shoe ricocheted off the side of James's head, hit Andre's cheek, and landed on its sole in the dead center of the console. After a brief awe induced silence, everyone burst into raucous laughter. They continued to talk and laugh all the way to the studio.

Chapter 24

Drew leaned back on his stool, catching his breath after the band's heavy metal mash-up. It was a full house as usual, and the audience was high energy—a group that hyped always got his heart racing. He looked out at the crowd to capture a mental picture of their well-entertained faces, then his heart rate spiked again.

"Holy shit," Drew blurted out.

Reid's head snapped up out of the note cards he was reading while he waited for his cue to introduce the first guest.

"What's wrong, Drew?" Shanice said in his earpiece.

He stared into the audience with his mouth hanging open.

"Drew! Do you hear me? What's wrong?"

"My dad's here."

Reid scanned the audience. "Holy shit," he said without moving his lips.

"Where is he?" Shanice asked.

"Right side, fifth row on the end by the stairs."

Shanice craned her neck to see over some equipment blocking her view of the first few rows. "The old white guy in the suit and tie with his arms folded, mean muggin'?"

"That would be him," Drew said.

"Got it. I'll have Missy grab him and bring him back after the taping."

"Ugh," Drew groaned.

"You don't want him in the back?"

Not at all, he thought, but it was protocol for Shanice to have a production assistant escort family members and friends to their dressing room after the show. She preferred having advanced notice, but she understood that people popped up sometimes without warning.

"It's fine. Thanks," Drew said because explaining why he didn't want to see his father would have been more excruciating than the unwanted interaction. "My stepmother is with him, by the way."

"Not a problem. Missy will bring them both back to you after the show," she said as she cued the light and sound techs. Then Drew cued the band.

Fifteen minutes after taping, there was a knock at Drew's door. Shanice agreed to tell Missy to give his father and stepmother a quick tour of the studio, so he could straighten up his dressing room. He only needed a few seconds to make sure one of the guys hadn't left him a joint for after the show, like they often did.

"Come in," Drew said, giving the room another quick once over as Missy slowly opened the door.

"Hi, Mr. Simon!" Missy exclaimed.

"Hey," Drew replied flatly. No matter how many times he told her to call him Drew, she wouldn't. He gave up reminding her weeks ago, but it still annoyed him. She made him feel old. But his annoyance quickly shifted to dread when his father stepped into the room behind his stepmother.

"Surprise!" Susan squealed, rushing in with open arms. Like always, she grabbed him around the neck and pulled him down to land a couple dozen rapid fire kisses on his cheeks as Missy backed out of the room and closed the door, smirking. "Did we get you?" she asked, releasing him.

"Oh, yeah, you got me, alright. I had no clue you were coming. I wish you would have told me so I could have gotten you better seats."

"I didn't know we were coming either. Your father surprised me with this trip for our anniversary."

"Oh, man," Drew slapped his forehead. "I completely forgot. Happy anniversary." He bent to hug Susan again and kissed her cheek. "Are you headed back after this, or are you going to have a nice dinner in the city first?"

"We're staying for a few days, actually. I understand we're seeing a couple of Broadway plays too. Isn't that something?" Susan asked, beaming.

"Wow! That is something. How'd you plan all that, Dad?" Drew said, addressing Simon for the first time since he entered the dressing room.

Simon shrugged. "Lia may have helped me a little with the planning."

Drew nodded. He figured Lia had something to do with it. Simon had never expressed any interest in seeing a taping of *The Latest*. And even if he had, he wouldn't have a clue how to get tickets. Drew made a mental note to speak to his sister as soon as his unexpected guests left. Or maybe he would pay her a visit and thank her in person—really hard.

"Why don't you guys have a seat? Can I get you somethin' to drink? I have beer and water in my fridge, but I can get you something else if you like."

"Oh, don't go to any trouble. Water is fine," Susan said. Then she flashed a mischievous look at Simon. "Make that a beer. It'll give me gas, but I'm on vacation, right?"

"That's right!" Drew agreed as he opened his mini fridge. "Dad? Beer?"

Simon nodded. "Sure."

"Well, I have to say, Drew, I was thoroughly impressed with the show," Susan said as he handed them their beer. "I had no idea what all goes into taping one of these shows or how much your band plays. It was like a rock concert. You still got it, boy!"

"Thanks," Drew said, as he sat on a chair across from them with his own beer. "We play a lot for the studio audience, but most of it gets cut in editing."

"And the show we just saw will air tonight?" she asked.

"Yep."

"I'm excited to watch! I wonder if we'll be able to see ourselves," she said, nudging Simon. He responded with a less than enthusiastic half smile, to which Susan narrowed her eyes. An awkward smile spread across his face.

"Happy?" Simon asked.

Susan rolled her eyes.

"I'm glad you enjoyed the show," Drew said, ignoring their exchange. There was no need to ask his father if he enjoyed the show. He knew he hadn't. With all the loud rock music and liberal celebrity guests making liberal celebrity comments about things like gun control and taking a knee during the national anthem, Simon's expression had vacillated between bored to death and utter fury.

The trio sat in silence for several seconds.

"This is a lovely dressing room," Susan said, looking around. "Isn't this a lovely dressing room, Simon?"

"How am I supposed to know? I've never been in a dressing room before," he grumbled.

"Patrick! I have had it with you. This was your idea to come here. Now, if you don't go ahead and tell your son what you wanted to say to him, you can take me back home right now, and we'll forget about the anniversary this year—and possibly any future ones."

Drew eyed his father. His bright red skin made it hard to tell if he was embarrassed or enraged. Drew figured it was both, but from the way Simon glared at Susan, he was clearly more mad than embarrassed. As usual, Susan was not intimidated, evidenced by her raised eyebrows and stern expression.

With his jaw clenched, Simon took a deep breath and turned his face toward Drew. "Andrew, I'm sorry," he said.

Drew's eyelids fluttered involuntarily as his brain tried to process the foreign words coming from his father's mouth. "Excuse me?"

Simon clenched his jaw again; this time he flared his nostrils too. "I'm sorry," he repeated slower and louder.

While Drew had an extensive list of grievances against his father, Simon had never apologized to him for anything before— ever. "You're sorry for what?" he asked, with a perplexed chuckle, not sure if he was dreaming.

Simon looked at Susan, shaking his head.

"Don't look at me like that. You didn't think this was going to be easy, did you?" She gestured for him to continue.

Simon took another deep breath and looked Drew in the eyes. "I'm sorry for telling you and Lia that your grandparents were dead. That was wrong. I should not have done that."

"Oh. That," Drew said as he leaned forward in his chair, resting his elbows on his knees. "Okay. So, you're sorry. Care to tell me why you did that?"

Simon rubbed the back of his neck. "I... I don't know. I don't have an explanation."

"BullSHIT! You and I both know why you did it."

Simon reared back on the couch. "We do? Well, if *we* know why *I* did it, then why are you asking me?"

"Because I want to hear you admit it. I want you to say it."

Simon narrowed his eyes. "Say what?"

"That you're a fucking racist."

"And there it is," Simon huffed. "*That's* why I didn't want your grandparents in your life. You start talkin' to that woman, and in a matter of weeks, she's already poisoned you against me. Now you're speaking to me like you've lost your goddamn mind!"

"What! You think Grandma turned me against you?"

"I don't think it, I know it! They tried it with your mother. They tried everything they could to keep us apart."

"Of course they did, Dad! You beat their daughter! Wouldn't you do the same thing if Lia got mixed up with some abusive asshole? I sure would if it was Paige."

Susan gasped. "Patrick! You didn't!"

"No! I most certainly did not!" he said, shaking his head vigorously. "Is that what that woman told you? That I beat your mother? That's a bald-faced lie!" he shouted as he scooted to the edge of his seat like he was preparing to jump to his feet.

Drew glared at Simon while Susan looked at him in horror. He closed his eyes and blew out a long breath. "Okay, I grabbed her a couple times," he said. "But I loved your mother more than anything; I never meant to hurt her. I just got carried away. The incidents were ten years apart, and I never did it again after the second time. Boy, did she really let me have it that time." He ran his hand back through his hair.

"I guess you think that makes it better? That it was only twice. That you didn't haul off and punch or slap her. I saw one of those times you *just* grabbed her. I will always remember the look on her face. She was terrified. And I knew exactly how she felt because you used to grab me like that right before you beat the crap out of me. A nine-year-old should never be able to relate to his mother in that way. That's what turned me against you, Dad. I hate you for what you did to us."

Simon lowered his head. "I'm sorry you feel that way, son. I know you think my discipline was too harsh, but—"

"Harsh? You were brutal. Remember what you did to me when we got arrested in Virginia?"

"Andrew, you were fifteen and got arrested four states away from home for breaking and entering and assaulting a man who had enough guns and ammo to arm the military of a small country. You don't think you deserved to be punished for that stunt?"

"You beat me at the police station—"

"What?" Susan hissed. "The police down there let you do that?"

"Are you kidding!" Drew said. "Once they found out they had a cop's kid, they were practically salivating waiting for Dad to get there and deal with me. Gave him a private room and everything."

Susan shook her head, glaring at Simon. He refused to look at her.

"And you beat me again when we got home," Drew said. "Remember that?"

Simon cleared his throat. "That's enough, Andrew."

"No, that was more than enough." He closed his eyes and took a breath. "I'm not saying I didn't deserve to be punished. We all got the belt for what went down that night, even Chris, but I didn't deserve all that, Dad. I wasn't a bad kid. I just made a bad choice."

"I know you weren't a bad kid."

"Then why? Did you hate me that much?"

Simon's face twisted with confusion. "Hate you? You think I hated you?"

Drew cracked his neck.

Susan reached over and rubbed Simon's back. "Tell him."

He shook his head.

She nodded. "Tell. Him."

Simon stared at the floor, twisting his wedding band around his finger.

"My mother died when I was ten years old, and my stepfather beat me every single day after her funeral until I left home at seventeen. He didn't like me too much and reminded me of that with all new kinds of torture. I lived in fear, and I hated him so much, I thought about killing him constantly." He sighed. "I never wanted my kids to feel that way about me, and I tried to do better, but... I guess... I guess I didn't know how. I'm sorry," he said and looked up at Drew, anguish and regret swirling around his face.

He had never seen his father that way. Simon was not one to concede to accusations of wrongdoing, nor did he ever come close to admitting he was afraid of anything. That was weak. Drew knew that was the hardest conversation his father ever had, and that he was looking for forgiveness. He dug his right thumbnail into the center of his left palm, hoping the pain would distract him from the conflicting emotions. Some of the anger and resentment he held onto so tightly for Simon was slipping from him and transferring to a man Drew had never met, and that wouldn't do. That man didn't owe him anything. His father did.

"I'm sorry your stepfather did that to you." Drew wiped quickly at his eyes. "I can relate to you losing control. It's not like I'm winning any husband or father of the year contests myself. And maybe that explains why you were so hard on me, but it doesn't excuse it. It sure as hell doesn't excuse you for keeping us away from our grandparents. How could you do that, Dad? They're our family, our only other family!"

"I told you. I. Don't. Know."

"Not good enough. Why?"

Simon clenched his jaw tightly and grunted.

"Dad!"

"BECAUSE THEY MADE ME FEEL LIKE TRASH!"

"Simon, sshhhh," Susan said, rubbing his back.

"I fell hard for your mother. She was smart, beautiful, talented, and the sweetest person I had ever met. And for some reason she liked me too. I felt like the luckiest man on the planet. When she asked me to meet her parents, I was excited because I knew how much she loved them and valued their opinion—especially your grandfather's. He was a war hero, political activist, accomplished in his career. And according to your mother, 'the best daddy a girl could ever have.'

"When the day arrived that I was supposed to meet them, I was so nervous, my stomach was in knots. I had been through a war and by then I was a sergeant, an MP, but I still always felt like a trailer park orphan that barely finished high school. I wanted to impress them so badly, but I kept saying the wrong things. It was written all over their faces. They didn't think I was good enough for Beth. Then the conversation turned to politics, which led to the war. And an uncomfortable meeting quickly became a disaster. It was like you and me talking about politics. Your grandfather had really strong opinions about the war, and I didn't have a problem with that. I had strong opinions too. It wasn't the first debate I had gotten into about Vietnam. But then he started getting angry and made a comment about kids being sent over there to get slaughtered for nothing—that they died in vain." He shrugged. "I hated it when people said that. I lost a lot of friends over there. They weren't just some kids to me; they were soldiers, and my brothers. It was like he was saying their sacrifice was worthless and that all we went through meant nothing. I snapped. Said things I shouldn't have. And your grandfather threw me out."

"I can't believe Mom kept seeing you after that."

"Only for a little while. She broke up with me when she couldn't take the guilt from sneaking around behind her parents' backs anymore."

"I guess that didn't last too long."

He nodded. "About a month later, she came to see me." He glanced at Susan, and then back at Drew. "Unfortunately, I had an, uh, old girlfriend over."

Drew's brow shot up.

Simon shook his head. "Nothing was going on. I was talking to her about your mother, hoping to get some advice. But Beth didn't exactly... well... she went nuts. Ran the girl outta there and started throwing my things around. I didn't have much, so it wasn't a big deal, but when she started throwing my plates and glasses at me, I had to stop it. I could have gotten in serious trouble for that kind of domestic disturbance. Before I knew what I was doing, I grabbed her and pinned her against the wall. I held her there until she stopped trying to fight me."

Drew's breathing had become shallow. He took a deep breath and closed his eyes as Simon continued.

"I let her go and she collapsed in my arms, crying. She was inconsolable for nearly an hour. When she finally calmed down, she told me she was pregnant. And that she was scared to death to tell her parents."

Drew studied the floor. "And what about you? What was your reaction to that... news?" he asked, glancing up at his father.

Simon smiled. "I got down on one knee, asked her to be my wife, and I promised her I would make things right with your grandfather. We decided to get married first to show your grandparents how committed we were, thinking that would help them accept the pregnancy better."

Drew tilted his head. "You really thought that would work? Would that have worked with Lia?"

"I didn't have a daughter back then. And I told you, I barely finished high school." He smirked. "So, yeah, I really thought it would work. But, of course, it didn't. But Beth stuck with me, and you were born, then Lia came along. I know she missed her parents terribly, but she loved being a mother and traveling the world." He shrugged. "It wasn't perfect, but I thought we were happy. I didn't know how wrong I was until you guys didn't show up in California. After three days of calling every police department and hospital between Fayetteville and Barstow, it finally occurred to me to call your grandparents. Your mother told me she was staying there, and it felt like somebody had pulled the rug from under me. I had no clue she was thinking about leaving me. I panicked."

Drew blew out a breath as he rubbed the back of his head. "So, you threatened to take us away from her and tell everyone Grandma and Grandpa were passing for white if she didn't come back."

Simon furrowed his brow. "Your grandmother tell you that?"

"No. I overheard Mom and Grandpa arguing about it. How could you manipulate her like that?"

"You were all I had. I did what I had to do to get my family back," he said and got up from the couch. "You got a toilet in this shoebox?"

Drew pointed to the door behind him.

"Drew," Susan said, after Simon closed the bathroom door. "I know you're hurting, sweetheart, and it is neither my place nor my intention to tell you how to feel about any of this. Your father made some unbelievably bad choices, but I know he loves you. He just doesn't know how to show it."

"You're right." He nodded. "It's not your place," he said as he stood and walked to the door. "I'm gonna go out and get a car for you guys."

Drew returned to his dressing room after escorting his father and stepmother out of the studio and collapsed on his couch. He lay there, his face buried in the cushion, for a long time trying to process everything that had happened that day. And right when he thought he might go insane, there was a knock at the door.

"Come in," he said, without turning around. The door didn't open. "Come. In!"

The door creaked and a draft blew in, cooling the sweat misting on his neck. "Are you takin' a nap, man?" Reid asked as he sat on Drew's chair. Then the door closed.

Drew looked over his shoulder. "Hey, Shanice," he said, sitting up. "No. I wasn't."

"Are you okay, Drew? I heard shouting," Shanice said as she sat next to him on the couch.

He ran his hand through his hair. "Great. How much did you hear?"

"Not much. Your voices were muffled. You wanna talk about it?"
Drew shook his head.

"We're about to grab something to eat. You wanna come?" Reid asked.

"Not hungry," Drew said, then a phone buzzed, and they all pulled their phones out of their pockets.

"Uh oh," Shanice said, frowning at her screen. "I can't go either now. I've been summoned."

"Do they want me too?" Reid asked as Shanice hopped up.

"Nope. It's only me getting called into the principal's office this time." She tossed her long braids over her shoulder and pecked playfully at Reid's lips, giggling in between. "Are you coming over later?"

"Mmmmhmmm," he hummed with an intense look in his eyes and pulled her closer as he planted a long, hard kiss.

Drew looked away. As the only one who knew they were dating, he often had a front row seat to the new couple's blossoming relationship. It was interesting to see them swap personalities right before his eyes, Shanice instantly more carefree and Reid more serious in each other's arms. But they had gotten a bit too comfortable expressing their affection for one another in front of him.

"You sure you're alright, man?" Reid asked as Shanice rushed out the door. "Because you look like shit."

"I feel like shit."

"What happened?"

"My dad apologized to me."

"For what?"

"For... everything?"

"Whoa, dude! That's huge. Did you accept his apology?"

Drew rubbed his face with his hands. "I don't think I did."

"Are you going to?"

He sighed and lay back down. "I don't think I can," he said as he rolled over to face the back of the couch.

Reid gave Drew's shoulder a pat. Then the door closed. He was alone, finally, to sort out his thoughts and feelings. He tried replaying the conversation with his father to make sense of it all, but his mind refused to focus on that. Instead, it took him back to a different place and time. A better place and time, however brief.

Chapter 25

Long Island, New York
1988

"Amelia, didn't I tell you kids to stay out of that room?" Grandpa asked at the top of the steps. He wasn't yelling, but his deep, booming voice reached Drew easily all the way down in the living room.

"But Drew went in there this morning," Lia whined.

Drew slapped his hand over his mouth to keep from spewing a mouth full of milk all over the coffee table.

"Andrew!" Grandpa barked as he charged down the steps. His tone made the hairs on the back of Drew's neck stand at attention. He was already on his feet, trembling, by the time his grandfather reached the bottom of the stairs.

"Did you go into your mother's room this morning?"

Drew flashed a dirty look at Lia as she slowly descended the stairs on her spindly legs. Then he looked back up at Grandpa standing in front of him with his hands on his hips and a frown on his face. His mother's blue eyes glared at him from behind Grandpa's glasses.

"Um, yes, sir," he said as he folded his arms behind his back.

"And when I asked you if you had been in her room today, what did you tell me?"

Drew hung his head. Grandpa placed his finger under his chin and lifted his head. "I said I didn't go in Mommy's room."

"So, you disobeyed me and then lied to me?"

"Yes, sir," he said, resisting the strong urge to look at the floor.

Grandpa shook his head, rubbing his chin. "Come with me," he said as he walked to the dining room. Drew followed slowly. "Sit." He pointed at one of the dining room chairs. Drew sat as Grandpa sat in the chair next to him.

Just then, Grandma came out of the kitchen and sat at the head of the table. Drew jumped at the sight of her. He hadn't noticed her leave the living room where they were watching *The Young and the Restless*. Then he realized the television was off. A lump formed in his throat. Grandma only watched two things on television— the news and *The Young and the Restless*. If she had turned the TV off in the middle of her favorite soap opera, he was in serious trouble. His leg started bouncing.

"Andrew, when I tell you to do something or *not* to do something, I expect you to listen to me. I also expect the truth when I ask you a question. Do you understand?"

"Yes, sir, but—" he started to explain, but stopped short. His father didn't allow that.

"Go on," Grandpa said.

Drew looked over at Lia, who had taken cover behind the door frame. He could only see half of her face, but he could tell she was as confused as him.

"But what, Andrew? What were you going to say?"

"Um, I was gonna say I haven't seen Mommy in two days. I just wanted to check on her."

"I know you're worried about her, but she's fine. I told you she needs to rest right now. When she's ready to come out, she will come out. And until then, you are to do as I say and stay out of her room. Am I understood?"

"Yes, sir."

Grandpa nodded. "Now, what would your parents do to punish you for disobedience and lying?"

Drew shrugged.

Grandpa raised his eyebrow and cocked his head back. "Don't know, huh? Amelia! Do you know?"

Lia jumped out from behind the door frame. "He'd get a spanking for sure, Grandpa," she said without hesitation or a hint of remorse.

Drew flashed an even dirtier look at his sister. And being heavily influenced by an obsession with old cowboy movies, he vowed to himself to get vengeance for her betrayal by sunset.

"Is that right, Andrew? Would you get a spanking for this kind of behavior?"

Drew lowered his head. "Yes, sir."

Grandpa lifted his head. "Well, I'm not going to do that because I think we have an understanding now. But you can be sure I will take you across my knee faster than you can blink if this happens again. Am I clear?"

"Yes, sir," Drew said, nodding adamantly. "Crystal clear," he added. As a wave of relief washed over him, Grandpa grabbed him in a tight hug. Drew's body tensed up. While his mother always hugged and kissed him after she had punished him, his father never hugged him when he was in trouble, or ever. He pulled away, but Grandpa held him tighter.

After a minute, Grandpa kissed the top of his head. Drew looked up and smiled. "Hey Grandpa?"

"Yes, sir?"

Drew giggled like he always did when his grandfather called him "sir" with his booming voice. "Would you teach me that song you were playing after dinner last night?"

Grandpa reared back in his chair. "You like jazz, boy?"

Drew nodded vigorously.

Grandpa smoothed down his mustache, doing a poor job concealing his grin. "I tell you what. If you practice for an hour like your mama wants you to, I'll teach you a little ditty. Deal?" he said, extending his hand.

Drew grabbed it and Grandpa shook his hand so fast it made his whole body wiggle, triggering a giggle fit. Grandpa kissed Drew's head again and stood. Drew moved to follow suit.

"Where do you think you're going?" Grandpa said, holding Drew down in his chair by his shoulder.

"I thought we were done."

"You and I are done, but it looks like your Gran might have a few things to add." He nodded at the bar of Ivory soap that had appeared on the table out of nowhere. "She has a real pet peeve about lying." He gave Drew a pat on the back and turned to Lia. "Let's go for a little walk while your Gran and your brother have a little chat," he said as he ushered her out the front door.

Drew looked up nervously at his grandmother's stern expression and his leg bounced up and down again like a jackhammer.

* * *

Grandma put her hand on Drew's bouncing knee. "You're shaking the table, dear."

"Sorry, Gran."

"No apology necessary, Andrew." She smiled. "Now, Eric, why don't you go on and ask me what you want to know before this boy gives himself a stroke."

Drew looked across his grandmother's dining room table at EJ and watched him shift around in his chair as he wiped the sweat glistening on his forehead.

Drew expected to be nervous, sometimes even normal social interactions made him uneasy. EJ, on the other hand, never seemed nervous about anything. But now that all the pleasantries and small talk were out of the way, there was nothing left to discuss other than the elephant in the room. And it wasn't just any regular zoo elephant. It was one of those circus elephants with makeup and jewelry, making it stand out even more. The only one who didn't seem rattled was Grandma.

EJ cleared his throat. "Um, well, I don't really know where to start, Miss Cheryl," he said, calling her by the name they had agreed was most appropriate under the circumstances. "I appreciate you agreeing to see me, and I definitely don't want to offend you. I wasn't raised like that."

"I know." Grandma nodded. "I know exactly how you were raised."

EJ's forehead wrinkled. "Ma'am?"

Grandma smiled. "Andrew, will you do me a favor and get the large plastic container in the front closet?"

"Sure," Drew said as he got up and went to the foyer. At the bottom of the closet was a large gray storage container. He prepared himself to lift it, but it wasn't very heavy. He could tell it was full and had some weight, but it wasn't unmanageable.

"Where should I put it?"

"Put it on the table and open it up. There's a blue scrapbook. Hand it to me, please."

Drew nodded as he opened the box to find it filled with scrapbooks neatly filed so that the bindings showed. "Uh, Gran, there are like four blue ones in here."

"The cobalt blue one with gold trim," she said.

Drew pulled out the book and opened it. His eyes shot wide open. "Ha! Is this you, dude?" He turned the book around to show EJ an old school picture of a six or seven-year-old boy with a short afro and broad jack-o-lantern smile wearing a plaid shirt and bowtie.

EJ's jaw dropped. "Give me that!" he barked, reaching across the table.

"Not a chance." Drew stepped back out of his reach as he leafed through the pages of the scrapbook. He laughed harder with each page turn. "Oh my God, E, these are the worst school pictures ever!"

EJ slumped back in his seat, grumbling under his breath.

"Andrew, give Eric the scrapbook, please," Grandma said. He could tell she was serious, despite the giggle that slipped out.

"Okay, Gran, I will. I just gotta see if this horror story has a happy ending," he said, continuing to laugh as he turned the pages.

Grandma narrowed her eyes. "Eric, do you see a green scrapbook in that bin?" she said. "Army green."

EJ pulled out the army green scrapbook and opened it. "What? Ha!" he roared and showed Drew the picture of himself as a toddler standing stark naked in the kitchen, covered in flour.

"Hey, man! Give me that!"

EJ flashed a sly grin, chuckling as he held out the scrapbook. Drew reached for it. "Psych!" EJ said, snatching the book back out of Drew's grasp.

Drew frowned. "Here!" he said, handing over the blue scrapbook. EJ smiled and happily exchanged books. Drew continued to scowl as he leafed through his own scrapbook. "Why am I naked in most of these pictures, Gran?"

Grandma snickered. "Your mother said you hated wearing clothes. Whenever she dressed you, it was only a matter of time before you were completely naked. And your little tooshie was too cute to resist taking pictures."

EJ nodded. "I can't blame her. That is definitely a cute tooshie," he chuckled, flipping through his scrapbook.

Drew growled as he skipped several pages to get to his school pictures and found his own toothless first grade picture. "Check this out!" He turned the book to show EJ. "Mine's as bad as yours, man."

"Runs in the family, I guess," he said with a shrug. "Nice 'fro, bruh."

They continued looking at pictures and laughing at themselves as well as their siblings for the next hour and a half. Grandma had made scrapbooks for all eight of her grandchildren with pictures sent to her by Beth and EJ's grandmother. The books also had pictures and articles she had cut out of magazines or printed off the internet. While there were plenty of pictures of Drew and

EJ from big magazines like *Rolling Stone* and *Forbes*, she also had tons of articles about all her grandchildren from local and school newspapers going back to their childhood.

"Miss Cheryl, why'd you give my mother away?" EJ asked, snatching Drew's attention away from the twelve-year-old *New York Times* article about Lia and Peter's engagement. EJ apologized as soon as the question fell out of his mouth, but it was too late; the fancy elephant in the room had already trampled across the dining room table.

"Don't apologize, Eric. That's why you're here, isn't it?" she said as she pushed her teacup aside and slowly removed her reading glasses, letting them hang from a pearl chain around her neck. She opened her hands on the table in front of EJ. He looked at them, then at her, and put his hands in hers.

"Giving a child up doesn't mean they were unloved or unwanted. Leaving my baby with James and Rocelia was the hardest thing I have ever had to do. So believe me when I tell you, I would never have done it if I didn't think it was the best thing for her."

"Best for her or for you?" he asked softly, looking down at the table.

Grandma placed her finger under EJ's chin and gently lifted his head. "Best for her," she said, looking him squarely in the eyes. "Your grandfather and I didn't leave Geneva with his family so that we could have an easier life living as white people. We did it because things were different back then. They were 'Black and white,' or rather 'Negro and white.' John and I both had difficult childhoods because we looked different from our families. We didn't want our child to face the cruelty we endured."

"Well, why even have children? You had to know there was a possibility your baby would be brown like my mother?" EJ asked.

Drew stared at Grandma, waiting for her answer. He wondered the same thing.

"Please don't take what I'm about to tell you the wrong way, either of you. Because unplanned does not mean unloved or unwanted either." She gave Drew a meaningful look, then she closed her eyes. "Geneva was the result of John and I being careless. Beth was the result of a failed tubal ligation. We weren't planning to have any children at all. But you know what they say, we make plans and God laughs. And now the world has eight of the finest human beings ever made because God knew better than Cheryl and John Jones," she said as she opened her arms wide and gestured for them to come to her. They both left their seats and kneeled on either side of her chair as she wrapped her arms around their necks and squeezed as hard as an eighty-nine-year-old woman could.

After a minute or two, Drew and EJ returned to their seats and resumed flipping through the scrapbooks. They eventually made their way to their mothers' books. They each took their time, studying every page, then they exchanged them. Drew marveled at how much EJ's mother looked like his. He let out a sigh as he stared at his Aunt Geneva's picture.

"What, man?" EJ asked.

"I wish they could have met."

"They did meet," Grandma said as she flipped through one of EJ's sister's books.

Drew's and EJ's foreheads crinkled with confusion.

"Eric, will you get the red scrapbook out of that bin for me, please?" she asked as she surveyed the table filled with colorful scrapbooks. "It's probably the only one left in there."

"Thank you, dear," she said as he handed her the scrapbook. It was much older than the other books from the patches of worn leather and the cracking sound the binding made as she carefully opened it. Drew and EJ moved closer to her as she flipped page after page of black and white pictures of her and Grandpa at their wedding and shores of different bodies of water. There were also pictures of people Drew didn't recognize.

"Hold up. Is that my great-grandmother?" EJ asked.

"Yes, it is," Grandma said, brushing her finger across the woman's cheek. "This is your grandfather's mother, Lillian, the most gifted pianist I have ever known. You have her to thank for your musical talents. She taught all her children to play, and they taught theirs."

Drew leaned in for a closer look at the sepia portrait of a beautiful, young, brown-skinned woman with bright eyes and a smooth, round face, and he made a vow to himself to get serious about teaching his kids to play the piano. He had shown them some things over the years, and April made sure they had formal lessons. But taking piano lessons from a stranger wasn't the family tradition. He stared at his great grandmother Lillian's picture as Grandma turned the page, then his jaw dropped.

On the next page was a picture of his grandparents standing by an old Ford. Grandpa had one arm around Grandma. The other arm held a very upset, one-year-old Beth. His head was turned toward the screaming baby, puckering his lips as he leaned in to kiss her cheek. Grandma smiled at the camera with her arm across a five-year-old, pigtail-wearing Geneva, holding her close. Geneva grinned, showing all her teeth as she held onto Grandma's forearm with one of her tiny hands and a fistful of Grandpa's slacks with the other.

"This is the only picture I have of all four of us together. After this was taken, we never went back for formal visits."

"Why not?" EJ asked.

"Geneva was smart as a whip. By the time she was five, she was asking a lot of questions and putting things together like a little detective."

EJ nodded. "She never lost that trait, by the way."

Grandma chuckled. "Well, she was an amazing investigator at five. I'm sure you kids didn't get away with too much with Miss Geneva for a mother." She took a sip of tea. "So, we thought it would be better if we stopped visiting. But make no mistake," she pointed at EJ and Drew, "we were always a part of her life, even if she didn't know it. One of us would go down to see her piano recitals or dance performances—we always made sure to stay out of sight. And we paid for her to go to nursing school. Your mother was somethin' else." She caressed EJ's cheek. "We were so proud of her."

EJ tucked his lips into his mouth between his teeth as his eyes filled with tears. He dropped his head, sobbing softly into his hands. Grandma pulled him to her and let him cry on her shoulder as Drew slipped out and retreated to the back porch.

A breeze blew across the backyard, and his nose filled with the fragrance of autumn flowers from Grandma's small but lush garden. He closed his eyes as the memory of lugging bags of soil and mulch across his parents' yard year after year came back to him. Helping his mother with her garden was his most dreaded chore. It took hours and, on top of his regular yard work, meant his Saturday was shot. As a teenager, he would have given anything to get out of spending the day planting flowers with his mom. He released a long sigh. He'd give anything for one more sweaty, back-breaking day with her.

"Sorry about that," EJ said as he joined Drew on the porch. "I didn't mean to hijack your grand—our grandmother."

Drew smiled. "It's cool, man. I guess I better get used to sharing her. There're eight of us, right?"

EJ nodded. "Yeah, that's going to be an adjustment for you, but I'm used to sharing grandparents. I'll walk you through it," he said with a wink.

"Thanks." He glanced at his watch. "We better get going."

"Grandma invited us to stay for dinner."

"I know, but we're recording tonight. We don't wanna be late. I hear the producer is kind of a dick," Drew said and punched his cousin in the gut as he bolted back into the house.

Chapter 26

Grandma Cheryl smiled as she patted Drew's cheek. He responded with a sheepish grin and placed his hand on hers.

"Thanks for hosting our little viewing party, Drew," Gabe said as he stepped out of Drew's half bath, extending his hand.

"It was my pleasure," Drew said as he shook Gabe's hand and handed him his overcoat. "Thank *you* for going out of your way to bring Grandma and make sure she gets home safely."

"Oh, now that's the real pleasure, and it's all mine," Gabe said, shrugging on his camel-colored overcoat. "And one town over is hardly out of my way." He pulled down his matching fedora more securely on his head and offered his elbow to Grandma with a little bow. "Are you ready to go, madame?"

Grandma chuckled. "I certainly am, monsieur," she said as she blew kisses to EJ and April leaned against the wall across from the kitchen. Then she and Gabe strolled out of Drew's apartment arm in arm, giggling like a set of elderly Bobbsey Twins, although grandma was at least fifteen years more elderly than Gabe.

"You'd think those two have known each other their whole lives how they're always tee-heeing all the time," EJ huffed.

Drew nodded. Grandma and Gabe had gotten very close over the last few months, preparing for their *Bloodlines* interview. They still talked regularly, even though they had finished taping the episode weeks ago.

"It's nice he lives so close he can check in on her," Drew said. "And they have tea together every Sunday. I went once. All they did was talk about books I never heard of before. I felt like a third wheel. But they seem to really enjoy each other's company. They're like best friends now, I guess." He shrugged.

EJ's brow shot up. "Best friends, huh? You sure they're *just friends*? I know how you struggle with the definition of that term." The corners of his mouth twitched up in amusement at the same time Drew's face pinched in disgust.

"Um, drink this, please," Maya said as she came out of the kitchen and handed her husband another glass of wine. "We need to occupy that mouth of yours with something other than talking."

"Thank you, Maya. My thoughts exactly," Drew said, brushing past the three of them into the kitchen. "Nobody wants to think about Grandma and Gabe—"

"Lighten up, man. It was a joke," EJ grumbled and drained his glass, then he refilled it with the remainder of the bottle.

Drew opened the last bottle of wine, filled three glasses, and handed two of them to Maya and April. The group of four drank in silence, staring off into some distant place of their choice, shellshocked after watching the special preview of their two-hour episode of *Bloodlines*. Eventually, Drew pulled out a bottle of Jack Daniels from his liquor cabinet and four shot glasses; the wine wasn't helping one bit.

EJ swept Maya's long fluffy hair off her shoulder and sighed as he rested his head on the smooth brown skin at the crook of her neck. His chin fit into the curve like a puzzle piece. "You need some cuddle time, baby?" she said, cradling his head. EJ nodded. She kissed his temple. "I should get this one home. But let us help clean up before we go." She gathered their glasses and headed for the sink.

April took the glasses from her and placed them in the sink. "Drew and I can handle this, Maya."

The tiny diamond stud in Maya's nose sparkled as she wrinkled her nose. "Are you sure?"

"Of course. There's barely anything to clean up. You guys have been excellent guests! Right, Drew?"

Drew nodded.

Maya's long lashes fluttered over her big brown eyes as they darted from April to Drew to EJ and back again. "Okay, we'll go on and get outta here, then. But promise you won't tell my mama we left without helping," she said with a wink.

April laughed, holding up her pinky. "Promise."

The women hooked their little fingers together and leaned into a hug. Drew and EJ took the cue and gave each other a quick bro hug.

"I'll see you tomorrow," EJ said as Drew handed him their coats.

"Bright and early," Drew said with a grimace, rolling his stiff shoulders. The tour design company Python hired included a group of choreographers everyone was convinced were sadists. To be fair, they had a lot to do in a short period of time to fulfill their mission: turn a motley crew of not-so-young and not-so-coordinated musicians into a well-oiled machine by October. And they took their mission seriously, which left Drew feeling like the Tin Man caught in the rain every morning.

EJ and Maya headed out the door hand-in-hand, and April followed Drew back into the kitchen. They transferred the leftover hors d'oeuvres to containers and cleaned up without saying a word. They didn't have to. April had a step-by-step process for putting food away and cleaning up the kitchen. It had been easier for Drew to apply April's system to his own place than to come up with a new one. Speaking of well-oiled machines, the choreographers could learn a few things from April; she and Drew moved around his compact kitchen like long time dance partners. The only change in their routine was the glances April kept stealing at Drew.

"Quit looking at me, April," Drew said as he slid a glass container of cubed cheese into the fridge and closed the door with a little more force than necessary.

"Just making sure you're okay," she said, placing the last wine glass on the drying rack.

Drew's eyes rolled up to the ceiling. Kelvin and Gabe had both pulled him to the side before they left to ask him "how he was feeling after seeing the show." April was the third person to inquire about his emotional well-being in less than an hour. Fourth, if the way Grandma had studied his face with concern before she left counted.

"Why does everybody think I'm going to fall apart?"

"The show was pretty intense, Drew..." she trailed off. There was no need to say more. Although "intense" was probably not an intense enough of a word to describe the show. There were no surprises. Gabe had shared all the information they used on the show during the taping a few weeks ago. But all the starts and stops and retakes made it a little easier to digest. Seeing it all together, edited and polished, from start to finish was undeniably overwhelming.

"It was heavy," Drew agreed. "But not only for me." A flashback played in his mind of the article about the well-publicized lynching of Grandma's two great-uncles. They had the audacity to run a successful printing business in the Mississippi Delta at the turn of the twentieth century. Their shop printed all kinds of publications, including a local newspaper called the *Colored Chronicle* that reported on the crimes committed by the KKK and identified its members by their government names and affiliations. "Nobody asked Grandma or EJ if they were okay," he said, shaking away the images of "strange fruit" from his mind's eye.

"They don't..." she trailed off again.

"They don't what?" he barked, meaning for her to take the sharpness in his tone as a challenge to spit it out.

April narrowed her eyes. "They don't have your mental health challenges," she said. Challenge accepted.

Drew leaned back against the peninsula and dragged his hand down his face. "I'm fine, April."

As she opened her mouth to probe further, Drew's cell phone vibrated in his pocket. He had been ignoring calls all afternoon, but he couldn't pass on the opportunity to get out of the conversation about his feelings April was tiptoeing around. He held up a finger, then tapped the green circle instead of the red one.

"Hey, Kim. Are you on the plane... Good... Yeah, it went well, really well. Gabe and his crew did an amazing job making us all look good. I didn't sound nearly as dumb as I thought I would." Drew chuckled, hoping the smile in his voice didn't sound as forced as the one plastered on his face. "I can't wait for you to see it either... Gabe said it'll be the show's season finale in two months... So when do you get in... That late, huh... Yeah, everybody just left." He glanced at April. "Nah, you don't have to come over. I know you're exhausted... Yes, I'm sure. I'll see you at the rehearsal space in the morning... Love you too, babe..."

Drew ended the call and met April's pursed-lip expression. "What's that look for?" he asked and immediately regretted it. That simple question was enough to yank the door to his innermost thoughts wide open, and the spark of victory flickering in April's eyes told him she intended to slide inside before he had a chance to slam it shut and lock it up tight.

"Why'd you tell Kimmie not to come over, Drew?"

"She's been in L.A. for the last few days working on a top-secret project. She doesn't get in until almost midnight. She needs her sleep—"

"And *you* need to talk to someone. Your whole identity has been turned upside down practically overnight, Drew. You have to unpack your feelings about everything... about your mom and dad keeping this from you—"

Drew shook his head. His resentment against his parents seemed insignificant when he looked at the big picture. And he had plenty of medication for the anxiety those feelings triggered. But there were no pills to combat the racism his cousins still faced on a regular basis. Not even EJ's success and fame shielded him from occasional microaggressions. He related to their family history on a level Drew couldn't. And deep down, no matter how many hundreds or thousands or hundreds of thousands of people watched *Bloodlines* and learned the truth about his family history, Drew knew he would never experience the world the same as his cousins because the world would always treat him differently. And it wasn't fair. But talking about it wasn't going to change anything, nor could it help him know for sure if his mother was trying to protect them from the reality of that, and the guilt, or if she was simply ashamed of who she really was.

April stepped closer to him. "It's okay to be confused or even angry right now, Drew... It's okay if you need cuddles too," she said, running her fingers through his hair.

He closed his eyes as she wrapped her arms around his shoulders and pulled him into a hug. The scent of her favorite perfume that had been teasing him all afternoon, filled his nose. He tensed up, reminded of how far he had crossed the line the last time she tried to console him. But he couldn't resist the comfort of her embrace. He wrapped his arms around her waist and exhaled, grateful Gabe had made up a flimsy excuse to invite her to the viewing party after he found out Kimmie couldn't come. Something about it being good for her to see the show in advance so she could prepare the kids. Gabe was the smartest man Drew had ever met, but his heart was even bigger than his brain. He must have known Drew would need a warm hug.

But "warm" wasn't an adequate word. The heat radiating from underneath April's thin, form-fitting sweater was hot enough to melt the imaginary snow fort he had built around himself to survive the day. He surrendered and buried his nose in the curve of her neck, slowly inhaling each layer of the floral scent she had carefully applied.

A series of intermittent buzzing vibrated from April's skinny jeans, just in time to extinguish the countless reels of April lathering her naked body with the expensive shower gel starting to replay in Drew's head. She broke away and fished her phone out of her back pocket. "I didn't realize it was this late," she said as she tapped the screen and Drew reclaimed his spot against the peninsula. "Heeeey, babe... Yeah, everyone's about to leave now." She cut a glance at Drew. "I'll be home in about an hour." A smile pulled at her lips. "Sure. I'll stop and get you some ice cream."

"Tony's looking for his lady?" Drew asked, fiddling with his electric bottle opener as she ended the call. He didn't bring up the almost identical lies they had told their partners. There was no more need to discuss that than there was to tell their current significant others that they were alone with their former significant others, especially when they both knew nothing was going to happen and that there was zero chance anyone could record it and put it on the internet.

Her eyebrows knitted tightly. "More like he's looking for his nurse."

"How's he doing, by the way?"

She shrugged. "Honestly, he's been a pain in the ass."

"Well, he just had knee surgery, April. He's probably in a lot of pain."

"I know, I know. Don't get me wrong; I really don't mind taking care of him. But he's been so grumpy since we pushed the wedding back to next year."

Drew's eyebrows shot straight up. "Why'd you do that?" Drew said, fighting the urge to do a touchdown dance. "He should be on his feet again by May, right?"

"The doctor told him he'd probably need to use a cane for several months. And hobbling around on a cane does not fit

Tony's vision for our wedding and that elaborate first dance he has his heart set on," she said with a flip of her wrist.

Drew nodded, struggling to maintain a neutral expression. He completely understood Tony's disappointment, but he couldn't muster up one ounce of sympathy for him. He was elated to hear they weren't getting married this year. Then he looked at April. There was a dimness seeping through the normal bright glow of her hazel eyes, a clue he started noticing way too late in their marriage. The happiness ping ponging inside of him slowed to a stop.

"I'm sorry Tony's injury threw a monkey wrench into your wedding plans. Are you alright?" he asked, finally remembering she had feelings too.

April flicked her hand again. "May 2020 will be here before we know it, and Tony will get the big fancy wedding of his dreams!" she said, smiling ear to ear. The brightness in her eyes turned up several notches, snuffing out the hint of sadness around the edges.

Drew held his even expression, hoping she understood she didn't have to do that with him anymore. She didn't have to pretend to be happy and strong with him. Her smile faded as she wound the end of one of her French braids around her finger, making her look more and more like an angsty teenager with every twist. He took a half a step toward her.

"April—"

"Well, I better get going," April said abruptly, taking a full step back.

When the Uber pulled up to the curb, she threw her arms around Drew's neck and squeezed tight.

"Thank you for coming," he said as he opened the back door of the black Tesla.

April slid into the back seat. "I wouldn't have missed it for the world."

He planted a peck on her cheek. "Get home safe," he said, shooting a hard look at the driver spying on them in the rearview mirror. The driver averted his eyes, but not before responding to the warning in Drew's eyes and tone with an earnest nod.

As the car pulled away from the curb, the back window came down and April stuck her head out. "Talk to somebody, Drew!" she shouted, winning the last word on the subject as the Tesla sped down the street.

Drew chuckled and shook his head, turning toward his building. He pulled out his phone while he waited for the elevator and stared at the screen. His thumb hovered over the keyboard for a few seconds before tapping out a series of text messages to Kimmie.

> *If you're still up for it*
> *Come over when you get back*
> *Let yourself in*
> *You have the codes*

Chapter 27

Drew hurried down the corridor backstage at Madison Square Garden, fully dressed to perform. He looked at his phone. It was five o'clock. The show started at nine. Four hours is a substantial chunk of time, but pre-performance time runs differently than in the real world. It creeps by, then suddenly four hours turns into four minutes. You could easily end up late to the stage, miss your first cue, and throw off the entire show.

Drew's usual pre-show ritual involved a couple of hours of meditation and warming up. But this wasn't a usual show; it was the mother of all shows chock full of some of the music industry's highest grossing artists of all time. Any of the acts in the lineup could, and had, sold out the Garden; all of them in one live broadcast had stirred up an unbelievable media frenzy. They were in high demand, and interviews filled every free minute.

Drew took two deep breaths—all the meditation time permitted—and entered the conference room at the end of the corridor. He squinted at the bright lights behind Lena Rocha from *Vibe* magazine now. For unstated reasons, she parted ways with *Rolling Stone* not long after the 2010 Grammys. The rumor mill got churning immediately, spitting out different reasons for her abrupt departure, but the one that stuck was her awkward interview with Drew on the red carpet. For over a week, all the entertainment news shows replayed the fleeting yet menacing look he gave her when she asked about Chris and Randy. Their fans went on the attack and berated her mercilessly for months. He always felt bad about that.

"Hey, Drew! Come on in. Have a seat," Lena said, waving him over. "We're gonna get started in two minutes." Her big smile and warm welcome relieved him of his apprehension. Either he had nothing to do with her leaving *Rolling Stone*, or she harbored no hard feelings.

Drew took a seat in the empty director's chair between EJ and Kimmie on the front row. Reid and Von each gave him a hardy back pounding from their elevated perches on the second row.

"What took you so long?" Kimmie whispered as an assistant hooked up Drew's mic.

"I couldn't find my belt," he whispered back.

Drew had a special belt he wore for every performance. The one his mother had gotten for him not long before she died. She said it was calling her name, and she had to get it for him because "every good rock star needs a rockin' belt."

Kimmie's eyes went big. "Ooops. Where'd you find it?"

"Somewhere between you ripping it off me and taking advantage of me, you managed to toss it on top of a shelf."

"My bad. I guess I got a little carried away." She shrugged.

Drew winked. "So aggressive."

She giggled and went back to texting on her phone like everybody else. Drew followed suit and pulled out his phone.

April: I know you'll be too busy to text soon, so BREAK A LEG!!!! The kids and I can't wait for the show to start!

Thanks. See you guys after the show

"Alright, guys, thanks so much for agreeing to sit for an interview so close to showtime," Lena said, signaling the group that everything was set up and ready to go. They all put their phones away simultaneously, as if part of their well-rehearsed choreography.

"So, EJ, is this everything you imagined it would be, your vision for this major collaboration project?" she asked, her eyes twinkling with excitement.

EJ leaned forward, resting his elbows on the arms of his chair. "Lena, let me tell you, this is way bigger than anything I imagined or even hoped for. I had this idea to call up some old heads and see if they wanted to come out and jam, maybe record some raw stuff for YouTube or whatever. To tell you the truth, I wasn't sure anybody would show up—"

"Wait." Lena reared back in her seat. "You didn't really think they'd blow you off, did you? You're EJ Wallace!"

"Heh. If I recall, I got blown off quite a few times," he said, shooting dirty looks at Drew and Lady Lovely. "But eventually all the right people said yes, and the rest is history."

"History indeed," Lena said. "Your *Undefinable* tour is selling out in every city, and you haven't even done the live show yet. You are sure to shatter concert sale records to go along with your record-breaking album downloads. What do you think has people going bananas over this collaboration?"

EJ shrugged. "I don't know. I just think people love good music."

"You mean people love great music, don't you?"

"Nope. I mean good music. People love the memories of great times, great friends, great loves, and great feelings that good music triggers. It's like a little spark of magic. Every musician on this tour is a ridiculously talented artist, but they also each have a talent for making good music for the soundtrack of people's life experiences. It could be as simple as hangin' out with your boys talkin' smack about girls you ain't never gonna get with Wiretap playing in the background," he slapped Drew on the back, "or practicing Kimmie's sexy dance moves in your parents' basement with your girlfriends. And it could be as profound as hearing Kwayk rap about racial profiling and police brutality on your car radio as a cop asks you to step out of your vehicle for the first time—"

"Don't forget about all the first wedding dances to Von's jazz?" added Marisol Cruz, a Dominican singer, who blasted on the scene during the Latin explosion, but never fully emerged from the shadow of J-Lo.

EJ nodded. "Right! I think we had Von's music playing at our wedding."

Von cleared his throat. "Um, you know I was there, right? I actually performed at your wedding."

"For real?" EJ shot a surprised look over his shoulder at Von on the back row. Von replied with an unimpressed smirk. "I'm just messing with you, man."

"Whatever, man," Von huffed, shaking his head.

Everyone burst into laughter.

"Well, I know that working with family is nothing new for you, EJ. So, let me ask you, Drew, what's it like collaborating with your long-lost cousin?"

Drew smiled. It was only a matter of time before she asked that. Since *Bloodlines*, every reporter asked about it. From highbrow questions about race and identity that even people who studied the subject for years couldn't answer, to less intellectual questions like whether his DNA profile had any effect on the size of his penis, to harmless softballs like Lena's, it was clear people hadn't lost interest in the months since their family's episode had aired. Early on, one guy asked Drew what it was like to find out he was African American. He was taken aback. Not once during the process had he thought of himself as African American, or that he had a right to. Even though his Black family members had welcomed him with open arms, and even though if he had been born a generation or more earlier, because of the one-drop rule, he would have been classified as colored or Negro or Black. If his mother had made a different choice, he might have considered himself a person of color, but she hadn't, so he didn't. Nor did he think of himself simply as a white person with a colorful family tree. It was more complicated than traditional or contemporary definitions of race and ethnicity.

The only thing he knew for sure was that finding out about the Black side of his family was the most profound experience of his life, and a source of immense pride. It was like finding a secret room in your house that increased the value of the property. But the truth had come with a fair amount of pain as well, leaving Drew with a level of ambivalence he hadn't anticipated at the start of this journey. His lineage on his mother's side was equal parts tragedy and triumph. Gabe and his team painted a vivid picture of his family history, highlighting the more remarkable stories of survival and achievement despite unimaginable degradation and disadvantage along their family's timeline until finally reaching the big reveal. Through their grandfather, he and EJ were descendants of Thomas Jefferson and Sally Hemmings, the enslaved half-sister of his deceased wife. That was huge, but only one of many examples where pride and shame intertwined on his family tree. Sally Hemmings was sixteen, only a few years older than Paige, when the forty-six-year-old, third President of the United States fathered the first of several children with her.

Drew wrapped his arm around EJ's shoulders. "Lena, it is a dream come true working with my awesome big cousin. I love it!" he said, planting a juicy kiss on his cheek.

"Ugh, man!" EJ groaned, pushing Drew off while everyone else nearly fell out of their chairs laughing.

"No, but it really is a dream come true," Drew said sincerely. "I've always wanted to work with EJ... Who hasn't? He's an amazing producer, everybody knows that. I was ecstatic to find out he was family. But him being my cousin doesn't really factor too much into our working relationship, because he's more like a big brother to me. In fact, we've all gotten very close." He glanced over his shoulder at his fellow artists. "I think of them all like brothers and sisters."

"Awww!" Everyone cooed as Reid, EJ, and Rick pounded him in the back extra hard, making him grimace.

"That's beautiful, Drew," said Lena. "One more question about that. How's Grandma Cheryl?"

"She's great!" EJ said. "She's pissed she can't be here tonight because of a cold, but she's watching at home with her great grandkids who're too little to come out tonight. Thanks for asking."

"I love Grandma Cheryl!" Lena gushed. "I follow her on Twitter. Do you guys help her with that?"

Drew chuckled. "She helps me with Twitter!"

EJ rolled his eyes. "That's terrible, bruh. She's like ninety."

Drew shrugged. "Her tweets are epic. I have more followers, but she gets waaayyy more likes and retweets than I ever do!"

The group laughed again.

"So, Reid, how do you guys deal with egos in the group?" Lena asked.

"Why are you asking me that question?" he asked with wide-eyed innocence.

Lena shrugged, flashing a sheepish smirk.

"I don't think we have ego problems, *per se*. Everybody's pretty chill. Sure, we've butted heads and had a few... enthusiastic debates—"

"Heated arguments," Kimmie corrected him.

Reid nodded. "Heated arguments too. But we always work it out. We all committed to doing what's best for the project, and that means checking egos at the door."

"That's what the sign says," Bret reminded him.

"Oh, yeah. There's a sign on the door of the studio that says, *Phones and Egos Off.*"

"That's a great sign," Lena said to EJ. "Seems effective, too."

"Thanks. My mother had it made for me years ago. It's a take on a similar sign she had by the front door when we were growing up: *Shoes and Attitudes Off.*"

"Was it as effective for you and your siblings?"

EJ rubbed his chin. "There was probably a 50/50 success rate for both the shoes and the attitude. But she had plenty of other ways to make us remember. All of them a lot louder and way more painful than just doing what the sign said in the first place."

"Ha! Sounds like my mom. La chancla right to the back of the head," she said as she pretended to fling an invisible flip flop.

The interview continued for a few more minutes as Lena got everyone to weigh in on at least one of her thoughtful questions. They finished a couple of hours before showtime and everyone scattered, heading back to their dressing rooms to warm up and for any other rituals.

"Hey, Drew!" Reid called out from behind.

"What's up?" Drew asked as Reid caught up to him outside his dressing room.

He looked up and down the hallway. "Can I talk to you for a minute?" he whispered.

"Sure, come on in," Drew said, trying not to sound as annoyed as he was.

Reid followed Drew into the room and closed the door behind him.

Drew checked the strings on his guitar and tuned it again, watching Reid pace the floor from the corner of his eye. Then Reid sat on a folding chair and rubbed his sweaty palms on his jeans. Next, he cracked his neck. Then he jumped up and started the process all over again—three times.

"You know, you would be a lot less nervous if you went back to your dressing room and warmed up," Drew said, making no effort to conceal his annoyance.

Reid jumped like he had forgotten Drew was there. "What? Oh, yeah. I already warmed up."

Drew narrowed his eyes. "When could you have done that? You were on my heels right after the interview."

"I did it before—Hey, am I disturbing you or something?"

"Well, now that you mention it."

A deep scowl darkened Reid's face even more than it was before. "Fine. I'll leave," he grumbled and stormed toward the door.

Drew jumped up and grabbed Reid by the arm. "What's wrong with you, man? I've never seen you this nervous before a show."

Reid shook his head and turned to leave again. Drew yanked him back. "Dude, spill it. What's goin' on?"

He took a deep breath as he shoved his hand into his pocket and pulled out a burgundy ring box. He opened it slowly, showing Drew a brilliantly sparkling, five carat, diamond engagement ring.

With his mouth fully agape, Drew took the box from Reid and sat down. "Reid... I don't even know what to say." He rubbed the back of his neck. "This is completely out the blue. I mean, what am I gonna tell Kimmie?" he said and collapsed back into the couch, laughing hysterically.

"You're a jerk, man," Reid muttered, snatching the box out of Drew's hand.

Drew flew at Reid and attacked him with a bear hug, nearly knocking him over. "Dude! How long have you been thinking about asking Shanice to marry you?"

Reid shrugged. "Truth?"

Drew nodded.

"Since I met her," he said as he opened the box and looked at the ring.

"Wow. So, you're gonna do this again, huh?"

Reid grimaced. "I'm crazy, right?"

"Hey, man, you know what they say. Third time's the charm. And Shanice is a great chick. Nothing like the other two." He gave Reid a firm pat on his shoulder. "So, when are you gonna do it?"

"Tonight. After the show. I was gonna do it before, but I thought I better wait, in case she says no. Don't wanna ruin the show with my sobbing." He smirked.

"She won't say no." Drew shook his head. "She won't say no."

The tension on Reid's face melted into a smile. "So, what about you? You thinkin' about doin' it again?"

"Why? Are you trying to have a double wedding?"

"No, man. I'm serious. You and Kimmie have been together for a while now. You been thinkin' about it?"

Drew smiled. "Don't you think there's enough life-changing stuff going on tonight?"

Reid dropped it and left to finish getting ready. Drew went back to checking his guitar, and then he ran through the scales, warming up the lowest and highest parts of his natural singing voice. Then he ran through them again, adding some grit. After twenty minutes of that, he sang a couple of verses, paying close attention to how it felt and where exactly each note sat in his throat. Then he popped in his ear buds and cranked up the volume. He recorded himself playing and singing along until he was confident that he would be able to perform well whether or not he could hear himself on stage.

An hour before showtime, Mike and Travis were at his door with a few crew members they knew from back in the day. He invited them all in and it was 2009 all over again. They joked and laughed, taunting each other like old times until one of the stage managers came in with her people like a tornado touching up makeup, gathering instruments, and shepherding musicians to a huge open area not too far from the stage.

Drew whistled as they arrived at the gathering spot. "Whoa." He had never been part of any show or tour as huge as *Undefinable*.

In addition to the collaboration group, there were the dancers, backup musicians, and singers, and dozens of crew members. He knew there were a ridiculous number of people involved, but he hadn't ever seen them all together in the same room.

As he took in the massive crowd of entertainers and support staff stuffed into the small area behind the stage, the nerves churned in his gut, and he smiled. The weed he had smoked earlier was wearing off just in time to give him the right amount of jitters. He put his head down and closed his eyes as he took several deep breaths to settle his nerves.

"Okay y'all!" EJ shouted, causing everyone to quiet down and circle around. "I just wanna say a quick prayer before we take our places—wait, who's missing?" EJ asked, looking around the enormous circle of people, three rows deep, now all holding hands.

"Who do you think?" Von said.

"Somebody better get on a radio or a cell phone and tell Kimmie and Marisol to get their asses out here right now," EJ said.

"¡Tranquilo, papí!" Marisol said as she pushed her way through the crowd to the eye of the circle, sashaying over to Von in a short, silver dress covered in shimmering fringe and taking his hand.

"Where the hell is—"

"I'm here!" Kimmie shouted.

Travis nudged Drew. He looked up as Kimmie emerged into the eye of the circle wearing a sparkling, nude-colored bodysuit that made her look like she had diamond encrusted skin.

She made a beeline for Drew and broke his grasp on Mike as she wiggled between them. "What'd I miss?" she whispered, squeezing Drew's hand.

"Nothing much. Just EJ about to blow a gasket. What held you up?"

"Wardrobe malfunction. I am literally sewn into this skin-tight monstrosity."

"You look beautiful." He smiled.

Kimmie blew the long-hanging bangs of her platinum blond wig out of her eyes. "Stop, Drew. I know how much you hate this stupid wig and all this makeup. I don't look anything like myself—"

"You stop. You look amazing," he said as he lifted her hand and kissed the back a few times. "Take some deep breaths, Kim. You're trembling."

She closed her eyes and breathed in through her nose and out through her mouth. Drew and Mike joined her.

EJ cleared his throat, and everyone bowed their heads. "I want to thank you, God, for every single person in this room. It is a blessing to work with the most talented and dedicated people in the world. I pray that everybody knows how much I love and appreciate them. We thank you, dear God, for allowing us to come together in this time and place to honor the gifts you have bestowed upon us. And heavenly Father, I ask that you keep us all healthy, keep us all strong, and keep us all crazy enough to do this thing we love over and over and over again for the rest of our lives! Amen?"

"AMEN!" The show people roared, and a thunderous ovation of cheers, whistles, and laughter reverberated throughout the space.

"Aiight! Let's do this!" EJ shouted as everyone scattered to their places.

Drew gave Mike and Travis bro hugs and took off to get into position. Arriving at the wing of the stage, he found Reid nodding as EJ talked in his ear.

"... and light this bitch up!" EJ barked as he hit him with three rapid, hard slaps to the ass. Then Reid charged down the narrow stairs leading under the stage. In a matter of minutes, he would be lifted through a hole in the floor, shredding his axe as lights and lasers bounced around the stage. A normal show has at least one opening act to warm up the audience for the headliner. But this was a live televised concert with many high-profile acts. By unanimous decision, Reid was selected to set the tone for the concert. He was the opening act, and he would have only two and a half minutes to get the crowd properly hyped. It was a heavy burden for a single musician. Failure could mean disaster for the entire show.

EJ gave Drew a quick head nod and took off to get into position. There was no need for a deeper interaction. They both had a "do or die" expression that only performers recognize. There was nothing to be said.

A glimmer of light from above caught Drew's eye. He looked up to see Kimmie in position on a platform, puffing her cheeks in and out with quick breaths as she shook out her hands and bounced away nervous energy with the same intense expression. He couldn't see any of the others, he didn't need to. He was as connected with this group of musicians as he had been with Chris, Randy, Mike, and Travis all those years ago. All the tiny hairs on his body stood on end, and he knew his brothers and sisters were all in position, ready to take the stage.

As Drew stood, tapping his foot furiously, his guitar appeared over his head being lowered across his torso by faceless hands while other faceless hands adjusted his clothes and touched up his makeup. The adrenaline simmered under his skin like a powder keg as Reid dropped the final note of his solo. Silence and darkness fell abruptly across the stage and a cacophony of screams, applause, and whistles erupted from the audience. One of the hands tapped Drew's shoulder three times, signaling he had exactly six seconds to get into place. He was on stage in half that time. Then in three... two... one, a spectacular explosion of fireworks and music lit up the stage.

Chapter 28

"I'm sorry, Dad," Zach said as Drew pulled the corners of his bow tie.

"How's that look?" Drew said and turned Zach around to face the full-length mirror attached to the closet door in the large guestroom of EJ's beach house. "And stop apologizing to me." He sat on the bed and bent over to tie his shoes.

"But I really feel bad, Dad! I'm your best man. I wanted to give you the bachelor party you deserve."

"First of all, I don't think I qualify as a bachelor. Second, the party you arranged at Uncle Travis's restaurant was nice. I had a great time. Third, you're twenty. Your mom would have killed you and then me if you threw me some wild bachelor party."

"Well, whose fault is that?"

Drew sighed. "What are you talkin' about, Zach? You're starting to piss me off." He went over to the dresser and grabbed his cufflinks. "Here. Help me with these."

"I'll be twenty-one in like six months. This couldn't have waited until after that?" He fixed Drew's cuffs and fastened the cufflinks.

"You're asking if we could have pushed the wedding back so that you could buy strippers and liquor for your old man?"

"Well, when you put it that way, it sounds crazy." He chuckled.

Drew threw his head back and let out such a loud laugh, he almost didn't hear the knock at the door.

"Come in!" he yelled between laughs.

A large group of well-dressed men filed in the door. Suddenly, the room was abuzz with the loud conversations and raucous laughter of Drew's friends and family, many of whom were also fairly buzzed themselves.

"Aiight, everybody! Shut up!" shouted EJ. Silence fell over the room. "We don't wanna hold you up too long from getting ready, but we thought we should send you off with one last toast—"

"Before the slaughter!" James blurted out.

"Why is it always the assholes that ain't never been married talkin' the most smack?" EJ asked.

"I might be an asshole, but I'm a smart asshole with full control of my money and my balls," James retorted.

"Man, shut up," EJ's brother, Corey, said as he slapped James in the crotch.

"Ugh!" James groaned, doubling over in pain.

"Anyway, Drew, like I was saying, we wanted to give you a proper send-off," EJ continued while Corey and Mike passed out little plastic cups. Then Travis filled them with Patrón. He stopped short when he got to Zach, and they both looked over at Drew with sad, pleading eyes.

"Fine. One shot. But you better not tell your mom," Drew said.

"Thanks, Dad!" Zach and Travis said in unison as Travis poured Zach his first drink—his first authorized drink.

"Can I have one too, Dad?" Cole squawked from across the room.

"NO!" rang out a chorus of tenors, baritones, and basses before Drew had a chance to answer, causing Cole to turn beet red as he hung his head in defeat.

Reid threw his arm around Cole's shoulder. "Come on, little dude. You can have one of my special shots."

"I'm not a little dude... little old man," Cole snarled as he shrugged out of Reid's embrace and stood up tall, putting them nearly eye to eye.

Everyone laughed, except Drew. Puberty had crash-landed on Cole. Along with a recent growth spurt, making him unequivocally tall for a thirteen-year-old, came an incredibly short fuse that caused him to mouth off with little provocation.

Drew walked over, placed a firm hand on his youngest son's shoulder, and whispered a few not-so-gentle reminders in his ear. "Are we gonna have to have this conversation again today?" Drew asked loud enough for everyone to hear.

Still having a few inches to go before he would be eye to eye with his dad, Cole looked up at Drew. "No, sir," he replied, shaking his head. His red hue had returned with a vengeance.

Drew grabbed Cole by the shoulders and turned him around to face Reid. "Well?" he said, giving him a little shake.

"I'm sorry for being disrespectful, Uncle Reid," Cole said, his eyes downcast.

"Already forgotten, little—I mean, Cole. You want this shot or not?" he said with a smirk, holding out a little plastic cup of apple juice.

"Yes, sir. Thanks," he said as he took the cup.

"Sir?" Reid scoffed. "That's worse than 'old man!' I'm not your pops. 'Uncle Reid' is fine," he said as more of the non-drinkers gathered around to get one of Reid's special shots.

"Does everybody have a beverage?" EJ asked, surveying the room. "Aiight. I know y'all are sick of hearing me talk all the time—shut up, James—" he said as James opened his mouth. "So, I'm gonna turn over the floor."

EJ stepped back and Mike came forward, clearing his throat. "Um, I'm not much of a talker. So, I'm not exactly sure how I got voted to do this—"

"Because you've known Drew the longest," Travis said.

"Oh, yeah!" Mike snapped his fingers as if a light bulb clicked on in his head. "I guess I have known you the longest out of everyone in this room."

"Even Uncle Travis?" Zach asked.

"Yep. Trav and Randy had already gone home when Chris came up to me after school with this tall, skinny kid trailing behind him. He was real quiet too." He scrunched up his face. "Well, maybe he wasn't that quiet. I was pretty worked up ranting about a fight I got in after school. Luckily, no teachers caught us, and I didn't have any bruises, but the jerk destroyed my shirt. It was literally hanging on me by threads.

"So, I'm freakin' out, because my mom warned me that if I got in another fight, I was in for a world of pain when she got a hold of me. Drew just drops his backpack, takes off his T-shirt, and hands it to me. He said, 'Give me your shirt; it's similar to mine'—they were both faded black Metallica T-shirts. 'I'll tell my mom I got jumped on my way home. She always thinks I'm gonna get beat up on my way home from school anyway.'" Mike shook his head. "I think me and Chris even punched you in the face a couple of times, didn't we?"

"Yep," Drew said. "The first of many, many stupid things we did together." He chuckled.

Mike smiled. "He's gotten a bad rap over the years, but that's the Drew I know. The guy who literally gave me, a kid he had known for three minutes, the shirt off his back. And he's had my back during some of the worst times of my life—" Mike cleared his throat as tears formed in his eyes. Travis moved closer and placed his hand on his shoulder. Drew closed his eyes in vain, trying to keep his tears from falling.

"Drew, you risked your ass to have my back during the hardest time in my life. And I know you'd do it again without a second thought. You are my friend, you are my bandmate, you are my brother, and I love you, man. I wish you all the happiness in the universe. Nobody deserves it more than you." He raised his shot. "To everything."

"To everything!" the men cheered, shot cups up and empty in two seconds.

A celebration of congratulatory hugs, back-slaps, and laughter died down and the sea of men parted to reveal Drew's father standing in the room. "Hey, Dad," he said, shooting a look at Zach, but he had already slipped his shot cup into EJ's hand. The smooth exchange went unnoticed by Simon. His focus was locked on the shot cup in Cole's hand.

"What are you doing with that?" He snatched the cup from Cole.

Whoa, Mr. Simon. It's only juice. This is the no-drinking section," Reid said as Zach eased closer to that side of the room.

"Well, isn't that nice," Simon said. "Get 'em acclimated to the tools of alcoholism early, so he'll know exactly what to do to get himself plastered, right?"

"Uh, I, well, I," Reid stammered and shot Drew a look of desperation.

Drew sighed. "Hey, thanks, guys. I really appreciate you all coming up and making me cry before the ceremony even starts," he said sarcastically as he gave EJ a head nod.

"Aiight, let's go, y'all!" He pushed as many of his brothers and cousins out of the room as he could reach. The rest of the men filed out behind them.

The room cleared out in five seconds. Only Zach, Cole, and Simon stayed behind.

Cole looked around the room, shaking his head. "Damn, Grandpa, you're such a freakin' buzz kill."

Simon's head snapped up. "What did you say to me, boy?" he snarled, moving quickly toward Cole.

Drew jumped between them. "Cole, get out. Zach, take your brother downstairs and find him a corner to stand in until it's time to start."

"But that's not fair!" Cole shrieked. "I was only kidding! Why can't anybody in this family take a joke!"

Drew replied with a scary dad face loud and clear enough to let Cole know that the punishment was not up for debate.

"Come on, Dave Chapelle. You can work on your standup routine standing up in the corner," Zach said as he guided a crestfallen Cole out of the room.

As they went out the door, Drew walked back over to the full-length mirror to check his hair.

"That boy is fast getting out of control," Simon said. "He needs a kick in the pants before he talks himself into a punch in the mouth one of these days."

Drew moved on from checking his hair to examining his face.

"Do you hear me, boy?"

"I hear you, Dad," Drew said as he calmly adjusted his tie. "What do you expect me to do, flog him before my wedding?"

"No, but he needs something more impressive than standing in a corner in order to nip this behavior in the bud."

Drew turned to face his father. "Cole is on top of the world right now. He's on the basketball team, a decent guitar player, has a ton of friends that idolize him, and the girls are starting to take notice. And I'll give it to him, he's pretty smooth with them. His quick wit and acid tongue that gets him in trouble with us makes them giggle. He's like the king of the eighth grade. Parking his overgrown body and ego in a corner is exactly what he needs to knock him down a few notches. Trust me." He placed a couple of firm pats on his father's shoulder. "We've been down this road a few times in the last six months or so. He'll be on his best behavior for the rest of the day because he knows corner time means he's cracked the thin ice he was already treading on," Drew said with a shrug as he grabbed his tuxedo jacket off the back of the chair. Simon helped him put it on.

"How do I look?" He turned back around to face his father.

"Very nice. Beautiful. Like your mother," he said, smiling wistfully.

Drew frowned. Simon started seeing a therapist a couple of years ago. The upside was that he had gotten much better at controlling his emotions and expressing his feelings. And because Drew had gone with him several times, they had gotten the help they needed to repair their relationship. The downside was that sometimes he said things like "You're beautiful, like your mother."

"Did I say something wrong?" Simon asked.

"I was hoping for *ruggedly handsome* or something along those lines."

"So, you want me to lie?"

"Yes!"

They laughed together.

"Dad, the wedding planner said it's time to go down now," Zach said as he came back into the room.

Drew closed his eyes and breathed in slowly, hoping the flood of oxygen would calm the dragonflies swarming around in his stomach.

Simon put his hand on Drew's shoulder. "You're ready," he said.

Drew opened his eyes to Zach's and Simon's smiling faces, and the nerves subsided. "I am ready," he agreed and led the way out the door.

As they descended the stairs, the scent of the massive amount of flowers filling EJ's humongous foyer filled his nose. Reaching the bottom of the stairs felt like entering an indoor garden on steroids. Flowers and tulle sat, hung, and draped everywhere. Except for the labored sighs of a tuxedoed thirteen-year-old, standing motionless facing the corner between two large hydrangea arrangements, the room was quiet and serene. All the guests had been invited to take their seats outside, where the ceremony would be held.

"Okay, Cole, you're done," Drew said.

Cole stepped out of the corner and trudged over to Drew, Simon, and Zach. "I'm sorry for talking to you like that, Grandpa. I really didn't mean anything by it."

"It's alright, Cole. I'm proud of you for apologizing and taking your punishment like a man. You are so much like your father was at your age." The corners of Cole's mouth turned up slightly as his chest poked out. Drew's chest rose a little as well.

"But I want you to start thinking before you speak," Simon continued. "Not everyone you encounter is going to love you as much as your dad and me and the rest of your family. Some people won't think twice about hauling off and punching you in the face. And these days, people are prone to shoot first and calm down later. I don't want anything bad to happen to you because of your mouth, so promise me you'll try harder."

"I promise, Grandpa," he said as Simon pulled him into a hug.

Cole turned to Drew. "I'm sorry you had to punish me at your wedding, Dad. It won't happen again. I promise," he said, looking down at the floor.

Drew lifted his chin and gave him a bear hug. "Thanks, bud, I love you. Do you know where you're supposed to be right now?"

"Yes, sir."

"I think you better get moving then."

Cole beamed. "I'll see you guys soon! Wish me luck!" he shouted, already halfway across the foyer. Then he disappeared down a hallway.

Drew looked at his father through narrowed eyes.

"Why're you lookin' at me like that?"

"I'm proud of you, Dad," Drew said, patting him on the back. "You've come a long way."

Simon blushed. "Thanks, son. I'm proud of you too. I always have been, by the way," he said. "And I love you."

Drew smiled. Simon started saying those words regularly soon after he started therapy. At first, they were as awkward to hear as they were for Simon to say. But Drew had gotten used to it and didn't turn tomato red anymore when his father directed the sentiment at him. "I love you too, Dad."

"Ugh!" Zach groaned. "Are you guys done yet? 'Cuz I'm real close to puking all over these pretty flowers."

"Awwww! Zachy's not getting enough attention? I'm proud of you too, and I wuv you so much!" Drew said, grabbing Zach's head as he peppered his face with kisses.

"Dad! Stop! You're messin' up my hair!" Zach growled as he shrugged Drew off and rushed over to the mirror in the foyer. He spun around in circles, looking at his hair from every angle, while intermittently shooting daggers at his father and grandfather as they laughed.

"Excuse me, Drew. Are you ready?" the wedding planner asked as she approached the men.

Drew cleared his throat. "Yes, Priya. I'm all set."

"Mr. Simon, your wife has already been escorted to her seat. Would you like me to escort you to her? We are about to start."

"No, no, no, I can manage. You take care of these boys," he said. Then he walked across the living room and out the door to the deck.

Priya led Drew and Zach out the same way and down the stairs to the pool, where EJ's brother, Damon, an ordained minister, waited with his Bible in hand and a cheesy grin on his face.

"Lookin' good, cuz!" Damon said, transferring the Bible to his left hand and extending his right. Drew grabbed it as they leaned in and bumped shoulders. Damon repeated the action with Zach.

"Let's get you married, man," Damon said as he stepped onto the lush grassy area just beyond the pool where the guests were seated.

Drew and Zach followed Damon to the flower-covered arbor placed right at the edge of the yard where the grass met the sand. Murmurs and whispers floated around the air along with the soft classical music from the string quartet as Drew walked down the aisle, but his gaze fixed on the ocean a few feet away. The sight and sound of the waves crashing against the beach gave him a tingling feeling, and goose bumps rippled over his body despite the warm, mid-September air. He closed his eyes to concentrate on the sound and smell of the ocean. It always calmed him.

Relaxation washed over him, and he slowly opened his eyes to an even more beautiful sight. His family and friends sat before him grinning—a sea of humans in every size, shape, and color. All generations were represented as well, from ninety-three-year-old Grandma Cheryl, sitting proudly in the front row, down to two-month-old Reid Cox Jr., cradled snugly in Shanice's arm. Drew smiled back at them; his heart so full, he thought it might burst.

The murmurs and whispers resurged as Paige appeared on the deck and made her way down the stairs, past the pool and down the aisle. Drew's heart skipped a beat. He stood breathless, mesmerized by his sixteen-year-old daughter. But that wasn't an unusual state for him. Paige was the captain of her championship-winning soccer team. Some of the stuff she did on the field defied the laws of physics. She was amazing, and Drew always thought she was beautiful, even in the sweatpants and sneakers she usually wore. But he hadn't prepared himself for how grown up she would look all dressed up in her satin sunset-colored bridesmaid's dress. He was even less prepared for how much she suddenly seemed to resemble his mother.

Drew glanced at his grandmother. For a second, her eyes widened like she had seen a ghost, then they filled with tears. Simon, on the verge of tears himself, reached over Susan and offered Grandma his handkerchief. She took it. Although they would never be friends, Grandma and Simon had buried the hatchet over tea and decided to leave the past in the past. "I'd rather use what little time I have left holding onto my grandbabies and my great grandbabies than some old grudge," Grandma had told Drew when they talked about her unexpected change of heart.

"Hey there, gorgeous," Drew said as Paige reached the arbor. He kissed her blushing cheek, and she took her place on the other side of Damon.

Then the music changed, signaling the moment had finally arrived. Looking up at the deck, Drew's heart pounded hard and fast. Priya and her assistant opened the French doors, and Cole emerged from the house. He held his right elbow up and looked over his shoulder, smiling as his mother stepped out and took his arm. The guests' chatter turned into *Oh's* and *Aw's* as the bride and her giant baby boy made their way around the pool to the grassy area. Then they all rose from their seats.

Drew didn't hear or see anything except April until he got a creepy feeling that someone was staring at him. While everyone's full attention was on the bride, Lia pierced Drew with a smug look as she held up her hand and rubbed her fingers together. "Pay up," she mouthed to him. He quickly looked away, resisting the urge to react to his sister, who had taken that moment to remind him of their friendly wager.

The minute Lia got wind that April had called off her engagement to Tony all together after the Covid-19 Pandemic thwarted their wedding plans for a second time, she blew up Drew's phone, texting him "I told you so!" in every language she knew and several she didn't. Then, when he and Kimmie decided they were better as friends a few months later, Lia predicted he and April would marry again. Drew balked at the idea and confidently agreed to pay her five thousand dollars in addition to forever referring to her as "Your Highness, All Knowing Queen of Everything" if she was correct.

Having never reneged on a bet won fair and square, Drew had the money in his pocket ready to hand over to his sister immediately after the ceremony. It would be the best bet he ever lost. But she could forget about her new title—he'd gladly pay another five thousand to get out of that part of the bet.

Thoughts of his loss vanished as his focus returned to April. There was nothing more important than her. He said a prayer to himself that he would never again forget to make her his first priority, and he reminded himself of the vows he would soon say to her out loud: *I know everyone is responsible for their own happiness, but I also know that, for me, happiness means nothing unless I can share it with you. I vow, before God, our family, and closest friends, that when times get tough, I will always, always, always turn to you and not on you. And I will always remember that the answer to any important question and the solution to every single problem I have had since I was eighteen can be found in your smile, in your love...*

"Hey, babe," April said with a wink as she and Cole reached the end of the aisle. Drew could not have imagined it possible for April to be more beautiful than he already thought she was, but standing before him, she was positively stunning. He would have bet another five million dollars that she was the most beautiful woman in the world. Her cream-colored dress hugged her body perfectly from the lace straps and bodice accentuating her slender neck and sculpted shoulders, around the curve of her hips, down to her toned thighs, right to her pretty, suckable toes peeking at him from the hemline.

A sudden magnetic surge made Drew reach for his bride as April took a step forward, reaching for her groom.

"Wait a second, April," Damon said, causing her to stop short. Her and Drew's hands hung suspended in midair. "I have been asked to add something to the ceremony."

April stepped back and flashed a confused look at Drew. He shrugged. There was a surprise in store, for sure. The kids would sing a song he had written for their mother, but that was planned for much later than this unexpected interruption. Drew and April looked at Damon. The matching his-and-her question marks etched in the creases of their furrowed brows begged for an explanation.

"Who gives this woman and this man to be married to each other?" Damon asked with a booming voice that rivaled their grandfather's.

Paige stepped forward and hooked on to Cole's free arm as she took April's right hand. At the same time, Zach took Drew's left hand and placed it in April's.

"We do!" all three kids shouted in unison, smiling proudly as applause and whistles erupted from their family and friends. And at the end of the summer, on the edge of the ocean, from that moment to the close of the ceremony, there were no dry eyes.

The Results
MIXTAPE

*Songs mentioned in the book or that inspired
characters and scenes*

"Lose Control"
TEDDY SWIMS

"Single Ladies"
BEYONCE

"What Makes You Sad"
NICOTINE DOLLS

"Pour Some Sugar
on Me"
DEF LEPPARD

"If I Ever Fall In Love"
SHAI

"If I Ruled the World"
NAS (FEAT. LAURYN HILL)

"Too Close"
NEXT

"I Keep Forgettin"
MICHAEL MCDONALD

"F*ck Tha Police"
NWA

"Come Together"
THE BEATLES, COVERED
BY GARY CLARK, JR. AND
JUNKIE XL

"Rough Riders"
DMX

"Celebrity Status"
MARIANAS TRENCH

"Look What I Found"
LADY GAGA

"Little Things"
JESSICA MAUBOY

"I Choose You"
SARA BAREILLES

Girl Group

Except for the sound of Maya's stiletto tapping rapidly against the tile floor, she and Gene rode up the elevator in silence. The doors slid open, and Gene charged down the corridor. Maya followed at a slower pace a few feet behind.

"Don't be nervous, Maya. EJ may be a big-time music exec, but he's down to earth. He really is a good guy," Gene said over his shoulder as they approached the presidential suite. "I promise nothing bad is going to happen to you in here... And I'll be with you the whole time."

Ignoring the bell, he pounded on the door with his fist and flashed a reassuring smile at her. It didn't work. Gene was a genuinely nice guy. He hadn't been in the business long enough for it to have damaged his soul, and certainly not long enough for him to know his presence could not protect her from the danger hers was in, but she nodded anyway and took a deep breath. That didn't work either. Her anxiousness did not subside.

Then she caught a glimpse of the two of them in the oversized mirror over the antique console table to her right, and her heart sank. She looked more out of place than she imagined, standing next to Gene in his tailored charcoal-gray suit and crisp white shirt. The Daisy dukes with a one-inch inseam and bright red push up bikini top that seemed like an acceptable costume choice for an audition with a music executive, was now wholly inappropriate for a one-on-one meeting with said executive, regardless of their history, or maybe because of it. She tugged on the shorts and top in vain, hoping to generate more fabric with the sheer force of her will as she quickly surveyed her surroundings for a more viable option.

She contemplated pulling a Scarlet O'Hara and fashioning a toga out of the ceiling-to-floor-length shears covering the window at the end of the corridor when the door swung open. EJ's gigantic security guard stood before them, filling most of the frame.

"Hey, Dre!" Gene greeted the big guy with a standard handshake-one-arm-hug-back-pound-dap. "This is—"

"Maya!" Andre exclaimed as he grabbed her in a bear hug, lifting her onto her tippy toes. "Come on in!" he said, leading Maya and Gene through the foyer into the living room of the suite.

Gene's eyebrows knitted. "You guys know each other?"

Before they could answer him, EJ's cousin, James, came rushing into the living room.

"Maya, Maya, Maya!" he sang as he pulled her into another bear hug. James's tall, thin build made for a less engulfing hug than Andre's, but not less warm, especially with the skin of his smooth milk chocolate arms against her naked back, cradling her so close that his bushy beard tickled her neck. "Damn girl. I nearly had a heart attack when I saw you up there. You and your girls are hot as shit, by the way! I already started mappin' out some things for y'all. Wooo!" he yelped, bringing his hands together in a loud clap and rubbing them together like he had something good coming his way. "I'm excited! Can you tell?" He let out a hearty laugh.

"Yes, I can see that now. It was harder to tell when you up and ran out of the room in the middle of our audition, though," Maya said. Her right brow arched up to her hairline.

"Aw man... that *was* rude, wasn't it? But we were all shocked to see you, Maya. Your boy lost his shit and shot outta there like a cannon ball," he said, nodding toward the balcony. "I had to go see about my cuz."

Maya looked through the balcony door. EJ was out there, leaning against the railing with his arms folded, resting his elbows on the ledge, and gazing out across Beverly Hills. He looked so good earlier in his Yankee's cap and the navy-blue blazer; she had literally stopped in her tracks. But his simple blue jeans and the white T-shirt that looked almost like it was painted onto his muscular frame made her bite her bottom lip. The short sleeves showed off his bulging biceps and the tip of the tail of the python tattoo that snaked across his trapezius and down his deltoid. From that angle, she could only see his profile and the deep waves of his flawlessly groomed Caesar haircut and beard along his chiseled jawline, but she could tell he was brooding.

"...Make sure you let your girls know how sorry I am for being so rude..." James continued, but Maya's attention had already left the living room. She drifted toward the balcony on shaky legs.

"...you right, Maya. I need to go back down there myself and apologize..." James called out as Maya opened the balcony door and stepped out. "You go on ahead out there. Don't let me hold you up. And don't worry. I'll explain everything to Gene on our way down, so he can hurry up and pick his jaw up off the floor—" he said, chuckling as she shut the door, snuffing out his chatter completely.

EJ looked over his shoulder as Maya closed the door behind her, and his eyes went wide for a fraction of a second. People that didn't know him as well as she did would have missed it. He worked hard to maintain his "cool-under-pressure-hip hop-mogul" persona. But the flicker of excitement in his eyes revealed he had not yet conquered his weakest weakness: Maya.

"Hey Maya," he greeted her with cautious tenderness.

"Hello, Eric," she said, less tender, but equally cautious.

He grinned. "You and my mom are still the only people who ever call me Eric."

They stared at each other for a few seconds. Goosebumps rippled across the vast surface area of Maya's exposed skin as the gap between them closed slowly. They embraced. It was like her body had no idea fourteen years had passed since they last touched. The physical attraction between them was as strong as the day they met at Juilliard when EJ came to lead an alumni panel discussion on contemporary music theory.

He tilted his head down until his lips were less than half a pucker away from hers. Her lips quivered in anticipation, but she turned her head abruptly and broke their embrace. A kiss would have made a liar out of Gene. Something bad would surely happen if they got to kissing.

"E.. don't..." Maya whispered, shaking her head as she turned around and reached for the door.

"Maya, don't go." He gently grabbed her wrist. "I won't try that again... I promise. I can control myself. I just wanna talk."

"Okay," Maya said, but it wasn't him she was afraid would lose control. When they met, she was barely twenty, and he was twenty-five, but they came together like a chemical reaction. They were two things drawn together to make one new thing. Their love was an entity all its own, but after three years she couldn't shake the fear that she was losing herself in the shadow of his blinding talent and passion before she even really knew who she was as an artist or a person. She realized she wasn't ready to give her life to a man because she hadn't lived her own life yet, so she left. She moved out of the tiny closet of an apartment they shared while he was at an out-of-town gig. It was cowardly. She never denied that. Or that he deserved better than to come home and find the engagement ring he had started saving for the day after they met on the counter next to his mail.

Maya slipped her stilettos off. She rested her elbows on the railing and looked out at Beverly Hills like EJ had been doing when she came out. "This is an awesome view."

EJ leaned on one elbow, facing her. "It's beautiful," he said, looking her up and down.

Maya pursed her lips and sucked her teeth. "Eric..." she sighed.

"What? I'm not tryna kiss you," he laughed. "Okay. I'll stop. Yaaas, girl! Beverly Hills is gorgeous," he said as he flicked imaginary hair off his shoulder and made a popping sound with his tongue like a girl from the hood. "Better?" He smirked.

Maya shook her head. "I see some things never change. You're still the same smart ass you were fourteen years ago." They both laughed.

"So, what you been up to, Maya," EJ asked when he finally stopped chuckling.

"In the last fourteen years? Well... after I spent most of it bustin' my butt in New York with little success, I decided to come back home last year to teach drama at Hamilton. Been in this, as my mother calls it, 'lil singin' group' for about a year. And now I'm standing on the balcony of the presidential suite in the Beverly Wilshire with the most talented and successful music producer in the world." She shot him a side eye.

"Heh, heh, heh, well, you know, what can I say?" EJ said, smoothing down his already smooth beard. "But for real, you're a teacher? That's what's up. I can see that. You were always good with kids."

"*Was* a teacher. I resigned to focus on the group." She grimaced. "Stupid, right?"

"Why would I think that's stupid?" He shrugged. "I gave up a teaching position at Carnegie Mellon to start a band with a Jamaican dude I met on the train."

"Yeah, well, look where you are and look where I am," Maya said.

"What do you mean? You're standing on a balcony of the Beverly Wilshire's presidential suite with the most talented, successful, and handsome—you said handsome, right—music producer in the world, baby!" He laughed.

"Stop, Eric, you're so silly." She covered her mouth to suppress a giggle. "I'm being serious right now."

"Okay. I'll be serious," he said. "But you need to relax. You realize it took me a lot longer than a year to get to this presidential suite. When I was on the road, we stayed in some pretty disgusting places. You remember that hotel in Phoenix with all those stains on the sheets? And the roaches in the bathroom?"

"Ugh. Yeah. I still have nightmares about that place. They tried to tell us they were designs on the sheets!" she said, rolling her eyes.

"Right, well, we stayed in places like that, and worse, for years. My brother, Corey, was our drummer for two years, and he literally cried every time we checked into a hotel—Don't tell him I told you that. But y'all aren't gonna have to go through that. 'Cause you got me. I take care of my artists."

Maya frowned. She suddenly remembered what a good person EJ was. An overwhelming wave of guilt washed over her, making her queasy.

He stepped closer. "What's wrong?" His hand hovered over her shoulder for a second before he shoved it in his pocket.

She inhaled and exhaled slowly. "Eric, I'm sorry... about leaving you the way I did. I know I was wrong. I know I really hurt you... and I truly am sorry. Believe it or not, I honestly thought I was doing what was best for both of us."

EJ shook his head. "It wasn't the best for me. It really messed me up for a minute," he admitted. "But that's old shit. I'm over it now." He smiled, trying to sell his lie to Maya and himself. "At least I got a few Grammys out of it. Nothing sparks creativity better than pain."

Maya offered a half smile, then her full frown returned. "How we gonna do this, E?"she asked with a sigh.

"Don't worry about that, Maya. Like I said, I'm over it. Besides, I don't have much direct contact with the artists on the label anymore. You'll rarely see me."

"Alright," Maya said, not completely convinced.

Acknowledgments

To my parents, Roceal and James, you are my first readers and editors, my loudest cheerleaders, and the hardest working members of my marketing team! Thank you for your relentless support in everything I do.

To my wonderfully brilliant, lifelong sister-friends, thank you for checking on me, asking how my book was coming along, listening to me lament over word choice and formatting concerns, offering counsel and comfort, and getting me out of the house when I needed a break, but didn't know it.

To my amazing new sister-friends from the writer community, thank you for taking the time out of your busy lives to read my book and offer such valuable and constructive feedback on craft and creativity. Your work and your generosity inspire me every day.

To my editors, thank you for diving deep, going page by page with me. Your willingness to discuss your suggestions and critiques was invaluable, and I am eternally grateful for the care you took with me and my book.

And to my readers, thank you for selecting my first book, *Passing Notes*, telling me how much you loved it, encouraging others to read it, and inviting me to your book clubs to chat about my story. Your excitement about the second book was the fuel that helped me make it to the finish line.

COURTNEY DUKE FOSTER, the author of *Passing Notes*, enjoys writing stories that show the good, the bad, and the wondrous aspects of life and love with characters you wish you could hang out with. She lives in Maryland with her two daughters, where she loves to encourage and support them in their creative pursuits and in every other way.

Website: courtneydukefoster.com

Instagram: bycourtneydukefoster